P9-DCD-132

Thereby Hangs a Tail

Also by Spencer Quinn

Dog on It

THEREBY HANGS A TAIL

A CHET AND BERNIE MYSTERY

SPENCER QUINN

ATRIA BOOKS
New York London Toronto Sydney

ATRIA BOOKS
A Division of Simon & Schuster, Inc.
1230 Avenue of the Americas
New York, NY 10020

This book is a work of fiction. Names, characters, places, and incidents either are products of the author's imagination or are used fictitiously. Any resemblance to actual events or locales or persons, living or dead, is entirely coincidental.

First Atria Books hardcover edition January 2010

ATRIA BOOKS and colophon are trademarks of Simon & Schuster, Inc.

Manufactured in the United States of America

10 9 8 7 6 5 4 3 2 1

Library of Congress Cataloging-in-Publication Data
Quinn, Spencer.
Thereby hangs a tail : a Chet and Bernie mystery / Spencer Quinn.—1st Atria Books hardcover ed.
p. cm.
1. Dogs—Fiction. 2. Private investigators—Fiction. 3. Dog owners—Fiction. 4. Show dogs—Fiction. 5. Kidnapping—Fiction. 6. Pet theft—Fiction. I. Title.

PS3617.U584T48 2010
813'.6—dc22

2009011014

ISBN 978-1-4165-8585-5
ISBN 978-1-4165-8593-0 (eBook)

This book is dedicated to Diana.

Thereby Hangs a Tail

ONE

The perp looked around—what nasty little eyes he had!—and saw there was nowhere to go. We were in some kind of warehouse, big and shadowy, with a few grimy high-up windows and tall stacks of machine parts. I couldn't remember how the warehouse fit in, exactly, or even what the whole case was all about; only knew beyond a doubt, from those nasty eyes and that sour end-of-the-line smell, a bit like those kosher pickles Bernie had with his BLTs—I'd tried one; once was enough for the kosher pickles, although I always had time for a BLT—that this guy was the perp. I lunged forward and grabbed him by the pant leg. Case closed.

The perp cried out in pain, a horrible, high-pitched sound that made me want to cover my ears. Too bad I can't do that, but no complaints—I'm happy the way I am (even if my ears don't match, something I found out about a while back but can't get into right now). The perp's noises went on and on and finally it hit me that maybe I had more than just his pant leg. That happened sometimes: my teeth are probably longer than yours and sharper, too. What was that? Yes, the taste of blood. My mistake, but a very exciting one all the same.

"Call him off!" the perp screamed. "I give up."

Bernie came running up from behind. "Good work, Chet," he said, huffing and puffing. Poor Bernie—he was trying to give up smoking again but not having much luck.

"Get him off! He's biting me!"

"Chet wouldn't bite," Bernie said. "Not deliberately."

"Not deliberately? What are you—"

"On the other hand, round about now he usually likes to hear a confession."

"Huh? He's a goddamn dog."

"Language," said Bernie.

Those nasty eyes shifted around, looking wild now. "But he's a dog."

"True," Bernie said.

I wagged my tail. And maybe, on account of the good mood I was in—what was better than a job well done?—shook my head from side to side a bit.

"Aaiieeee! I confess! I confess!"

"To what?"

"To what? The El Camino jewel heist, for Christ sake."

"El Camino jewel heist?" said Bernie. "We're here about the Bar J Guest Ranch arson."

"That, too," said the perp. "Just get him offa me."

"Chet?" Bernie said. "Chet?"

Oh, all right, but how about that taste, human blood? Addictive or what?

Hours later we had two checks, one for the arson, one for the jewel heist, and a good thing, too, because our finances were a mess—alimony, child support, a bad investment in some company with plans to make Hawaiian pants just like the Hawaiian shirts Bernie wears on special occasions, and not much work lately except for divorce cases, never any fun. We run a detective agency, me and Bernie, called the Little Detective Agency on account of Little being Bernie's last name. My name's Chet, pure and simple. Headquarters is our house on Mesquite Road, a nice place with a big tree out front, perfect for napping under, and the whole canyon easily accessible out back, if it just so happens someone left the gate open. And then, up in the canyon—well, say no more.

"This calls for a celebration," Bernie said. "How about a chew strip?" Was that a serious question? Who says no to a chew strip? He opened the cupboard over the sink, where the chew strips were kept; at one time, a very nice time, they'd been on an open shelf, lower down. "And while we're at it . . ." Uh-oh. Bernie reached for the bottle of bourbon, standing by the chew strip box.

We sat out back, watching the light change on the far side of the canyon as the sun went down, Bernie at the table sipping bourbon, me under it, trying to take my time with the chew strip. This wasn't any chew strip, but a high-end bacon-flavored rawhide chew from Rover and Company, an outfit owned by our buddy Simon something or other, whom we'd met on a missing-persons case, our specialty. Bacon smell—the best there is—rose all around me, like a dense cloud. I glanced up at Bernie through the glass tabletop. Could he smell it? Probably not. The puniness of his sense of smell—and the sense of smell of humans in general—was something I've never gotten used to.

He looked down at me. "What's on your mind, boy? Ten to one you're thinking about how you chased that guy down." Wrong, but at that moment he reached over and scratched between my ears, right on a spot I hadn't even realized was desperate for scratching, so I gave my tail a thump. Bernie laughed. "Read your mind," he said. Not close, but I didn't care—he could believe whatever he wanted as long as he kept up this scratching, digging his nails in just so, an expert. He stopped—too soon, always too soon—and said, "How about Dry Gulch? Hell, we earned it."

I was on my feet, gulping down what was left of the chew strip. The Dry Gulch Steakhouse and Saloon was one of our favorites. They had a big wooden cowboy out front—I'd lifted my leg against him once, not good, I know, but just too tempting—and a patio bar in back where my guys were welcome. We went in the Porsche—an old topless one that had replaced our not-quite-as-old topless one after it shot off a cliff on a day I'll never forget, although I've actually forgotten most of it already—brown with yellow doors, Bernie driving, me riding shotgun. Loved riding shotgun: what was better than this? I stuck my head way up, into the wind: smells went by faster than I could sort them out, a kind of nose feast that I'm afraid you'll never—

"Hey, Chet, a little space, buddy."

Oops. Way over on Bernie's side. I shifted closer to my door.

"And ease up on the drooling."

Drooling? Me? I moved over as far as I could and sat stiffly the rest of the way, back straight, eyes forward, aloof. I wasn't alone in the drooling department, had seen Bernie drooling in his sleep more than once, and Leda, too, Bernie's ex-wife, meaning humans drooled, big time. But had I ever made the slightest fuss about it, or thought less of them? You tell me.

We sat in the patio bar at the Dry Gulch Steakhouse and Saloon, Bernie on the end stool, me on the floor. The big summer heat—not just heat but pressure, like a heavy blanket is always weighing down on you—was over, but it was still plenty hot and the cool tiles felt good. Bernie pointed across the street with his chin. "What's that?"

"What's what?" said the bartender.

"That hole in the ground."

"Condos," the bartender said. "Ten stories? Fifteen maybe?"

Bernie has dark, prominent eyebrows with a language all their own. Sometimes, like now, they grew jagged and his whole face, normally such a nice sight, darkened. "And when the aquifer runs dry, what then?" he said.

"Aquifer?" said the bartender.

"Any idea of the current population of the Valley?" Bernie said.

"The whole valley?" said the bartender. "Gotta be up there." Bernie gave him a long look, then ordered a double.

A waitress in a cowboy hat came by. "Is that Chet? Haven't seen you in a while." She knelt down, gave me a pat. "Still like steak tips?" Why would that ever change? "Hey, easy, boy."

Bernie had a burger and another bourbon; steak tips and water for me. His face returned to normal. Whew. Bernie worried about the aquifer a lot and sometimes when he got going couldn't stop. All our water came from the aquifer—I'd heard him say that over and over, although I'd never laid eyes on this aquifer, whatever it was. I didn't get it at all: there was plenty of water in the Valley—how else to explain all that spraying on the golf courses, morning and evening, and those beautiful little rainbows the sprinklers made? We had water out the yingyang. I got up and pressed my head against Bernie's leg. He did some light scratching in that space between my eyes, impossible for me to get to. Ah, bliss. I spotted a French fry under the stool next to Bernie's and snapped it up.

A bourbon or two later, Lieutenant Stine of the Metro PD—a trim little guy in a dark suit—walked in. Bernie had worked for him sometime in the distant past, before my adventures in K-9 school (washing out on the very last day, a long story, but it's no secret that a cat was involved) and had played some role in Bernie and me getting together, the exact details a bit foggy.

"Hear you cleared the El Camino case," Lieutenant Stine said. "Nice job."

"Luck, mostly," Bernie said.

"And a full confession to boot."

"Chet's doing."

Lieutenant Stine glanced down, saw me. He had a thin face and thin lips, didn't smile much in my experience, but he smiled now, somehow ended up looking a little dangerous. "He's a good interrogator," he said.

"The best," said Bernie.

I thumped my tail.

"Understand a tidy reward went along with that," the lieutenant said. A few stools down the row, a guy in a Hawaiian shirt glanced over.

"No complaints," Bernie said to Lieutenant Stine. "What are you drinking?"

A minute or so later, Bernie and the lieutenant were clinking glasses. I'd lost count of Bernie's bourbons by now; counting isn't my strength, not past two.

"Glad I ran into you," Lieutenant Stine said. "There's a little something that might be up your alley."

"Like what?" Bernie said.

Lieutenant Stine glanced down at me. "Up your alley for sure, come to think of it," he said. "And potentially lucrative besides."

"You have our attention," said Bernie.

Lieutenant Stine lowered his voice, but nowhere near out of my range. Have I mentioned the sharpness of my hearing yet, or was that just about my teeth? At that very moment, for example, I could hear a woman huddled over a cell phone at a table clear across the room saying "They're upping my medication." That sounded so interesting, I missed the beginning of the lieutenant's remark, tuning in in time to catch ". . . Great Western Dog Show."

"Never heard of it," Bernie said.

"I'm surprised," said the lieutenant. "There's been a lot of publicity." Bernie shrugged. I loved that shrug of his. If only I could do that! I gave it a try, but all that happened was the hair on my back stood up on end. ". . . coming to the Arena end of next week," the lieutenant was saying. "Used to be in Denver, but the mayor lured them here."

"Why?"

"For the money it'll bring into the Valley, what else?"

"What money?"

"Hotel bookings, food and drink, all the tourist shit," said Lieutenant Stine. "The flowers alone come to a quarter mill."

"Flowers?" Bernie said.

"Exactly," said the lieutenant. "The Great Western crowd is a certain class of people—happens to be the mayor's favorite class, actually."

"I thought he was the reform guy."

"You're not alone."

"So what does he want me to do?" Bernie said, knocking back more bourbon. "Give the welcoming address?"

Lieutenant Stine laughed. There was something metallic in the sound; it gave me a bad feeling, deep inside my ears. "Not quite," he said. "In fact, he didn't single you out per se—it's even possible he's never heard of you, believe it or not—he just wants someone like you."

"To do what?"

The lieutenant lowered his voice some more. "Bodyguard duty."

"Nope."

"Nope? Just like that?"

"We don't do bodyguard duty."

"What about the Junior Ramirez case?"

"That's why."

"This is different. First, it pays two grand a day. Second, next to a psychotic like Junior Ramirez, this client's a walk in the park." Lieutenant Stine laughed that metallic laugh again. "Just about literally," he said.

"Two grand?" Bernie said.

"And a bonus at the end wouldn't be a stretch."

"Who's the client?" Bernie said. And, despite my memories of guarding Junior Ramirez—especially that incident with the ice cream and the razor blade—I was glad. Our finances were a mess, and two grand was two grand, and a whole week of two grands was . . . well, I'll leave that to you.

Lieutenant Stine reached into his jacket pocket, took out a photo.

"What's this?" Bernie said.

"That's her long name on the back," the lieutenant said. "'Kingsbury's First Lady Belle.' But for every day I think they call her Princess."

"The client is a dog?"

I sat up. Bernie was gazing at the photo. I could see it, too. One of my guys was in the picture? Where? And then I spotted her: a tiny fluffball with huge dark eyes, reclining on a satin pillow. I knew satin pillows on account of Leda having had one, although it got chewed up in a kind of frenzy, the details of the episode not too clear in my mind. But that satin taste: so strange and interesting, a vivid memory. I glanced around the Dry Gulch bar: no satin in view.

"Not just any dog," said Lieutenant Stine. "Princess is one of the top dogs in the country. She won best in show at Balmoral."

"What's that?"

"You don't know Balmoral? It's on ESPN2 every year, Bernie—the biggest dog show in the country."

"Never heard of it," Bernie said.

Lieutenant Stine gave Bernie a sideways look. I'd seen other friends of Bernie's do the same thing, Sergeant Torres at Missing Persons, for example, or Otis DeWayne, our weapons guy—but didn't know what it meant. "So you don't want the job?" the lieutenant said.

Job? What job? Making sure that a fluffball on a satin pillow stayed out of trouble? That was free money, not a job. Come on, Bernie.

"Who's the owner?" Bernie said.

"Woman name of Adelina Borghese."

"Where from?"

"Italy, I think. But she owns a spread over in Rio Loco."

"Rio Loco?" Bernie said. "I'll talk to her."

The lieutenant nodded. "Knew you wouldn't say no to that kind of green."

The Hawaiian shirt man glanced over again.

Bernie's eyebrows went a little jagged. "I'll talk to her, that's all. I can still say no."

Lieutenant Stine went away. I polished off my steak tips, stretched out on those cool tiles, chilled out. What a life! The final chase through the warehouse ran pleasantly through my mind. And then again. After a while, I grew aware that the Hawaiian shirt guy had moved next to Bernie and struck up a conversation, at first about Hawaiian shirts, then about something else.

"What I run," he was saying, "is what you might call a hedge fund for the little guy."

"Little guy?" said Bernie.

"Not little in terms of intelligence or ability," the Hawaiian shirt man added quickly. "But for one reason or another, men of distinction who don't happen to be Wall Street insiders. I've had some nice play in commodities lately. You're familiar with the basics of tin futures?"

Bernie motioned for another drink, overturning the salt and pepper. "Can't be that complicated," he said.

"Exactly," replied the Hawaiian shirt man. And to the bartender when Bernie's drink came: "I'll get that." Then came a lot of back and forth about tin, puts, calls, Bolivia, and other mysteries. My eyelids got heavy, way too heavy to keep open. I let them close, drifted off. Harmless talk was all it was. As long as the checkbook didn't come out of Bernie's pocket, we were in good shape.

Sometime later I awoke, feeling tip-top. I got up, gave myself a good shake, looked around. The bar was empty except for me, the bartender, the man in the Hawaiian shirt, and Bernie. The only completely sober one was me. Then came the bartender, the man in the Hawaiian shirt, and Bernie, dead last. Also, the checkbook was coming out.

TWO

In the old days, when Leda was still around, I used to sleep out in the front hall, my back against the door, on account of Leda not wanting me in the bedroom for some reason. Now I like to sleep at the foot of Bernie's bed, on this nubbly rug we got at a yard sale, me and Bernie. Those nubbles feel great in a way that's hard to describe. But on nights when Bernie snored—such as the night after our dinner at Dry Gulch—I moved back to the front door, which was why I heard a car pulling up outside just as the first light of day pushed in at the darkness.

I got up, went right to the tall, narrow window by the door, looked out. A limo was parked on the street, long and black. The driver, dressed in black, got out and opened a rear door. A blond woman got out. She wore black, too. Lots of blackness, all of a sudden. I started barking, not sure why. From next door came a high-pitched yip-yip-yip. Hey! Iggy was up. I barked louder. So did he. Iggy was a great pal. The fun we'd had, back before the electric fence guy had made a sale at Iggy's place—I could tell you a story or two. Iggy had had trouble getting used to the electric fence, now stayed indoors most of the time. No electric fence at our place, mine and Bernie's, of course. Bernie had grabbed the collar from the electric fence guy and walked right through the zapper, taking the shock, and had then shaken his head and sent the man on his way. Who needed an electric fence? I wasn't the wandering type, except if it just so happened the back gate was open, or the smell of fox or javelina was in the air, or a strange car went down the street, or I picked up the sound of—

The woman in black was coming up the walk. She moved fast; the sun, popping up over the rooftops, glittered on her jewelry. That sparkly one on her finger—wow! Leda had a ring like that, but not nearly as big. Leda had *had* one like that, I should say. Just before the breakup with Bernie, there'd been a bad incident where I got blamed for losing the ring. Why would I want to bury a ring? Did I have even the slightest memory of ever doing anything remotely like that? No. My mind was absolutely guilt-free on that subject.

The woman leaned forward to press the bell, but it had stopped working sometime back and was on Bernie's list of things to fix. Every so often the toolbox came out and he took a crack at shortening the list. Those were exciting days! That time the toaster blew up, for example, or when the toilet—

Knock knock. The woman in black had figured out about the bell, quicker than most. Something about the way she knocked rubbed me the wrong way. I barked again. Iggy picked up on me and did his yipping thing. The woman knocked harder, not a heavy knock, exactly, more a sharp ratta-tat-tat, like high heels on a polished floor. She spoke, and there was sharpness in her voice, too. "Anyone in there? Open up."

I turned and ran down the hall, past Charlie's room, empty, meaning this wasn't every second weekend or Thanksgiving or whatever Bernie and Leda had agreed on lately, and into Bernie's room. Bernie lay on his back, one arm flung over his eyes, the covers all twisted up. I smelled bourbon and cigarette smoke, plus the smell of Bernie when it was time for a shower.

I barked, but not too loud; the poor guy. I knew what he needed, had seen the whole routine plenty of times—a lot more sleep, then Advil, coffee, cold wet towel on his forehead. Knock knock knock. There wasn't time for any of that. I barked again, louder this time.

"Uh," said Bernie, his voice weak. "Gah."

I moved to the side of the bed, pulled at a corner of the sheet. From down inside the twisted covers, Bernie pulled back. Bernie was a big, strong guy, but not at the moment. I ripped the sheets right off him.

Bernie, arm still over his face, groaned, "Chet, what the hell?"

Somehow I'd got all tangled in the covers. I couldn't see—and that's a thing I hate. I struggled, clawed, rolled around—nearby something came crashing down on the floor—and burst free at last. Bernie was sitting up now, one eye open. It had turned red overnight.

"Sleep," he said, his voice a bit stronger now, maybe what you'd call a croak. "I need more—"

Knock knock knock.

Bernie's other eye opened, this one even redder. "What?" he said. And then: "Who?"

I barked.

"Someone's at the door?" He turned to the bedside clock, maybe a painful movement because he winced and said, "Ow." Then he squinted at the clock, rubbed his eyes, squinted again. "But it's only—"

Knock knock knock knock—and even more knocks. That sharp ratta-tat-tat was driving me crazy, and maybe Bernie, too.

He put a hand to his head, rose, leaning sideways slightly as though the room was spinning in the other direction, and staggered into the bathroom. Then came peeing sounds—which reminded me I had to go too, in fact, pretty soon—running-water sounds, and the interesting clitter-clatter that happens when a bottle of pills gets spilled. Not long after that—and meanwhile more knocking, plus Iggy's muffled yipping—Bernie emerged wearing his polka-dot bathrobe, face scrubbed and hair combed, except for a small stick-out hornlike thing on one side, not very noticeable. Then, holding the robe together with one hand—the belt, I remembered, had been part of a fun tug-of-war game we'd played on Charlie's last visit, me, Charlie, and Bernie ending up in a heap on the floor (but I had the belt, meaning I was the winner, right? Wasn't that the point of tug-of-war?)—then—where was I?—oh, yeah: Bernie moved toward the front door.

Knock knock knock. "Christ Almighty," Bernie said. "I'm coming." He turned the knob and pulled—maybe more forcefully than he'd intended—flinging the door open; Bernie lost his grip and the knob thumped hard against the wall. At the same time, he also lost his grip on the polka-dot robe, which fell open.

The blond woman's eyes, pale green, I thought, but don't take my word for it—Bernie says I'm not too good with colors—dipped down, widened very slightly, then rose up and took in Bernie's face, her eyes now narrowing fast. "Perhaps I've made a mistake," she said. Once on the Discovery Channel Bernie and I watched a show about polar bears—hoo, boy—and there'd been this picture of a long, pointy icicle, slowly dripping. No icicles in the Valley, of course, but for some reason, the sound of the blond woman's voice made me think of that picture. Funny how the mind works.

Meanwhile, Bernie was blinking and saying, "Um."

"I was looking for a private detective named Bernie Little," the woman said.

"Bingo," said Bernie.

"I beg your pardon?" the woman said.

"Meaning you found him. Me. I'm Bernie Little. And this"—he turned and gestured at me, polka-dot robe opening again, but only for a moment—"is Chet." She gave me a look, actually quite a careful one. My tail started wagging. "What can I do for you?" Bernie said.

"I'm Adelina Borghese," the woman said.

"Pleased to meet you," said Bernie, extending his hand. Adelina Borghese's hand remained at her side.

"Didn't that policeman mention me?" she said. "I thought this was all set up."

"Ah," said Bernie. "The client with the ridic—" He stopped himself. "Uh, come in. Please. The office is—" He motioned down the hall. Adelina's gaze followed the movement, paused on a pair of boxers lying on the floor. Bernie noticed. "Um, on vacation," he said. "The maid."

We had a maid? So many things I liked about Bernie, and that was just one of them: you learned something new every day. But no time to think about that now. I bolted outside, raced to the rock at the end of the driveway, and lifted my leg. At the same time, I heard that yip-yip-yip, and, leg still up, turned my head—I can turn it practically right around backward if I have to—and there was Iggy at his window. Good to see Iggy, but—uh-oh, what was that? He was lifting his leg, too.

Not long after, we were sitting in the office—Adelina Borghese in one of the client chairs, Bernie behind the desk, me beside it.

Bernie was dressed now—khakis, tucked-in shirt, loafers—and looked much better. He'd also brewed coffee; loved the smell of coffee, but the taste didn't do much for me. Water was my drink, although once, out in the desert with some bikers, I'd had a fun evening with beer. But no time to go into that now. Bernie was a great interviewer. His interviewing skills and my nose: if you want my opinion, that's what raised the Little Detective Agency above the rest. I settled in to watch Bernie work.

"Cream? Sugar?" he said, pouring coffee.

"Black," said Adelina Borghese.

"Me, too," said Bernie. "We have something in common."

See what I mean? Brilliant. Although maybe this woman was going to be a tough customer, because from where I was, her lips seemed to purse in a way that said, "Dream on."

Bernie sipped his coffee, his hand not quite steady. "Ah," he said. "Hits the spot."

Adelina Borghese sipped hers, said nothing, and didn't touch it again.

"I take it you're the owner of Queenie," Bernie said.

Now Adelina Borghese's mouth looked like she'd just tasted something bad. "Queenie?" she said.

"Uh," said Bernie, "wasn't that the name of the ri—" He stopped himself. "What am I saying? Princess, of course. I take it you're the owner of Princess."

"Correct," said Adelina Borghese. "Although I don't really think of the relationship in that owner-slash-possession way."

"More like a team?" Bernie said.

There was a pause, and when Adelina spoke again, her voice wasn't so icy. "You might say that," she said. "Princess is very special. She's a great competitor."

"At what?" said Bernie.

"Dog shows," Adelina said, her voice refreezing fast. "What kind of briefing did that policeman give you?"

"A good one," Bernie said. "The competition angle didn't come up, that's all."

"What other angle is there?" said Adelina. "Dog shows are about competition and Princess is like . . . like Michael Jordan."

Bernie loved hoops, had lots of old tapes, so I knew about Michael Jordan, but was Adelina expecting us to believe that the little fluffball in the photo could dunk? A basketball was a very difficult kind of ball for me and my kind, as I'd learned, maybe more than once.

"What kind of prize money's involved?" Bernie said.

"Prize money?" said Adelina.

"If Princess wins."

"She gets a blue ribbon."

"No money?"

"What could be better than a blue ribbon? She loves them."

Bernie smiled, a little smile there and gone very fast. He took another sip of coffee, his hand now steady, I was glad to see. "I look forward to meeting her," he said. "But I have to warn you, Chet and I don't do much bodyguard work and we've never guarded a dog before."

"Chet?" said Adelina.

"We're a team, too," said Bernie.

Adelina bent forward, stared down at me. "Can he be trusted?"

Now Bernie's voice got a bit icy, too. "What do you mean?"

"Around small dogs," she said. "He looks big. I don't recognize the breed. And what's the story with his ears?"

My ears again? How rude. I didn't think hers quite matched either. And so what about the odd notch nipped out here and there? Getting into a scrape now and then went with the job, and you should see the other guy. Bernie's voice grew icier. "There are many private detectives in the Valley," he said. "I can recommend some if you wish."

"There's no goddamn time for—" Adelina caught herself. "No need for that," she said. "You come highly recommended. They've even heard of you in New York."

I twisted around to see Bernie's face: eyebrows up, a look of complete surprise. But he said nothing.

"Are the terms satisfactory?" Adelina said. "Two thousand a day from now till the end of the show?"

Plus expenses. Come on Bernie: plus expenses. But he didn't say anything, just nodded.

"I suppose you'd like some sort of retainer," Adelina said.

"Not yet," said Bernie. *Not yet? Why not?* "First, we've got some questions." Did we? That was interesting. I waited to hear.

"What sort of questions?" Adelina said.

Bernie started numbering them on his fingers. I loved when he did that! Bernie was always the smartest guy in the room, even if some people missed that. "One," he said: "Is it customary for show dogs to have bodyguards?"

"No," said Adelina.

"Two: is it just your custom?"

"No," she said, "and please don't number the questions on your fingers. My husband does that and I can't stand it."

Bernie's hands folded up and sank down on the desk. "So there's a Mr. Borghese?" he said.

"Not exactly," said Adelina. "My husband is a count."

Bernie leaned forward. Maybe he thought she'd said something else. "Say again?"

"A count, Mr. Little. A member of the minor European nobility."

"Ah," said Bernie. "A *conte,* in Italian."

"Correct," said Adelina.

"Making you a contessa," said Bernie.

"Let's not get into any of that," she said. "You can call me Adelina."

"And I'll be Bernie," said Bernie, with a little laugh, as though he'd cracked a pretty good joke. No laugh from Adelina, and in truth I didn't get it either. Bernie cleared his throat—I can do that, too, much more noisily—a habit of his that usually meant the failure of whatever had gone before. "It's not your custom to retain a bodyguard for Princess, but you want one now," he said. "Why?"

Adelina bit her lip. Then, big surprise, her eyes filled with tears. The crying thing: always a bit of a mystery to me. Humans cried sometimes, women more than men—Leda, for example, had had a crying episode every day—but I'd seen Bernie cry once, if crying meant just the tears part with no sound: that was the day Leda packed up all of Charlie's stuff. Adelina's crying was the same—just tears, no sound. She opened her bag, took out some tissue, dabbed at her eyes; they seemed darker now. "Princess's life is in danger," she said.

"Why do you say that?" said Bernie.

Adelina dug into her bag again, handed him a folded sheet of glossy paper. "This came in the mail." I got up, watched Bernie unfold it, moved around the desk so I could see.

"A page from a magazine?" Bernie said.

"*Show Dog World,*" said Adelina. She glanced at me and blinked, as though not quite believing her eyes about something, exactly what I had no idea.

I turned my attention back to the glossy page. There was a bit of writing, useless to me, of course, but mostly just a big color photo of Princess on a satin pillow, maybe the same photo I'd seen last night. The difference was that someone had inked in a bull's-eye target over her tiny fluffball head. I had only one thought: we were in business.

THREE

Bernie says he hates guns, but he happens to be a crack shot. We've got a rifle and a shotgun locked in the office safe—it's behind a big framed photo of Niagara Falls, you'd never guess—and a .38 Special in the glove box of the Porsche. Bernie loves waterfall pictures, by the way; we've got a bunch. But back to the guns. Sometimes Bernie goes to the range for practice. I love the range, although the fact is I've only been once on account of the whole experience turning out to be a little too exciting. But that's how I know bull's-eyes—from watching Bernie at the range. He gets a look in his eye at the range—cool and still—and then bam! Bull's-eye! Bernie had a look like that now, as he gazed at Princess's picture.

"How did you get this?" Bernie said.

"It came in the mail," said Adelina Borghese.

"In Italy?"

"Italy?"

"Isn't that where you live?"

"We have a villa in Umbria, yes. But the letter came to our place in Manhattan."

"When?"

"Last week."

"Do you have the envelope?"

"No."

"Where is it?"

"An assistant opens the mail. He throws out the envelopes, junk mail, all that."

"Did you try to find it?"

"Too late—everything goes in the shredder."

"Did you show this to the police?"

"The Manhattan DA lives in our building. He told me not to worry about it—most likely just a mean-spirited joke, he said."

"But you didn't take his advice," said Bernie.

"He doesn't have a dog," said Adelina.

Bernie nodded as though that made sense to him. Personally, I was losing the thread, maybe because it was getting past breakfast time and there were no signs of breakfast happening. I rose, had a nice stretch—the kind where I get my front legs way out, head down, butt up, can't tell you how good that feels—wandered into the kitchen and nosed behind the trash bin. You can sometimes find the odd tidbit there, but today wasn't one of those times. All I spotted was a wine bottle cork. Not food, but I picked it up and started gnawing anyway, hard to explain why. Meanwhile, I tried to remember the last wine-drinking occasion. Had to have been on a night Suzie came over—she liked red. Wine smells are pretty interesting—even humans are on to that. I love when they stick their little noses in the glass and go on about blackberries and chocolate and lemongrass—trust me, they haven't got a clue.

Hadn't seen Suzie in a while, now that I thought about it. Suzie was the greatest! She always had biscuits in her car, for one thing. Suzie was a reporter for the *Valley Tribune*. She'd done a story on Bernie, back when we were working the Madison Chambliss case. Bernie hadn't liked the story much. What was the word? Shambling. What the hell's that? Bernie had said. She'd written that Bernie was a big shambling guy like an athlete past his prime, but she hadn't mentioned that Bernie had actually been an athlete, pitching for Army back in his college days. Pitching was about baseball and Army was about fighting, kind of confusing, and all of this before Bernie and I got together, but I can tell you one thing—he can throw a tennis ball a long way when he wants to; not so far that I can't get it in a flash, of course. We can play ball for hours—whatever those are, exactly—me and Bernie. Also Frisbees—what a great invention! Once old man Heydrich, our neighbor on the other side, not Iggy's, a neighbor who doesn't warm up to me and my kind, didn't quite see the Frisbee coming, nobody's fault really, but try telling that to old man Heydrich.

Back to Bernie and Suzie. The point was that although Bernie hadn't liked Suzie's story, he'd ended up liking Suzie. Plus she liked him. Everything was going along swimmingly—I love swimming, by the way, understand that expression perfectly—until an old, or possibly not so old—boyfriend of Suzie's showed up, name of Dylan McKnight. Don't get me started, but I can tell you that he and I didn't hit it off from the get-go, though I've liked just about every human I'd ever met, except for perps and gangbangers, and even some of—

". . . meet the plane," Bernie was saying. I looked up, saw him moving toward the front door, Adelina beside him.

"I'll let my husband know," Adelina was saying. "Sure you don't want a retainer?"

"Not necessary," said Bernie. "This'll be all over soon. We'll bill you then."

Oh, Bernie.

* * *

We had a late breakfast, bacon and eggs for Bernie, kibble for me. And some of Bernie's bacon, to tell the truth. Bernie had gotten this idea, no telling from where, that too much bacon was bad for him. The idea of too much bacon made no sense to me and I was happy to help him out.

After breakfast, Bernie went into the office and started tap-tapping at the computer. I sat by the tall, narrow window in the front hall, gazing out. Time passed and then I heard a truck coming. FedEx or UPS? An important difference, because the UPS guy always tossed a biscuit on the lawn as he blew by and the FedEx guy never did. The trucks sounded almost the same, except for a soft tick-tick-tick that meant FedEx, and a moment later I heard that damn ticking: no biscuit. Soon the FedEx truck drove past; I barely looked at it. But then, what was this, right on its tail? A motorcycle. Motorcycles were always interesting, and this one especially, since it stopped in front of our house.

The driver wore a helmet and visor, the dark kind. He turned, raised the visor, looked at the house and saw me. He yanked the visor back down so fast I didn't actually get a chance to see what he looked like beyond dark skin and a flash of blue, wasn't even sure he was a he. One quick whiff of the driver would have been enough on that score, but all I could smell of the outside was tail-pipe exhaust. Vroom vroom: the bike roared away. Iggy must have seen it, too. He went yip-yip-yip.

I watched out the window some more, but nothing happened. How about a good stretch and a nice yawn? Perfect. And several more times, also perfect, before Bernie started moving around. I went to find him.

Right away I saw he wanted a smoke. Not hard to put that together: I knew from how he was checking all the places forgotten cigarettes might be—the silverware drawer, under the La-Z-Boy in the TV room, in the laundry pile—but unlike some earlier attempts at giving up smoking, this time Bernie had been thorough and thrown them all out. I followed him around, although it was clear from the start there were no smokes hidden anywhere. Otherwise I'd have picked up the smell, except if they'd been in the safe, and even then, don't bet the ranch.

Bernie took a deep breath, let it out slowly. That was one of his techniques, for what I didn't know. "How about a walk?" he said. And then: "Hey, Chet! Down, boy."

We went out the back door, Bernie first changing into his jogging shoes, which meant he was going to force himself to run. The smell of those jogging shoes: wow. And how strange to me the way humans wear different shoes for different activities; and the shoes women sometimes wear! I remember one really nasty pair of Leda's: they'd actually scared me, which was how come I'd chewed them up. No way Leda would understand. The same footwear at all times works for me. I bet a lot of people would be happier with nice big paws like mine, thickly padded for those times silence is important, but with big sharp claws for when it's all about traction.

We went through the backyard, out the gate, and into the canyon. The canyon is one of the nicest things about living on Mesquite Road. It's actually in the middle of the Valley, this whole city, or maybe bunch of cities, I'd never been clear on that, that goes on and on in all directions but was practically invisible from where we stood. Is that cool or what? I've lived in other places, namely the Academy kennel and before that a falling-down apartment with some drunks, not too nice, when I was just a pup, but this, with Bernie, was the best, the best that ever could be. Right now he was bobbing up and down on his toes a bit, throwing punches at the air. Soon he started running, sort of, up the gravelly trail that led to the hill with the big flat rock on top and then wound along a high ridge.

Human running: not a thing of beauty, and all that effort to produce so little speed, kind of puzzling. To rev Bernie up a bit, I charged around him in circles, first one way, then the other, then this crazy thing I do of both ways at once, or pretty close.

"Chet." Bernie huffed and puffed. "You're making me dizzy."

He plodded on. I picked up a faint scent that reminded me slightly of bacon, but this had nothing to do with breakfast. Javelina! Anything better than hunting javelinas? Hard to imagine. I sniffed around a cactus, the round kind with the sharp needles—I knew about those needles, oh yeah, wasn't going to make that mistake again—and caught the javelina scent, much stronger. I left the trail, went into my trot, nose to the ground, rounded a tall red rock, and bingo, as Bernie would say: there he was, a big fat javelina, munching on a dead little something. He smelled me—javelinas are no slouches in that department, I admit—and looked up and snarled, a muffled snarl on account of the dead little something in his mouth. Did he think I was competition, that I'd actually eat the critter—maybe not completely dead, in fact: was its tail twitching a bit? I snarled back, more out of disgust than anything. The javelina dropped the critter—which scrambled right up in the dust and darted down a nearby hole in the ground—and bared his tusks. I showed him my teeth. He didn't like that sight, not one bit—I could tell by the way his hairy feet started shuffling backward, as though they didn't know what the tusks were doing at the other end. I rocked back, got ready to charge.

"Chet! Chet!"

I turned, gazed back at the trail, surprisingly distant and way above me, and there was Bernie, leaning out over the edge.

"C'mon, Chet. C'mon back."

I looked at Bernie, then back at the javelina, still standing with his tusks and his surly attitude. *Be right there, Bernie, as soon as I take care of this—*

"CHET! RIGHT NOW!"

I glanced up at Bernie again, tried not to see him. But there he was. What did right now mean, exactly? I took it to mean fairly soon, not a long time away but not—

"NOW MEANS NOW!"

Bernie had a very loud voice when he wanted. The ground seemed to shake all around me. Bernie couldn't make that happen, of course; it just felt that way. I turned back to the javelina once more. He was gone. Easy to follow his trail, a snap to run him down, but—

"CHET!" The ground shook; I was almost sure. I headed up to Bernie but moving my slowest, tail just about dragging on the ground. He sounded mad, no doubt about it. But when I popped up over the ridge, Bernie gave me a hug. "Too nice a day to spend at the vet's," he said. "Remember the last time?" I did not. Bernie gave me a biscuit anyway, not the gourmet kind from Rover and Company, just the cheap kind from the market; but I loved them, too. I gobbled it up, rose onto my back legs, and gave Bernie a big kiss. He laughed and said, "Let's get some exercise." And then he got going up the path again in that shambling—yes, I'm afraid it fit—way of his. Bernie might have been limping a bit, too. That happened sometimes, especially when he was tired, and came from his wound, a long-ago wound in a desert war, not our desert but some distant one. I walked at his side, taking in the smells.

We went around the bend, passed the flat rock and headed onto the ridge, Bernie huffing and puffing, me strolling along, occasionally sticking my tongue way way out for no reason. High above, a big black bird circled in the sky, the haze all gone, another sign that the big heat was over. I didn't like big black birds, or any other kind of bird, for that matter.

"Chet? What are you growling about?"

Me?

"You're tired? Want to stop?"

Me?

"Isn't there a bench up ahead?"

We went up a short rise, came to a lookout with a wooden bench. Bernie flopped down on it, said, "Ah." I stood beside him. From here, if you gazed in one direction, you could sometimes make out the downtown towers, but neither of us gazed in that direction. Bernie was studying the sky and I was studying Bernie. "What a day," he said. The big black bird was gone. Bernie took a bottle of water and a small bowl from his fanny pack. We drank, Bernie from the bottle, me from the bowl. I'd tried drinking right from a bottle a few times—much harder than it looks.

"Don't want to jinx it," Bernie said, "but things might be working out on the money side. That five grand I put into those tin futures last night?" I remembered the checkbook coming out, but five grand? "Guess what—it's up to six already. Overnight! Plus all this easy money from Adelina. I feel guilty taking it. The Manhattan DA's probably right—there's no threat here." Bernie turned his face to the sun, closed his eyes. He looked much younger all of a sudden, and I could see the resemblance to Charlie. "Life is good, Chet. Why is it so hard to keep that front and center?" Poor Bernie. I didn't know what the hell he was talking about, just pressed my head against his leg. He reached down and scratched between my ears. I closed my eyes, too, and did nothing much but feel the sun and the air, so soft and—

Crack! Zing!

What was that? A loud explosive sound rang across the canyon and I saw the strangest sight—my bowl spinning in the air, water drops sparkling in the sun. The next thing I knew, Bernie had dived off the bench and grabbed me. We rolled together in the dust, bumped on something hard—at that moment I heard another crack-zing—and ended up behind a boulder. At the same time came one more crack-zing, this one followed right away by a ping, and a chunk of boulder right above my head got turned into a tiny powder cloud.

Then it got real quiet, Bernie and I huddled behind the boulder. Time passed. The big black bird, or another one, returned to the sky, circled around. Bernie rose to his knees, pulled himself up, very slowly, took a peek over the boulder. I took a peek, too.

"Chet! Down!"

But I wanted to see. Across the canyon, not far from where a group of houses crept down the hillside, I caught a glimpse of a far-off bicycle, or maybe a motorcycle; and then it was gone. The big black bird swooped down over us—close enough so I could hear the beating of its wings—and flew away.

FOUR

Back home, Bernie took the rifle out of the safe. I tried not to jump up and down. Loved the rifle, hadn't seen it in ages. We went out, got in the Porsche, Bernie sliding the rifle behind the seats. "Had a drill instructor once," Bernie said. "Know what he told me?" No clue. First mention of a drill instructor, as far as I could remember; didn't even know what one was. We had a drill in the tool kit, of course, but had anyone ever come over to show Bernie how to use it? Might be a good idea. "He said, 'Don't bring a spoon to a knife fight.'" Hmmm. I thought about that the whole ride, once or twice got the feeling I was real close to figuring it out.

We drove toward the sun, through a few neighborhoods a lot like our own, then past a baseball field with a kids' game going on. I didn't understand baseball, but it always looked like fun, and the ball itself I loved. Who'd have guessed what the insides were like? At that very moment a kid swung his bat and the ball went soaring into the sky. We weren't going very fast. Would it be totally impossible to—

"Che—et?" Bernie had this way of sometimes saying my name real slow. The ball hit the grass and bounced toward the outfield fence in lovely long hops that made me want to—"Che—et?" We drove on.

And soon turned down a side street lined with faded little houses and the occasional low, dusty tree. All at once, I felt thirsty. The street dead-ended at a wooden fence. Bernie parked. We hopped out. There wasn't a soul in sight, a common human expression that actually just means not another human in sight. Bernie reached back in the car for the rifle. We walked around the fence.

On the other side lay the canyon, spreading into the distance. We followed a path that led in long switchbacks down the slope. I smelled exhaust right away, and not long after that, Bernie knelt in the dirt. "Motorcycle," he said. "Been and gone." He rose and we kept going. The path took us down to the canyon floor, then rose again, cutting up the side of a reddish hill. At the top stood a spiky round bush. "More tire tracks," Bernie said. I could see them myself; also picked up a smell I knew from cases we'd worked, me and Bernie, and before that from my days in K-9 school: pot. I trotted around a bit, sniffing here and there. Meanwhile, Bernie was gazing off in the distance, away from the sun. He grunted. Bernie has all these different grunts. This one meant he'd just understood something, something he didn't like. He raised the rifle, put one eye to the sight, closed the other. I went still, waited for the bang. But there was no bang. Instead Bernie went on looking through the sight, then said, "Yup, the bench, clear as day."

The bench?

Bernie lowered the rifle. "Funny, huh?" he said. Whatever the joke was, I didn't get it, and Bernie didn't look amused either.

"Time and space," he said. "We're in the exact same space as the shooter, just not at the same time, that's all. But—" He turned, came over, gave me a pat. "But aren't they curved, time and space? Isn't that what Einstein tells us? Therefore, the lines are blurred, and by extension, the shooter is still here, at least partly."

Did this make sense to me, any at all? Well, does it to you? Honestly, now. I opened my mouth real wide, stretched out my jaw, cleared my head, making it feel all nice and empty; and at that moment caught the pot smell again, stronger than before. I turned, followed the scent. It led me partway around the spiky bush and then under. I ducked down, felt a spiky jab or two and then: the butt end of a joint, on the ground in plain view.

I barked.

"On the other hand," Bernie said, "what about quantum mechanics?"

I barked again.

"And suppose string theory—" Bernie began.

I barked once more, sharply this time.

"Chet? Got something?"

Bernie came forward, crouched down, bent a spiky branch out of the way. "Ow," he said. "Christ." But then: "Hey. Good man." He took a surgical glove from his pocket, put it on, picked up the joint. "Still warm," he said. His face darkened. "Possible fire threat, in fact. I—" He cut himself off, peered under the bush. "What's this?" He reached in deeper, pulled something out, held it glittering on the palm of his hand: a shell cartridge.

"Thirty-ought-six," said Bernie. He laid the butt of the joint beside it. I knew what those were, baby: clues, two of them. "See?" Bernie said. "Einstein was right. He's still partly here."

Whoa. Meaning the shooter was some guy named Einstein? We headed back toward the car. How could Bernie have figured that out already? No way was Einstein the only pothead shooter in the Valley—we had them out the yingyang.

"Imagine the kind of detective he'd have been," said Bernie. "Einstein, I'm talking about." That just confused me more. We had competition—there was Len Watters in Pedroia, for example, and the Mirabelli Brothers in Sunshine City, but Einstein, PI, was new to me. Hey, bring the dude on—we weren't afraid of competition, me and Bernie. Except for finances, we were doing great.

Back in the office, Bernie sat at the computer and started tapping away. From time to time he muttered a few words, like "smokes pot," or "handy with a thirty-ought-six," or "ax to grind." I lay down on the rug. Ax to grind? I knew axes, remembered a real fun camping trip where Bernie showed Charlie how to take down a tree. Talk about excitement! Tim-ber! And a lucky thing no one was in the tent at the time. But where did axes fit in now? Joint, cartridge: that was it, right? Still, I trusted Bernie.

My eyelids got heavy. That happens once or twice a day, maybe more, a delicious feeling, hard to describe, that means a nap is on the way. Napping is a lot like sleeping. There's a difference, but what? Let's just say I'm a big fan of both, and leave it at that.

Tap tap tap. Pretty soon I was caught up in a dream that was all about camping. Right from the get-go I was chasing a squirrel, and then in that funny way dreams have, the squirrel turned into the fat javelina from the canyon. I chased that, too, and lots of other things, some of them animals I'd only seen on the Discovery Channel, like iguanas and water buffaloes. How weird was that? Funny how the mind—

"Chet? Up and at 'em, big guy."

Up and at 'em? Took me a moment or two to understand, what with iguanas and water buffaloes still on the loose, but then

I was on my feet, giving myself a good shake, the coat-rippling kind that starts at the front and ends with my tail going thrum thrum.

Bernie laughed. "Wish I could do that," he said.

Poor Bernie. No tail, for starters. I couldn't even imagine what that was like. You'd be off-balance every waking moment!

We got in the Porsche. No rifle this time, but before turning the key, Bernie opened the glove box and checked the .38 Special. "Way I see it," he said, "gotta be someone who wants payback, someone we put away." Fine, if Bernie said so, although I didn't quite get what he was aiming at. We backed out of the driveway, headed down Mesquite Road. "Remember Victor Prole?" Bernie said. Nope, but there was Iggy, yip-yipping at the window. I barked back. "Good boy," said Bernie.

"Hard to forget a creep like that. Dope dealer, Harley lover, gun nut—and he got out of Central State two weeks ago." Still didn't ring a bell. I barked again, couldn't think of anything else to do. Bernie gave my head a quick rub. Ah. Very nice. I moved a little closer.

We went on a long drive, all the way to the big downtown towers and beyond. The sky lost its blueness, turned no particular color at all, just a dull haze, swallowing up the tops of the towers, giving me a bad feeling, hard to explain. I almost wished that Bernie would put the top up; no longer possible anyway—something about a blown condenser.

"It's all one system," Bernie said. "Air, water, us. Why is everyone so clueless?"

I had no clue what Bernie was talking about, so I guess I was clueless, too. I squeezed over still closer to him, felt better.

Soon the towers were behind us and we were in a bad neighborhood with broken windows and people standing around doing nothing. Some of them turned to watch us go by. I kept my head up and my eyes straight ahead. We were on the job, me and Bernie, although what job, I wasn't sure. And, by the way, who was paying?

Bernie turned into a narrow street full of potholes and parked by a little square house with stained yellow walls and black grates on the windows. He took the .38 Special from the glove box and tucked it in his belt. I had my teeth with me at all times. Kind of a funny thought. I tried to think why, but couldn't, and by the time we got out of the car and were walking across the yard, all brown and weedy, I'd forgotten the whole thing, whatever it was.

Bernie knocked on the door. No answer. He glanced around. I'd already done that, spotting nobody. Bernie knocked again. Ratta-tat-tat. Hey! That reminded me of Adelina Borghese and the Princess job. Where were we with that, again? What had Bernie—

A voice came from inside the house. "Yeah?" A man's voice, rough, unfriendly, maybe even a bit familiar. I got a strange feeling in my teeth, like they wanted to press on something.

"Yo," said Bernie.

"Huh?" said the man behind the door.

Sometimes I have trouble understanding human speech, even get a bit frustrated; other times, I wonder what all the fuss is about. *Yeah, yo, huh:* this was one of those other times.

"That you, Victor?" Bernie said.

"Nope."

"Victor Prole?"

"No way."

"Sure sounds like the Victor Prole I knew," Bernie said. "With the prognathous jaw."

One thing about Bernie: he could lose me just like that. I

stood there, staring straight ahead, doing absolutely nothing. We were partners and that was that. Anything he wanted to try, no matter how hare-brained—and boy, in my experience is that one bang-on expression—was all right by—

The door opened and there stood a man, very big. He had a nice jaw, in my opinion, sticking far out as jaws should, a rare trait in humans. The rest of his face was nothing special—tiny eyes, flat nose, stubbly beard. I caught a whiff of him and remembered. Yes, I knew Victor Prole: a real bad guy we'd collared for something or other, but not before he sucker-punched Bernie in a downtown elevator. Don't like elevators myself—in fact, almost always avoid them—but I'd been in that elevator and good thing, too.

Those tiny eyes shifted from Bernie to me and back to Bernie. "You," he said.

"Do I look better in person?" Bernie said. "Or through your scope?"

"Scope?" said Victor Prole.

"On your thirty-ought-six," Bernie said.

Victor Prole screwed up his face, squeezed his eyes shut for a long moment: not a pretty sight. "Not makin' sense," he said, and started to close the door.

That trick never worked on Bernie. His foot shot out, kept the door from closing. One thing I've noticed about perps, gang-bangers, bad guys: it doesn't take much to set them off. In this case, that little foot move of Bernie's was enough. Victor Prole's face swelled up, his lips curling in a nasty way, but what I noticed most was one of his arms, reaching for something behind the door, out of sight. Then came a silvery flash, and Victor was swinging a heavy wrench at Bernie's head. I knew wrenches from the time Bernie had decided to install a new toilet, the kind that used less water, although an awful lot of water got used that day.

I sprang, aiming right at Victor's wrist, but when my teeth clamped down, the wrist wasn't there. Somehow Victor was already on the floor, Bernie on top of him. Things were happening fast. I loved that! I piled right on and we all rolled around until Victor cried out, "Stop, for fuck sake!" Bernie had Victor's arm twisted up behind his back in a way that always ended things.

"Where's the rifle?" Bernie said.

"Huh?"

"The one you used to take potshots at us out in the canyon."

"Potshots? Didn't take no potshots. Don't own no rifle, no weapon of any kind."

"That's not like you," said Bernie.

"You're breaking my arm," said Victor.

"Sorry," Bernie said. "Getting shot at undermines my composure."

Down on the floor, Victor looked confused. Meanwhile, I smelled pot. I followed the scent—it's easy, kind of like following a bubbling little stream—to a sofa near a TV. And under the sofa—a bit of a struggle to get in deep enough with my paw—a brick of pot, tightly wrapped in plastic. I carried it back to the front door, where Victor was saying, "Wasn't even in no canyon this morning. I had an appointment with my PO, downtown." Bernie's grip on Victor's arm relaxed a bit. "I swear," said Victor. "I'm going straight this time. I even started yoga." For some reason at that moment, they both looked at me. I dropped the brick beside them and wagged my tail.

Bernie called Victor's parole officer. Victor alibied out. We didn't bust him for the pot, or even seize it; all we took was the wrench, no idea why. Did it have something to do with not bringing a spoon to a knife fight? That was as close as I got.

Back in the car, Bernie was quiet. I could feel him thinking. His thoughts were like breezes, rising up and dying around us, very relaxing. After a while, he took a deep breath and said, "Have to look into this later." He checked his watch. I didn't like Bernie's watch, didn't like how humans were always attaching themselves to bits of machinery. I got a crazy urge to give the watch a little nip, was even starting to lean that way—although I'm sure I'd never ever actually do such a thing—when Bernie glanced at me and said, "Princess touches down in twenty minutes."

I sat up straight.

FIVE

When the rich get too rich," Bernie said, "is when the problems start." Problems? I suppose we had some, but I couldn't think of them at the moment. We were somewhere I'd never been—and that was always fun—an airstrip out in the desert, with lots of small planes on the ground, sparkling in the sun.

"Any idea what it costs to run one of those babies, never mind pony up in the first place?" Bernie said.

Ponies: don't get me started. I had a nice stretch, the walking kind, gave myself a shake, circled around a bit, and lay down on the shady side of the car. A little snack of some sort would have been nice, otherwise no complaints. I heard a distant buzz, very faint, that seemed to come from beyond some mountains, brown and bare.

"The ancien regime all over again," Bernie said, "minus the powdered wigs."

I glanced over at him, leaning against the car. When Bernie worried, he got lines on his face that weren't normally there. He had them now. What was he worried about? All I understood from that last remark was powder. There was gunpowder, of course, so . . . hey! I got it! Bernie was worried about how we got shot at. Was I cooking or what? All of a sudden my mind was running at top speed. Victor Prole alibied out, even though he looked and smelled right for the shooter role. So our next move had to be all about IDing the shooter. I was in the picture, understood the whole enchilada just like Bernie. And why not? We were partners, after all, although the only enchilada I'd ever tried—snapped up at a dead run in an alley while chasing a gangbanger weighed down by heavy gold chains—ended up disagreeing with me.

The distant buzzing got louder. I glanced up, saw a plane high over the mountaintops, shining like the sun—a very pretty sight. After a while Bernie said, "I think I hear something." He peered into the sky, spotted the plane, and said, "There it is." I took a close look at Bernie's ears. Not too tiny, in fact a reasonable size for human ears, so why didn't they work?

The plane flew in a big circle, landed with a bounce, and rolled in our direction. At the same time, a long black limo appeared on a dirt road that came out of some nearby low hills. It sped down, leaving a golden trail of swirling dust. Things were so beautiful sometimes I just wanted to gaze and gaze.

But this wasn't the right moment. We were on the job. I stood straight, head up, tail up, alert. The limo parked beside us. The driver got out: Adelina's driver, wearing black and, now I noticed, a diamond in one ear. He opened the furthest back door for Adelina. I almost didn't recognize her at first. She was dressed like a cowgirl, with a big white hat, fringed shirt, cowboy boots. I checked Bernie. Uh-oh. Mouth open. Only women—some women—could make that happen to Bernie. But he got it closed pretty quick, and we walked over to Adelina.

"You're on time," she said.

Bernie nodded. He had many different nods. This was one of the cold kind. I got it. We were always on time; we were pros, me and Bernie. "Any news?" he said.

"Like what?" she said.

"More threats. Anything we should know."

"Isn't one threat enough?"

"Wouldn't be here otherwise," Bernie said. "But this job is all about information. The worst thing the client can do is withhold."

"I'm not withholding anything."

Bernie nodded. I was pretty sure this nod, a slow one, meant he didn't believe her, but I couldn't be certain and there was no time to think about it. The plane came to a stop not far away. I barked. Didn't like planes, not one bit, hard to explain why because I'd never been in one.

Adelina's green eyes were on me. "Why is he barking?"

Bernie smiled. He has a great smile—did I mention that? Smiling is about as close as humans can get to a tail wag. "Hard to say," he said.

"Are you sure he's safe?" Adelina said. "He's so . . . so boisterous, and Princess is delicate."

Boisterous? A new one on me. Like a boy, maybe, Charlie, for example? Hey, not bad. Must mean Adelina liked me after all. That made me bark some more, maybe a bit too loud, because Adelina seemed to flinch. She started to say something, but at that moment the door of the plane opened and a staircase emerged and lowered itself down to the tarmac. Kind of weird. It made we want to dig a hole, so I got started in the dirt at the edge of the runway.

"Che—et?"

I looked up, one of my front paws poised high. Bernie gave me a quick little head shake. That was one of our silent signals. It meant no. I could always dig another hole later, even a bunch of them. All of a sudden I was in a digging mood.

"Che—et?"

Bernie gave me a finger wiggle. That meant come. I went over, stood beside him, a real team player, but at the same time wondering about the possibility of digging under the fence that separated our place from old man Heydrich's. Why hadn't I thought of that before?

A big woman with short dark hair, except for strange gray side wings, appeared in the doorway of the plane. She had the fluffball in her arms.

"Princess," called Adelina, waving her cowboy hat. She ran toward the plane. Bernie and I followed. The big woman came down the staircase. Princess, even smaller than I'd thought from the photo, had her nose in the air and eyes half shut, not looking at any of us. Right from the get-go I wanted to give her a quick little nip. We were off to a bad start.

"Oh, Princess," said Adelina, taking her the moment the big woman's foot touched the ground, "I missed you so so much." She kissed Princess's face a number of times. Did Princess actually turn away her tiny head? Maybe. And if a tail was wagging somewhere under all that fluff, I couldn't see it.

"This," said Adelina, turning to Bernie, "is Princess."

"Um," said Bernie.

"Say hi to the nice detective, Princess."

Princess was back to gazing at the sky.

"And this is Nance, our trainer," Adelina said.

"Bernie Little," said Bernie, shaking hands with Nance. The hands of most women got lost in Bernie's, but not this one's.

Nance had a deeply tanned face, also wore bright blue eye makeup, the combination having a strange effect on me, like I'd want to lick that makeup right off, something I'd never do, of course. She gave Bernie a long look and said, "Do you really think Princess is in danger?"

"No," said Bernie.

No? Just like that, no? What if we get fired? Bernie: two grand a day!

"Then—" said Nance.

"But every once in a while, a threat like this turns out to be real."

"Exactly," said Adelina. She turned to Nance, those green eyes narrowing. "I thought we'd been through this."

Nance looked down. Humans often had complicated relationships with each other. In our nation—the nation within the nation, as Bernie calls it—we can get pretty complicated, too, but we have ways of sorting things out much quicker. I was used to these awkward human moments, almost always found them interesting, even entertaining. I opened my mouth, unrolled my tongue, rolled it back in.

Adelina turned her attention to Princess. You'd be surprised how often humans use one of my guys to end their awkward moments, if Princess could be called one of my guys. "Does little Princess need some time to herself?" Adelina had two voices—a baby voice for Princess and the icicle voice for the rest of the world. I preferred the icicle voice. Now came more kisses. "Poor Princess, cooped up on the nasty plane."

Cooped up? Princess would have had plenty of room in a mailbox. I glanced at Bernie: his face was blank.

"Nance?" said Adelina. "Is it safe?"

Nance bent down, patted the tarmac with her hand. "Yes."

"Not too hot?" Adelina said. "Remember Barcelona?"

"It's just right," Nance said, her voice sharpening.

Adelina gave her a look, also sharp, and gently lowered Princess to the runway. Hey: she had legs. Princess extended them in a way that reminded me of that staircase coming down from the plane, a thought I thought would lead to another, but did not. Whew. Slow it down, big guy.

I slowed it down, kept my eye on Princess. Her paws, so small, touched the tarmac. She stood still, her eyes, huge and dark, on nothing in particular. What would I do in her place, at a time like this? Give myself a shake, no doubt about it. Come to think of it, why not now, even in my place? No reason I could see. I gave myself a restrained kind of shake, grew aware that those huge dark eyes seemed to be fixed on me. And guess what. The very next moment, Princess gave herself a shake. If you could call it that: the movement was so tiny, really just a slight trembling, as though a breeze had ruffled her fur, that I almost missed it.

"Have you ever seen her do that before?" Adelina said.

"Never," said Nance.

"Do you think there's something wrong with her?" Adelina said. "Oh my God—is she sick?"

"Looks okay to me," said Bernie.

The huge dark eyes shifted over to Bernie. For the first time that I'd seen, Princess began to move under her own power. Hard to describe it, exactly. Her little legs were going quite fast, a quick trot, you might call it, or even running, but she was hardly getting anywhere. She reached the edge of the tarmac—

"Not on the ground, Princess," said Adelina. "It's dirty."

—and kept on, around a dusty thick-leaved plant—where I'd have lifted my leg, for sure, and almost to the Porsche. Princess gazed at it, then trotted back, her legs almost a blur. And her eyes: was that an anxious look I saw? I was almost feeling sorry for her—how crazy was that?—when she regained the tarmac and stopped near Bernie. Then, eyes right on him but expressionless now, at least as far as I could tell—she squatted.

"Good girl," Adelina said.

A yellowish pool began to spread across the tarmac. It got bigger and bigger, shockingly so. The smell was—I'll admit it—fascinating. But that wasn't the important part. The important part was the fact of the yellowish pool expanding quickly, the lead edge closing in on Bernie's shoes, black leather lace-ups with an interesting smell of their own, speaking of smells. We'll save that for later. The point now was that growing lake on the tarmac and the way Princess kept her eyes on Bernie the whole time.

"A long flight," Bernie said, stepping away.

Princess did something I'd never seen before. Still squatting, with no interruption of flow, she shifted, kind of like a crab, in his direction.

"I think she likes you," Adelina said.

"Definitely," said Nance.

"Well, um," said Bernie, taking another step, raising one heel, and peering down at it: yes, damp.

At last Princess went dry. She straightened and stood still. For some reason, the tiny pink tip of her tiny tongue was sticking out, just barely.

"How about a treat for our little star?" said Adelina. "Any bacon bits?"

"I'm a little concerned about her weight," Nance said, "so close to showtime and all."

Her weight? There were dust balls under Bernie's bed that weighed more than Princess.

"Just one won't hurt," Adelina said. "She's had a hard day."

Nance reached into her pocket, took out a bacon bit of a kind I'd never seen before, nice and thick. She approached Princess, hand out, smiling; Nance had very white teeth, big and even. Princess stayed still, putting in no more effort than letting her mouth fall slightly open as the bacon bit drew near. As for what got into me, how to explain? The facts are that suddenly I was airborne, in full flight, ears flat back; airborne and snagging that bacon bit right out of Nance's hand at the exact moment of transfer, possibly knocking Princess over, but totally by accident. The whole thing was an accident, really. As for the bacon bit: delish. I tore across the runway, downed the bacon bit, skidded to a stop beside the plane's big wheels and lifted my leg. No idea why and I didn't absolutely need to go: but it felt good. And doesn't everybody like feeling good? Or am I missing something?

SIX

There have been times in my life when I've felt pretty bad. Take when a mobster named Gulagov had me locked in a cage; or the day Leda packed up Charlie's things and took him away, except for some weekends and holidays; or way back when I was a puppy in this apartment run by a drug dealer who liked to give me a kick when things weren't going well. But had I ever felt worse than I did on that runway, moments after that little bacon bit episode? I was out there by the plane, my leg still raised, when I heard Adelina say, "You're fired."

We drove away from the airstrip. I rode shotgun as always, but not sitting straight like normal, instead lying on the seat, curled up, my head against the door. An awkward kind of position, with my silver tags digging into my neck a bit, but I let them. We were off the case, and all on account of me. After a while Bernie reached over and adjusted the tags. Then he popped a CD into the player and soon we had Billie Holiday. Bernie loved Billie Holiday. He pressed a button until "If You Were Mine" came on. "If You Were Mine" was Bernie's current favorite. He sang along—Bernie has a very nice singing voice, have I mentioned that?—and cranked up the volume for the trumpet part at the end.

"Don't you just love that trumpet?" he said.

I did. I loved the trumpet. The sound of the trumpet did things to me.

"Roy Eldridge," Bernie said. "They called him Little Jazz, no idea why. Except, hmmm—hey! In contrast to Louis Armstrong, maybe, Satchmo being Big Jazz? Think that's it?"

I had no idea what Bernie was saying, and besides: two grand a day! We needed it. With our finances a big mess, how could we be thinking about anything else except that two grand? Two grand a day, and all those days on the case, not sure how many. But Bernie didn't seem to be thinking about the money. After "If You Were Mine" played for the umpteenth time—which is a lot—I felt Bernie glance over at me; couldn't see him with how I was curled up, my gaze on the inside of the door but actually seeing nothing. All of a sudden he started laughing, just laughing and laughing. Don't think I'd ever heard him laugh like that. It went on and on, left him wheezing and gasping, and still wheezing and gasping, he reached over and patted my back. It felt good. "They broke the mold," he said, and then more "ha ha ha."

Broke the mold. That was new. I knew mold, of course, from back in the Leda days. She'd been terrified of mold and had hired this guy to inspect the house, even though Bernie told her there was no mold out here in the desert. And the inspector didn't find any, just gave Bernie a little grin, along with the bill. So breaking the mold had to mean when you didn't find any, and Bernie was thinking back to that day and now finding something funny about it. I didn't get the joke, but I sat up and moved closer to him. He scratched between my ears, the way I liked. My tail wagged, the slightest bit, all by itself. Not right, I know—I'd messed up big-time, been bad, not a team player, not a pro, and worst of all I'd let Bernie down—but I couldn't help it.

"Good boy," Bernie said.

When we got home, the phone message light was blinking. Humans had a way of inventing all these things—phone message lights, alarm clocks, bills—that disturbed their peace of mind. Bernie went right over and pressed a button. Our phone has a voice of its own that sounds like the voice of a robot in a DVD Bernie and I once saw. Don't ask me to explain what the DVD was about, but at the end Bernie'd said, "Get it? The robot is the master." Whoa. The robot was the master? I'd gotten scared, but too late, the movie being over.

But forget all that. Bernie pressed the button and our phone voice said, "Two new messages."

Then: "Hey, Bern, my man." I knew that friendly-on-the-outside voice: the guy in the Hawaiian shirt from Dry Gulch. "Chuck Eckel here. How ya doin'? Slight development on the tin futures front—give me a call when you get this. Like ASAP."

And then: "Hi, Bernie." Another voice I recognized, this one friendly not just on the outside but through and through: Janie, my groomer, the best groomer in the whole Valley. She had a great business with a great business plan: Janie's Pet Grooming Service—We Pick Up and Deliver. Hadn't seen her in a while, now that I thought about it. "It's Janie. Just wondering what you heard from the vet."

"Huh?" said Bernie. He picked up the phone. "Janie? Bernie Little here. Got your message. What's this about the vet? Give me a call when you get a chance." He punched in more numbers. "Chuck? Bernie Little." Bernie listened. There's this painter Bernie likes, can't remember the name, who paints the human face—made a bundle, Bernie says—in a bunch of parts that don't quite fit together. Bernie's face started getting more and more that way as he listened on the phone. "An earthquake? I don't . . . in Bolivia? But how does that . . . ? Three grand? But . . ." More listening, more coming apart of Bernie's face, the nicest face around, in my opinion. "What does that mean, cover the position?" I could hear the voice on the other end, the friendly coating thinning out. "You never—" And thinning out some more. "Lose the whole investment? That's not how I understood the . . . you need it by when?" Bernie hung up, but not before I heard Chuck Eckel say, "Close of business today, my man."

When Bernie's upset, even feeling a bit overwhelmed—not that anything ever really overwhelms Bernie—he has this habit of rubbing his eyes very hard with the knuckles of both hands. He was doing it now. Despite how I know nothing ever really overwhelms Bernie, the truth is I can't stand seeing him rub his eyes that way. So I went over and bumped my head against his leg, and bumped it again when he didn't seem to notice the first time.

"Hey, boy," he said. He stopped rubbing his eyes, looked down at me. I looked up at him. Our eyes met. His face started going back together the right way. "How about a chew strip?" he said.

A chew strip? Had I done anything to earn a chew strip? My mind flashed back to that scene on the runway. I knew the answer to the chew strip question was no. I probably didn't deserve another chew strip for a long, long while, like a day or two. At the same time, I felt this sudden breeze from behind me, surprisingly strong, and realized my tail was wagging.

Bernie laughed. "Hard to turn down a chew strip, huh, boy?"

Impossible, I guess.

We went into the kitchen. Bernie opened the cupboard over the sink, took out the chew strips and the bourbon. He handed me a chew strip and I started chewing. Hard to explain how good that made my teeth feel. And the taste! Out of this world, whatever that means. Meanwhile, Bernie poured himself a glass of bourbon, a small pour, I was happy to see, until he knocked it back in one go and refilled. He carried the glass with him into the office. I followed, trying to make the chew strip last, although it was almost gone.

Bernie took down the Niagara Falls photo and spun the dial on the safe. Was the rifle coming out again? No idea why we needed it at the moment, but the rifle coming out was always a good idea to my way of thinking. Bernie reached in. Not the rifle; instead he removed a small black box. I knew that black box: inside lay Bernie's grandfather's watch, our most valuable possession, except for the Porsche. I gobbled up the last bit of chew strip. We were on our way to see Mr. Singh.

"Bernie! Chet!" said Mr. Singh. "How is our beautiful timepiece today?"

Bernie handed over his grandfather's watch. His grandfather once owned a big ranch where Mesquite Road and our whole neighborhood was now, but lost everything, possibly because of a drinking problem, although the drinking problem might have come from some other story Bernie had told me, a story about another relative. But not Bernie's father. Bernie never talked about his father, who'd been dead for a long time. Bernie's mother was still around. I'd met her once: a piece of work. She lived somewhere far away with a new husband, or an even newer one. She called Bernie Kiddo! What was up with that? But I still shouldn't have done what I did, a story perhaps for another time.

Mr. Singh held the watch in both hands, admiring it. "Do you know that only a dozen of these were made?" he said. "How I would love to take this on *Antiques Roadshow*." Mr. Singh had a strange way of talking, almost like music. I could listen to him all day. "Did you ever find out how it came into his possession?" he said.

"No," said Bernie.

"Thereby hangs a tale, I'm sure," said Mr. Singh.

A tail? Was Mr. Singh saying Bernie's grandfather's watch had a tail? Fun to listen to, Mr. Singh, but hard to understand. We left, a big wad of cash in Bernie's pocket and a bite or two of curried goat kebab in my mouth. I like ethnic food. So does Bernie. There are picky eaters out there, but not us.

We dropped by the bank, one of those places where I can't go in. No problem. I was cool about waiting in the car, most times. Bernie wasn't gone for long. He came back muttering about tin futures and earthquakes in Bolivia. "There's all this money flowing around, Chet, rivers and rivers of money. How to tap into it, that's the problem."

Rivers of money? The only rivers in the Valley didn't even have water in them. I curled up on my seat and closed my eyes. What were we working on right now? I could only think of one measly case, a divorce in Sunshine City. We hated divorce work, me and Bernie. Maybe I was wrong about those rivers of money, maybe they were real. Wouldn't that be nice? I could almost see myself diving in.

* * *

I woke up feeling tip-top. Where was I? In the car. There was a faint taste of curried goat in my mouth, not bad at all. Everything, or parts of everything, came back to me—the watch, Mr. Singh, nothing on deck but divorce work. I checked Bernie: hands on the wheel, face not happy. I sat up, shifted closer to him.

"Nice nap?" he said.

Very. I opened my mouth real wide, stretching my lips tight, clearing my head. We were on Mesquite Road, not far from home. And there was Iggy in his window. Always good to see Iggy. I heard his faint yip-yip-yip from behind the glass and barked back. He stood up on his back legs, front paws pressing against the window, and watched us go by. We turned into our driveway, and at almost the same time another car drove up, one of those Beetles. I'm no expert on cars—can always spot a Porsche, of course—but Beetles are easy, and this particular Beetle I knew very well. It was yellow, for one thing, and I'd ridden in it a bunch of times: Suzie Sanchez's car. A great car. There was always a box of biscuits in the glove compartment.

We got out of the Porsche. Suzie was walking toward us. She smelled like soap and lemons, had shiny black eyes that reminded me of the countertops in our kitchen. I liked Suzie a whole lot. She and Bernie exchanged a glance, complicated and awkward. Complicated: that was the problem. In our nation, the nation within the nation, we keep these things simple. Take a recent evening, for example, when I'd heard some persistent she-barking from across the canyon and—

"Hi, Bernie," she said. "Hey, Chet—looking good." She reached in her bag. "Can he have a biscuit?"

"He just ate," said Bernie. Huh? What was he talking about? Surely not the goat kebab, hardly more than a nibble, and quite some time ago, in my opinion. Suzie's hand emerged from the bag, empty. Human tension is an interesting thing. You can smell it; well, maybe not you, but I can. The smell was out there now, and it got ratcheted up much stronger when Bernie said, "How's Dylan?"

Yikes. Dylan McKnight was Suzie's ex-boyfriend, but maybe not completely out of the picture, something about a trip the two of them had taken to LA. I didn't know Dylan McKnight well, had only met him once, and we hadn't hit it off—a real pretty boy, and also a former jailbird. The day we met he'd ended up in a tree, the exact details not too clear in my mind, except for the sirloin tips Bernie gave me later.

Suzie's voice, usually warm and friendly, changed fast to something much colder. "I wouldn't know," she said.

"No?" said Bernie. "Is he still in LA?"

"I don't believe so."

"He's back in the Valley?"

Suzie took a deep breath. "Bernie?" she said.

Bernie got this stubborn look on his face. "Yeah?"

"Do we have to talk about him?"

"I don't know," said Bernie. "What do you want to talk about?"

"Actually," said Suzie, "I'm working on a story and your name came up."

Bernie stopped looking so stubborn. "What story?"

"About this woman." Suzie flipped open a notebook. "Adelina Borghese."

"What about her?"

"Seems she was abducted."

"Abducted?" Bernie flinched, almost as though someone had hit him. I'd never seen him do that before. "We just saw her this morning."

Suzie went back to the notebook. "Happened shortly after noon," she said. "Apparently she owns some sort of prize dog."

"Princess," Bernie said.

Suzie turned a page and nodded. "Yes, Princess," she said. "The dog is missing, too."

SEVEN

All this stuff was going by too fast. Princess was missing? And abduction: was that what we called a snatch in our trade, a kidnapping? I got too hot, started panting.

"Where are you getting your information?" Bernie said.

"A tip," Suzie answered.

"Who from?"

Suzie's face hardened and thickened a bit, reminding me very strongly of Bernie in one of his stubborn moods. "I don't reveal my sources."

Bernie's voice rose. That didn't happen unless he was really upset, and not even usually then. "I don't want to know your goddamn sources," he said. "I want to know if your information is accurate."

Most people backed down right away when Bernie got mad. The truth is Bernie could be—I don't want to say dangerous, not about Bernie, because he's the best—so let's say he could be real tough, but only on perps, and Suzie was no perp. Big surprise: she didn't back down at all. In fact, her chin came up in an aggressive sort of way. "My information is accurate."

They glared at each other. I didn't like the way things were going, not one little bit. I barked. They both looked at me. I was about to bark some more when the phone in the house started ringing. Bernie hurried inside.

I trotted after him. An angry voice was coming through the answering machine. "What the hell's going on?" I recognized the voice: Lieutenant Stine. "I thought you were working for these people. Snatched in broad daylight? Pick up, for Christ sake."

Bernie went to the phone. I could tell just from the way he moved, like he was walking through deep water, that he didn't want to pick up. Then, as I'd seen more than once before, his back got real straight, like somehow he was making himself stronger inside, and he reached for the phone. Bernie—and possibly this is a small difference between us—could force himself to do things he didn't want to do. But if you don't mind my asking, why bother?

"Yeah?" he said.

Lieutenant Stine's voice came over the answering machine. "What the hell happened?"

"You tell me," Bernie said.

"Some guys blocked her limo on the old Rio Loco Road, pistol-whipped the driver, snatched the Borghese woman. And the goddamn dog. But my question is why weren't you there?"

"She didn't hire us," Bernie said.

"Huh?" said the lieutenant. "She told me she had. It's not adding up, Bernie—you're not trying to put one—" Bernie pressed a button and Lieutenant Stine's voice shrank to a tinny version of itself coming through the earpiece of the phone.

Bernie said, "I'm not trying anything. She fired us so fast it was almost like never getting hired in the first place." Lieutenant Stine said something I couldn't make out, and Bernie replied,

"Couldn't tell you why. That's her right. But where are you on this? Was the trainer in the limo, too? What—"

I heard a loud click on the other end. Bernie put the phone down, glanced at me, then at Suzie. She was busy writing in her notebook.

"Suzie?" he said, very quietly. "What are you writing?"

Suzie looked up. The pen kept moving even without her watching what she was doing. Sometimes humans amaze me. "I'm writing—question for Bernie: why fired?"

Bernie gave her a cold look. Hey! What was going on between them? And the getting fired part: that was all on me, not Bernie. I barked. Suzie closed her notebook, came toward me, stroked my head. "Good boy," she said. The truth was I'd been bad, not good, but I guess the point wasn't getting across to Suzie. What could I do? And besides, the stroking felt so nice. I just emptied my mind and enjoyed every second.

"We had a personality conflict," Bernie said.

Suzie stopped stroking me. "You and Ms. Borghese?" she said.

"Correct."

"What were the circumstances?"

"I'm not going into that," Bernie said. "And all this is off the record."

"All what?"

"What I'm telling you."

"You haven't told me anything, Bernie. Maybe you don't realize how big this is. The Great Western Dog Show's the mayor's baby. He's beside himself right now. And you're part of the story whether you like it or not."

"Do I hear a threat?" Bernie said.

A threat? I'd missed that completely. And Suzie was our friend, right? She'd never threaten us. Maybe Bernie was tired. All at once, I was a bit tired, too. I lay down under the hall table. A roof over your head is always nice. I realized that the house had a roof, of course, so in fact I had two roofs over my head, even better. And what about the ceiling? Under the roof, right, but still a kind of roof, too? I got a bit confused.

"No threat," said Suzie. "Just a heads up, that's all. The mayor's pissed off at the chief, and the chief's pissed off at Stine, and they're all going to be looking for a fall guy, so maybe if you got out in front, made some comment that put things in a better light—"

"Meaning blame someone else?" Bernie said.

"Not necessarily," said Suzie. "Just an explanation of why you were off the case."

Bernie glanced over at me, lying under the table, one eye open. I gave my tail a thump, not very hard; sleep was on the way.

"I've got no comment," Bernie said.

They exchanged a look I didn't like seeing between them, cold on both sides. Suzie put her notebook away, took a few steps toward the door, then paused. "How's Charlie?" she said, her voice softening.

Bernie took a breath, let it out slowly. I could feel big human emotions in the air, hers and his. "Fine," Bernie said. "He's fine."

"Good," said Suzie.

Bernie nodded. Suzie's mouth opened as though she was going to say more, but she did not. Instead she moved toward the door. The eyelid over my one open eye got very heavy.

When I woke up, I heard Bernie's voice coming from somewhere in the house. I couldn't make out the words, but it was pleasant just lying there, listening to Bernie talk. After a bit, I got out from under the hall table, gave myself a stretch, the kind with my front legs way forward, my head down low, my butt up high—can't begin to tell you how good that feels—and followed the sound of Bernie's voice along the hall and into the office. He was on the phone, standing by the whiteboard and scribbling on it with a pen that had an interesting smell, although it wouldn't really turn out to be edible, as I knew from experience. I sat on the rug beside Bernie, breathed in the pen smell. The whiteboard was covered in writing, arrows, drawings, almost every blank space filled. We believed in hard work at the Little Detective Agency.

"I understand," Bernie said. "But I'd still appreciate it." He listened for a moment, then said, "Thanks, I know the spot." He hung up and saw me. "Got work to do, boy." I beat him to the door.

And once outside I beat him to the car as well, leaping into the shotgun seat. One time Bernie tried doing the same trick. That was a funny day. He turned the key, shifted the shift—I love watching the shifting—and we were off.

The Valley goes on and on in all directions—have I mentioned that? We got on a freeway, then another, traffic stop-and-go at first, which made Bernie's hands tense up on the wheel, but then it eased and we barreled along, the Porsche making a rumbling roar I loved and sights and smells zipping by so fast it would make your head spin. Mine doesn't spin, exactly, but I can turn it pretty far back if I want, like really, really far, so that my nose is actually touching my—

"Chet! What the hell are you doing?"

I whipped my head around straight, sat up tall and still, eyes front, a professional through and through.

We followed the freeway up through a mountain pass, past the last developments and strip malls—the air so cool and clean it made my nostrils twitch—and down the other side, into the desert. Soon we were on two-lane blacktop, pretty much all by ourselves. "What if we just kept going?" Bernie said. "Kept going and never stopped." I knew the answer to that one from experience: we'd run out of gas. I glanced over at Bernie. He was patting his pockets, searching for cigarettes. Eventually he found a bent one under his seat and lit up. Bernie took a deep drag, held the smoke in for a long time, then let it out and said, "Christ." I loved the smell of smoke but didn't like to see Bernie so worried. What was he worried about? I had no idea. All I knew was that when he worried, so did I. I scratched at the seat a bit with one of my paws and felt better.

After a while, the airstrip appeared in the distance, a few small planes gleaming in the sun and a big red flag—although Bernie says I'm no good with colors so don't take my word for it—fluttering in the breeze. Soon we turned off the two-lane blacktop onto a dirt road that twisted back and forth up a hillside. Looking back I could see dust clouds swirling behind us, and a faint memory came to me, a memory of Adelina's limo coming down, most likely this very same road. I knew what this was: tracking. We were good trackers, me and Bernie—he often said we could have done well as trackers in the old West, whatever that was.

The dirt road took us to the top of the hill, then rounded a huge rocky outcrop on the other side. A motorcycle was parked at the base of the outcrop, on a narrow shelf between the side of the road and a steep drop-off. Bernie slowed down and parked behind the motorcycle. Loved motorcycles, myself, had ridden with some bikers once, but that's another story.

A woman in jeans and a T-shirt stepped from the shadows of the outcrop. She was big and strong, deeply tanned, had short dark hair with gray side wings: Nance, Princess's trainer. She gave Bernie a hard look. "You said there was no danger."

"I was wrong."

"That's pretty clear," Nance said. "I don't understand what you want, why you're here."

"We want to help."

Nance looked at me for the first time. "You had your chance and blew it."

"Tell you what," Bernie said. "Let's hold the recriminations for later."

"Later?" Nance said.

"Meaning after we get them back safe," Bernie said.

"Them?" said Nance.

"Adelina and Princess," said Bernie. "Who else is missing?"

Nance's look softened a little. "No one," she said. "It's just that not everyone would care about Princess, too."

"Um," said Bernie. Um: something Bernie said when he was feeling awkward. Sometimes, like now, he added, "Well, um." He cleared his throat, gazed over the drop-off. "What we need first is your description of what happened, starting from when you left the strip."

Nance licked her lips. I'm always on the lookout for that, not sure why. Human tongues, feeble little things for the most part, were interesting. Nance's for example, had a pointy tip. Bernie's was much rounder, more pleasing to my eye. "We left a few minutes after the . . ." She glanced at me. ". . . incident with your, uh—"

"Chet's his name."

"Incident with Chet," Nance said. I wagged my tail. Hey! I was starting to like Nance. And the faint pot smell coming off her? So what? It's everywhere, amigo. "We drove up here," she was saying. "It's the shortest route to the ranch at Rio Loco."

"You, the driver, Adelina, and Princess?" Bernie said.

Nance nodded. "Adelina was in the back, Princess on her lap. I sat facing her, so I didn't really see how it all began. We came over the rise, around the bend to right about here, and slowed down and stopped. Slowed down fast—I was pressed against the seat. I heard Rui honk the horn and I glanced toward the front and saw a car blocking the road. You know, parked sideways. By that time, Princess was barking—she hates the sound of the horn. I think Adelina said something like 'Rui, what's going on?' but before he could answer, these men were all around, waving guns. Masked men—ski masks, I think—you couldn't see their faces. They flung open the doors—it was all a blur by then—and one of them, this really big guy, just grabbed Adelina and started to yank her out. I reached for her, got hold of her ankle, I think it was, but then somebody hit me from behind and I fell on the floor, with the wind knocked out of me. Couldn't move. A man shouted something about keys. Finally, I got up on my hands and knees, kind of crawled out of the limo. The pickup was already on the valley floor." Nance pointed over the drop-off. Her hands were wide and strong; I couldn't help wondering what kind of patter she'd be.

"Pickup?" Bernie said. "You said car before."

"Did I?"

"Which was it?"

Nance's eyes, the color of her blue makeup, got an inward look. "I'm just not sure."

"Perfectly understandable," Bernie said. "And then?"

"I saw Rui—slumped over the wheel with a cut on the side of his head. I said, 'Rui, Rui.' He opened his eyes, got out, and puked all over the place."

Puke: I caught that part. Hadn't puked in a long time, myself—the last incident having to do with what turned out to be a wad of chewing tobacco over at Nixon Panero's autobody. Puking itself was pretty interesting: you felt so bad before it happened and then right away after, you were good as new!

". . . checked the ignition," Nance was saying. "The keys were gone. I called 911." She shrugged. "That's about it."

"How many attackers were there?" Bernie said.

"I've been trying and trying to remember. Everything happened so fast." Bernie was watching Nance. The look in his eyes meant he was thinking something about her, but I had no idea what. Maybe she caught the look, too. "Sorry I can't do any better," she said.

"You did fine," he said. "Better than that. How badly were you hurt?"

"Physically?"

Bernie nodded.

"Just a bruise or two."

A bruise? Humans got bruises on their skin, always an interesting sight. Once or twice Bernie had even asked to see someone's bruise, but not this time.

"Anything you can tell me about the car or pickup, whichever it was—the color, for example?"

Nance shook her head.

"Anything that would help identify the attackers?"

"They were masked, as I said."

"But you might have caught a glimpse of skin color, or heard an accent."

She shook her head again.

"Anything distinctive about their clothes?"

Nance closed her eyes. Humans often did that when they were concentrating extra hard; made no sense to me at all.

"Sorry," she said. "Sorry I can't be more help."

"There's a way you can."

"How?"

"We need a client."

"I don't understand," Nance said.

"In order for me to talk to the police, to have standing in the case, we need a client, someone to hire us."

"You're asking me to hire you?" Nance said. "After . . . after . . ." She glanced at me. "Why would I want to do that?"

"Because we're good at this kind of case," Bernie said. "Missing persons. You can check us out—it's what we do."

"Besides," said Nance, "I don't have that kind of money."

"We'll work for a nominal fee," Bernie said.

Uh-oh. I knew nominal from experience: a big word meaning nothing.

"I couldn't even do that," Nance said. "Not without approval."

"Whose?" said Bernie.

"Mr. Borghese's," Nance said.

"Can we call him?" Bernie said. "Right now? In cases like this, time is with the enemy."

Nance's eyes, glittering in the sun, went to me again. I'd been standing, but I sat down, couldn't tell you why, and looked calm, steady, highly trained; reliable through and through. "I'll take you to him," she said. "He's at the ranch."

EIGHT

I'd been to a ranch once before—a real working ranch, as Bernie said—on a family trip back in the Leda days. Bernie bought cowboy boots for everyone—Charlie, Leda, himself. No footwear for me, thanks, as I may have mentioned already. The fun we had, starting with the looks the old ranch hands gave Bernie when he came down to breakfast in his cowboy boots and his favorite Hawaiian shirt, the one with the orange flowers. But those looks all changed when the hands put on a shooting contest, Coke bottles on a fence rail, and asked Bernie, with these little smiles on their faces, if he'd like to try his luck. Blam blam—smithereens! No surprise to me, but later he turned out to be pretty good with the lasso, too. And Charlie—he'd loved the lasso. He'd tried to lasso me, just for fun, and I'd let him come close, on account of him being Charlie. But no one puts the lasso on me, for fun or not.

All I hadn't liked about the ranch were the horses. What's up with them? Totally unreliable, always twitching for no reason, but humans don't seem to get that, go on and on about how beautiful they are until I just want to trot over toward one of those weird legs, the real skinny part, and give it the tiniest . . . but I would never do that, at least not again, after what happened that time at the ranch.

Why I'm going into this is because the first thing I saw as we drove up to the Borgheses's ranch was a big white horse prancing in a corral with a white rail fence. Something about him made a bad impression on me right from the get-go. A ranch without horses—now that would be just about perf—

"Chet! Knock it off!"

Knock what off? The barking? That was me? I opened my mouth real wide, let my tongue flop out, tried to look innocent. My lip got caught on one of my teeth; it took some time to straighten all that out.

We followed Nance on her bike. Hey, she could ride, leaning into the turns, revving the engine with a vroom vroom vroom that had me sitting straight up. Nance led us through a gate with a big sign above, stretching over the whole road. " 'Rio Loco Ranch, 1846,' " Bernie said. "They say Wild Bill Hickok stayed here." Wild Bill Hickok? Sounded like a perp, although I didn't remember him; but hard to remember them all—we'd cleared so many cases, me and Bernie.

Nance parked by some cars outside the corral, and we pulled in beside her. As we hopped out, the side door of the barn behind the corral opened up, and out walked Suzie, folding up her notebook. She saw us right away and hesitated. Hesitation—a human thing, and so interesting: it makes them quiver just the littlest bit. But as for what it's all about, don't ask me.

Suzie walked slowly toward us. "Hi, Bernie," she said. "Hey, Chet." Bernie nodded. He had a lot of nods. This one was of the wait-and-see kind. Suzie looked at Nance. "Are you Nancy Malone?" she said. "Princess's trainer?"

Nance nodded, a nod a lot like Bernie's. Nance was also

Nancy Malone? Humans got so complicated with their names, no idea why. For as long as I can remember, I've been Chet, pure and simple.

"Suzie Sanchez from the *Valley Tribune,*" Suzie said. "I've left a few messages in your voicemail."

Nance licked her lips. We always watched for that, me and Bernie, me because I liked seeing those tiny tongues—did I get into that already?—Bernie for reasons of his own. "Haven't had time to check," Nance said.

"Can you spare a moment now?" Suzie said.

"Sorry," said Nance.

"When?" Suzie said.

"I'll get back to you," Nance said.

"Soon, I hope," Suzie said. "I'm sure it's in everyone's interest that we get the story right."

"Are you?" said Nance. She turned and disappeared through the same door that Suzie had come out of.

What now? This was pretty confusing. I moved closer to Bernie. Suzie looked at Bernie through partly closed eyelids, as though cigarette smoke had blown her way. "So were you shading the truth a little when you said you were off the case?" she said. "Or is it something else?"

"Something else," Bernie said.

She gave him a long look. "Bernie," she said, "what is it? What's gone wrong?"

"Wrong where?" said Bernie. Ah-ha! Bernie was answering a question with a question. Not too sure in my own mind what was going on, but I loved when he did that.

Suzie maybe didn't love it; I could tell from the wrinkles that appeared on her forehead, and her eyes getting smaller. "Are you being purposely obtuse?" she said.

"Obtuse is purposeful by definition," Bernie said.

"Then why?" said Suzie. "What's your point?"

Hey! Were they arguing? That made me feel bad. Didn't Suzie like Bernie? Didn't he like her? I twisted my head around, nipped at my coat. Bernie opened his mouth to say something, but at that moment a man, trailed by Nance carrying a saddle, walked out of the big door of the barn and into the corral. The man wore gleaming boots and carried a short whip—the whip was actually what I saw first—and stood very straight, but he was much smaller than Nance. He whistled—a sharp, harsh whistle that hurt my ears—and the horse came trotting to him. It stood there, tossing its mane in a very annoying way.

Nance stepped up, began saddling the horse. I'd carried Charlie around on my back many times and that was lots of fun, but wearing a saddle? I don't think so. And that shiny thing Nance was sliding in the horse's mouth, a shiny thing attached to the reins? Forget it.

The man took the reins, stuck one foot in the stirrups. Nance crouched behind him, her hands curled under his other boot, and boosted him into the saddle. Each boot had a short metal thing sticking out the back; they caught my eye.

"The count?" Bernie said.

"Who else?" said Suzie.

"How's his English?"

"Not bad."

"As good as Adelina's?"

Suzie laughed.

"What's so funny?" Bernie said.

"Adelina was born and raised in Passaic," she said.

"Passaic?" said Bernie. A new one on me, too. Was it somewhere in the Valley? The Valley went on forever; and beyond it?

Once I'd had an adventure in New Mexico; another time, I'd been to San Diego. We'd surfed, me and Bernie! Sort of.

"Passaic, New Jersey, Bernie," Suzie said. "Good luck with the case." She turned and walked away; the yellow Beetle was parked by the far side of the barn. Suzie got in and drove away.

Bernie watched her go. "Christ," he said. He looked down at me. "Did I screw that up?" Bernie screwing up? No way. I bumped against him. "And come to think of it, I've got this nagging thought that maybe obtuse—"

Nagging thought? He'd lost me completely, but it didn't matter because we both got distracted by the heavy thumpity-thump of the horse on the move. I turned and saw the count leaning forward in the saddle, the horse headed straight toward what looked like a section of fence standing in the middle of the corral. A pretty high section of fence: was it possible that—

Wow! More than possible. And I saw what those metal things—spurs, I remembered, from a time when me and Bernie were into watching Westerns, although he'd kept on saying, "See how it used to be?" until finally the Westerns went to the bottom of the DVD pile and stayed there.

Where was I? Oh, yeah—the metal things: they were for sticking in the sides of the horse when you wanted to make him jump. I can jump, too, and all on my own; wouldn't have minded a crack at that fence myself. Was this a good time for that? Why not? I happened to look at Bernie. Was he shaking his head at me?

The horse landed, thumpity thump, and the ground beneath me shook. The count had a stern look on his face, like this wasn't fun; I didn't get that: making the ground shake had to be fun. The horse circled around the corral. Nance walked over to where we were, stood on the other side of the fence.

"Poetry in motion," she said.

Poetry? Bernie loved poetry. He knew all kinds of poetry by heart; sometimes, like on long rides in the car, it came flowing out of him. My favorite was: *Cannon to the right of them / cannon to the left of them / cannon behind them / volleyed and thundered,* but I also liked *Old dog Tray's ever faithful / Grief cannot drive him away / He's gentle, he is kind / I'll never, never find / A better friend than old dog Tray;* although I really didn't get that one, since the only Tray we knew was a nasty old growler who guarded a junkyard in Pedroia, a friend to nobody.

Bernie gave Nance a nod, the kind of nod that might have made Nance think he agreed with her about the poetry in motion thing. "He was an alternate on the Italian equestrian team six Olympics ago," Nance said.

"I didn't know horses lived that long," said Bernie.

Nance shot him a quick look. "I'm talking about the count," she said.

"Oh," said Bernie.

The horse trotted over to us, his head over the fence. "Whoa," said the count. I got my first good look at the count's face: thin, with a big nose, quick, dark eyes, a mustache. I didn't like mustaches, no idea why. The count gazed down at Bernie. The horse was looking at me. I looked right back, you better believe it. He whinnied, a horrible sound, and started sidestepping. The count made a clicking sound and the horse went still. I found myself inching closer to him.

"This is the detective," Nance said.

"Bernie Little," said Bernie. He raised his hand over the top rail, within shaking distance, but the count didn't seem to notice.

"What is it that you want?" he said. He had a funny way of talking, the sounds not quite right, hard to understand.

"To help find them," Bernie said. "Your wife and Princess."

"In this matter you have failed already, no?" said the count.

"If that's true," Bernie said, "then our motivation will be all the stronger."

"There is motivation," said the count, "and there is competence."

"You can check us out," Bernie said. "I can give you a list of references."

"References?" said the count. "This is not how I operate."

"How do you operate?" Bernie said.

The count didn't answer. He just stroked the side of that big nose with his finger. Was that supposed to mean something?

"One thing I know," Bernie said, "in situations like this, time is not on our side."

The count gazed down at him. I knew that Bernie wanted him to say yes. I also knew what humans look like just before they say yes. The count wasn't looking like that now.

"It's best if we have a client," Bernie said. "But the truth is we're going to work this case, client or not."

"This is a threat of some nature?" said the count.

"Just a statement of fact," Bernie said.

"Ah," said the count. "Statement of fact. *Asserzione di fatto.*" Hard to understand, the count, and now impossible. "And when you refer to 'we,' you are meaning—?"

Bernie gestured toward me. Oops. I seemed to have gotten myself through the rails somehow, within a short lunge of one of those skinny horse legs. I backed through the rails, not easy. "Chet and I," Bernie said, giving me a private look. I knew those private looks. This one meant . . . something, I forget.

Then came a surprise: the count slipped down out of the saddle, landed lightly on his feet, and stuck his hand through the railing. "Lorenzo di Borghese," he said.

They shook hands.

"Um," said Bernie.

"Let us go inside the shade and formalize arrangements," the count said. "Nance, you will be so kind to give Angel a little more exercise."

"Of course, Loren—Mr. Borghese." Nance stepped through the rails and took the reins. The horse was named Angel? What angels were exactly, I wasn't sure, but something good, right? So what was—

"Che—et?"

Hey! Another surprise: I was through the fence again, kind of crawling in the dirt. High above, Angel whinnied and shied away.

"Angel, easy," said Nance, tugging at the reins.

"Che—et? Let's go buddy."

Bernie was watching me. I rose and trotted after him and the count, brisk and innocent.

I liked barns. Lots of smells in a barn, plus interesting stuff all over the place, most of the time including food scraps. And in fact I'd already picked up the scent of peanut butter on my way in, but I'd never gotten the hang of eating peanut butter and besides who was this dude, sitting at a table by the door, cleaning a rifle? I'd seen Bernie cleaning our rifle plenty of times so I knew what was going on. This rifle looked longer than ours.

"My secretary, Aldo," said the count. "Mr. Little, the detective."

"Hi," said Aldo, rising. A big guy, as broad as Bernie and taller. He had one of those ponytails; hard not to look at anything else, for some reason. I tried to remember what a secretary was and almost did.

"Nice scope you got there, Aldo," Bernie said. "Is that a—"

"If you don't mind clearing up, Aldo," the count said. "Mr. Little and I must confer."

"Right away," said Aldo, stuffing all the rifle parts into a canvas bag and heading toward the door.

Bernie and the count sat at the table; I lay under it. The count peered down at me. "Interesting animal," he said. Who was he talking about? "In our world overbreeding is always the risk. Here the opposite seems to obtain." Could have meant anything; all I knew was I didn't like the count's breath, which smelled of fish. I'm not a picky eater, but the appeal of fish is lost on me.

Bernie gave the count a smile, the mouth kind, the eyes and the rest of his face not joining in. "A lot of people have underestimated Chet," he said.

"No offense intended," the count said. He took out a pack of cigarettes. "Smoke?" he said.

"No thanks," Bernie said, but his eyes were glued to that pack.

"Of course not," said the count, lighting up and taking a deep drag. "You Americans," he said.

Yeah, we were Americans, me and Bernie. So?

The count blew out a long, thin smoke cloud. Ah, wonderful smell, always sharpened my appetite for some reason. "The fact is," the count said, "I am a dog lover." He tapped ashes off his cigarette. They floated down past my nose, and all of a sudden I was sneezing. Hadn't sneezed in some time: it took me completely by surprise. When I came out of it, the count was saying, ". . . familiar with the dog show world, Mr. Little?"

"Call me Bernie," said Bernie. "And no, not really."

"And you call me Lorenzo," the count said. "Lorenzo the Magnificent."

"Excuse me?" said Bernie.

"Ha, ha, just my little joke," the count said. He held up his hand, thumb and finger touching; his fingernails were polished and shiny. "What I need you to understand about the dog show world is the ruthlessness."

"Ruthlessness?"

"I refer to the owners." The count patted his pockets, produced a checkbook and a gold pen. "What was your arrangement with Adelina?"

"Two thousand a day."

"Dollars or euros?" said the count. Euros? A new one on me: what was he trying to pull?

"Dollars," said Bernie. Whew. Not so easy to put one over on Bernie, amigo.

The count flipped open the checkbook and started writing. "Suppose we begin with a retainer of, say, three thousand?"

"Fine," said Bernie.

The count handed over the check. We were back in funds! "Allow me to advance a theory," the count said, not quite letting go of the check, he and Bernie holding it together. "Princess, not Adelina, was the target."

"What makes you say that?"

"Didn't I just explain? The ruthlessness of the show world. Are you familiar with the expression 'cui bono'?"

Bernie nodded. I knew Bono, too, from a period where Bernie played "I Still Haven't Found What I'm Looking For" over and over until I wanted to . . . I don't know, something bad. But how Bono fit into this whole—

"Then who would benefit more than Princess's rivals?" the count said.

"She has rivals?" said Bernie.

"Bitter, bitter rivals, Bernie. Do you know how badly they want to win next week? If you will pardon the pun—it is a dog-eat-dog world."

Oh, how I hated that one. I shifted closer to the count's nearest leg. That boot looked thick, and there was the spur to deal with, but still I—all at once, Bernie's foot slid in front of me, blocking any move I may or may not have been planning.

"I would begin," the count was saying, "if you don't mind my advice, with Babycakes."

"Babycakes?"

"Formally known as Sherm's Lucky Roll," the count said. "Owned by Sherman Ganz of Las Vegas."

"Did you mention this to the police?" Bernie said.

"I was not impressed with the police. Aldo can fill you in on the details." The count rose, letting go of the check.

Stick it in your pocket, Bernie, quick.

NINE

Most of our meetings with Metro PD took place in the parking lot of Donut Heaven. We'd park cop style, Bernie's door facing the driver's side door of the cruiser, steam rising out of the open windows from their paper cups.

"Chet like crullers?" Lieutenant Stine said.

Humans, at a moment like this, often say, "Does the bear shit in the woods?" Not totally sure why, and I've never seen a bear, except on the Discovery Channel, and that was close enough.

"He just had a treat," Bernie said. "I don't think he's really hungr—" But by that time I'd kind of left the shotgun seat and was more or less leaning over Bernie, my nose just about out his window. Lieutenant Stine tossed a cruller through the small space between the cars, and I caught it. I'm a pretty good catcher—Bernie and I have this great game we play with a Frisbee. Once we entered a contest, and if it hadn't been for this squirrel appearing at the most unlikely—but maybe I'll have time to get to that later. I took the cruller back to my seat and had some quiet time.

"Who's working the Borghese case?" Bernie said.

Lieutenant Stine, chomping on a big mouthful, pointed to himself. Bernie started telling him all about our get-together at the count's ranch. So complicated, even the second time around. I held on to the essential details: Adelina and Princess were missing, two grand a day.

"What is a count, anyway?" said Lieutenant Stine.

"Some kind of nobleman," Bernie said.

"Nobleman," said the lieutenant. "Christ."

"Yeah," said Bernie.

"That means he's rich?"

"Wild Bill Hickok stayed at that ranch," Bernie said.

"That makes him rich?"

"I'm just saying it's an important ranch in terms of our history," Bernie said. "But thirty thousand unspoiled acres, plus a co-op in Manhattan and a villa in Umbria, and God knows what else—that's what makes him rich."

"What does he do? Where does all that money come from?"

"Probably inherited it," Bernie said. "That's the nobleman part."

They sipped their coffee. I polished off the cruller. Delish.

"Did he mention a rival?" Bernie said.

The lieutenant flipped through his notebook. "Babycakes?"

"I was thinking of the owner, Sherman Ganz. You look into him?"

"Huh?" said Lieutenant Stine. "Guy sets up a felony kidnapping, possible life sentence, on account of he wants to win a dog show?"

"Exactly," Bernie said.

"Don't pull my chain," said Lieutenant Stine.

Once a very bad guy named Gulagov—now sporting an orange jumpsuit up at Central State—got a chain on me. Bernie was the best, but I sided with the lieutenant on this one.

"When someone rich gets kidnapped, I think ransom," the lieutenant went on.

"Any ransom demand?"

"Not yet," said the lieutenant. "Doesn't mean it's not on the way."

"Maybe you're right," Bernie said. "What else?"

"Nada," the lieutenant said. "Went over the limo. It was clean. Questioned the driver and that trainer lady. They didn't see diddley."

That caught my attention. Bernie was a big Bo Diddley fan, sometimes played "Hey Bo Diddley" on his ukulele around the campfire. Was Bo Diddley a suspect in the Borghese case? That was going to get Bernie upset.

A voice crackled over the lieutenant's radio. He spoke into his mouthpiece. Then came some back-and-forth I missed, partly from the sound being so unclear, partly because of how caught up I was licking cruller dust off the seat. The radio went quiet. "Get that?" said the lieutenant.

"Some gas station guy spotted a dark green pickup outside Rio Loco?"

"Going a hundred and ten." The cruiser's engine started up. "Wanna come check it out?"

"No sense both of us driving out there."

Lieutenant Stine tilted up his cup and drained it. "Meaning?" he said.

"We'll just poke around a little."

"Poke anything interesting, I need to know."

"Likewise," said Bernie.

"Likewise isn't the way it works," the lieutenant said. "You should know that by now. I'm the law and I've got needs. You're not the law and all you've got is wants." They gave each other a long look, not particularly friendly. "Enjoy the day," said Lieutenant Stine.

Of course I would. Went without saying.

We'd driven to Vegas before, me and Bernie. Ages and ages to get out of the Valley, then a stretch of open desert where Bernie's hands relaxed on the wheel, and maybe we had some music—in this case "Sway" by the Stones, over and over, Bernie singing at the top of his lungs, something about demon life, and then saying, "Mick Taylor, Chet, listen to that—they were at their best." All beyond me, and I would have preferred Roy Eldridge and his trumpet, but it was always nice to see Bernie having fun. Pretty soon the open stretch closed in, and we hit Vegas. The sun was setting and the sky turned all sorts of colors, not my strong suit. We drove down a broad street lit up even wilder than the sky. Bernie's hands were tense again. He hated Vegas. "All this is just a mirror, Chet," he said. "Reflecting what? Good question. Some horrible corner of the human soul—there's no other answer." I came so close to getting that! Mirrors I knew, of course, had barked at what turned out to be myself in them more than once.

Not long after that, we stopped at a gate in a quieter part of town, tile roofs showing over the tops of walls, tall palm trees everywhere. A guard let us in. We followed a long curving road, parked by a fountain in front of a huge house. Lit-up jets of water flew in the air, fell splashing down into a pool. Was that a big fat fish swimming around in there? I'd never actually caught a fish before—never even had a fighting chance, to tell the truth—so this seemed like a real stroke of—

"Che—et?"

The big fat fish flicked its tail and swam away, not fast, very catchable. But maybe this wasn't the time. Soon we were in the house, following a maid through a bunch of enormous rooms. I smelled one of my guys right away. The smell got stronger and stronger, and then we entered a room lined with books from floor to ceiling. A gray-haired man with a trim gray beard sat on a leather chair in one corner, a book in his hand, and one of my guys—one of my guys who looked a lot like Princess—in his lap. We'd found her already? We were getting good, me and Bernie.

"Mr. Ganz?" Bernie said. The gray-haired man nodded and said something back, missed by me, because at that moment I caught the scent of the little lap guy, quite different from Princess's, missing a peppery something in hers that I realized I kind of liked. I was taking a deep sniff or two when I got the feeling they were talking about me.

"Oh, yes," Bernie was saying. "Perfectly safe with small dogs."

"Babycakes?" Mr. Ganz said. "Want to play with the nice big doggie?"

Babycakes had big dark eyes, maybe not as a big and dark as Princess's but more liquid. They turned on me like deep shadowy pools; then Babycakes made a tiny little squeak and snuggled deeper in Mr. Ganz's lap. "Poor Babycakes," said Mr. Ganz, stroking that golf-ball-size head. He looked up at Bernie. "We can't have any sort of emotional upset," he said, "not with the show coming so soon."

"Understood," Bernie said. "Just a few questions and we'll be on our way."

Mr. Ganz's voice, soft to that point, got much harder. "Maybe you don't understand," he said. "I was referring to Babycakes's state of mind, not my own. You can ask *me* as many questions as you like—poor Adelina, I quite admired her—although I don't see how I can be of any help."

Bernie pulled up a footstool, sat near Mr. Ganz but not quite facing. One of his techniques, and he had a reason for that not quite facing part, but I couldn't quite dig it up. I sat on the floor next to him, my ears pointing straight up. Babycakes tried to retreat further into Mr. Ganz's lap but ran out of room. Mr. Ganz drew the corner of his book over Babycakes, leaving only that damp-eyed face showing.

"We're starting from zero, Mr. Ganz," Bernie said. "Almost anything you can tell us will be helpful. For example, the fact that you admire Adelina. Or admired her, as you put it." Bernie smiled. This was a real quick smile Bernie had sometimes, like a knife flash. Bernie had some violence in him, deep down. Me, too. "Know something we don't, Mr. Ganz?" he said.

Mr. Ganz's gaze, big and liquid, not unlike Babycakes's, met Bernie's. "A safe bet," he said. "But about the circumstances of her disappearance or her present whereabouts, I know nothing. As for the ugly implication of your question, please don't say you were just doing your job."

All of that blew right by me; I only knew one thing for sure: I didn't like Mr. Ganz. Was this interview going to end with me grabbing him by the pant leg? I was ready.

As for Bernie, he was still smiling, but now in a more friendly way. Kind of a surprise, but I don't claim to understand Bernie 24/7, whatever that means. I simply trusted him to be the smartest human in the room. My job was to take care of everything else.

"Just fishing," Bernie said. "Sometimes you get lucky in this business."

Fishing? Did that mean hopping into the pool for the briefest second would have been okay after all? Or maybe we could still do it later? Something to look forward to: I loved that feeling, and, to tell the truth, felt it almost every day.

"Not this time," said Mr. Ganz, scratching lightly at the back of Babycakes's head, looking like he knew what he was doing. Hey! I wanted some of that.

Bernie's smile faded. "Tell me about the rivalry," he said.

"Rivalry?"

"Between Princess and Babycakes."

"Who told you there was a rivalry?"

"Count Borghese."

"Is he really paying you?"

"Yes."

"Then you should be aware he styles himself Count *di* Borghese."

"Styles himself? Meaning he's not a count?"

Mr. Ganz shrugged. "Italian counts are a dime a dozen. Got fifty grand? You can be a baron."

No idea what that was about, but not to worry—whatever fifty grand added up to, we didn't have it.

"He bought his title?" Bernie said.

"I didn't say that," said Mr. Ganz. "His title is legitimate, as far as I know, may even be an old one. But the point is, there's nothing noble about him. Take this supposed rivalry, for example. It's all in his mind. And in Princess's."

"Not sure I follow," said Bernie.

"Isn't it obvious?" said Mr. Ganz. "Babycakes and Princess have gone head-to-head in ten shows in the past two years and Babycakes—ooo, you good little girl—has been champion every time. A one-sided rivalry is a contradiction in terms." Babycakes was gazing off into space, one tiny ear bent back in a weird way.

"I thought Princess won the Balmoral," Bernie said.

"The Balmoral?" said Mr. Ganz. "Don't talk to me about the Balmoral."

"Why not? Isn't it the biggest dog show in the world?"

"Oh, very much so, but what about the concept of fair play?"

"What about it?"

"I can see your employer hasn't given you the whole story."

"Fill me in."

"Amazed you don't know about this," said Mr. Ganz. "They kneecapped Babycakes at the Balmoral."

Bernie hardly ever looked surprised; so seldom that for a moment, I didn't recognize the expression on his face. "Say again?" he said.

"What word didn't you understand?"

"Kneecapped, for starters," said Bernie. "I'm not sure we can even say that dogs have knees."

Of course we don't. Human knees are pretty ugly, make their legs looks kind of weird. Our legs are—although it's not for me to say—elegant.

"It's a metaphor," said Mr. Ganz.

"For what?"

"Simply the single worst atrocity I've witnessed in my entire life."

"Which was?"

Mr. Ganz stroked Babycakes. "I don't even like to revisit the trauma, not in front of her."

"I understand," Bernie said.

"Do you?"

Bernie nodded, this tiny nod he had, hardly a movement at all, and my personal favorite of all the nods: it was real.

"I believe you do," said Mr. Ganz. He took a deep breath. "I suppose you've met the trainer, Nancy Malone?"

"Yes."

"She worked for me once—did you know that?"

"No," said Bernie. "How did it end?"

"Not relevant to this discussion," Mr. Ganz said. "The point is that on day one at Balmoral—hadn't even started, we were still backstage—Nancy Malone sidled over and—" He lowered his voice—"stamped down on Babycakes's poor little foot. Viciously. Knocked her out of the competition—she limped for days and days." Mr. Ganz's eyes seemed to get even wetter. And Babycakes's eyes, too. Plus her ear was bent back further. "So, yes, Princess won the Balmoral, if you call that winning."

"What happened after?" Bernie said.

"After what?"

"After Nancy Malone stepped on Babycakes."

"Crocodile tears, of course." Crocodiles, also on the Discovery Channel, but at Balmoral, too? The case was getting complicated. Had to be prepared for anything: we were in a tough business, me and Bernie.

"What do you mean?" Bernie said.

"She was all contrite, claimed it was an accident, apologized profusely—even had the gall, if you can believe it, to pick up Babycakes and try to comfort the creature. I put a stop to that."

"Any chance it could have been an accident?" Bernie said.

"Absolutely not."

"Did you actually see it happen?"

"As a matter of fact, no, my view was blocked—it was chaotic back there, giving her the opportunity in the first place. But I have it on excellent authority."

"Whose?"

"Someone with a clear view."

"Does that someone have a name?"

"I don't believe I want to get into that."

"Why not?"

There was a long silence, and during the silence, I noticed a small silver bowl over in the corner, and in the bowl what looked a lot like steak, cut into tiny bits, possibly for a tiny mouth. Or possibly, in a hospitable sort of way, for anyone who happened to be around, a guest for example. A few moments later I found myself still sitting straight and alert, but somehow much closer to the small silver bowl.

"I have no further comment," said Mr. Ganz.

"That's going to look bad," Bernie said.

"I'm sorry?"

"Let's go back to how you admire—or admired—Adelina Borghese," Bernie said.

"What did you mean—what's going to look bad?" said Mr. Ganz. His voice changed, got higher and thinner, always a sign that the interview was going well. No surprise—Bernie was a great interviewer, or have I mentioned that already?

Bernie shook his head. "You've made your choice on that," he said. "But can you elaborate on why you used to admire Adelina?"

Mr. Ganz's voice rose some more. "Forget the past tense. I admire her, period."

"Why?"

"She's down to earth," Mr. Ganz said. "People with her kind of money are usually out of touch, in my experience. Adelina enjoys all the trappings, of course, but she hasn't been spoiled."

"Maybe that's because the money came late," Bernie said.

"The money came late?" Mr. Ganz said. "I don't understand."

"Isn't she from New Jersey?"

"Yes, but what's that got to do with anything?"

Bernie opened his mouth to say something, but at that moment Babycakes made a whimpering sound, very hard on the ears.

"Oh, poor baby," said Mr. Ganz. "She's so sensitive to mood, to tension. We'll have to continue this some other time."

"What are you tense about, Mr. Ganz?" Bernie said.

"I didn't say I was tense."

"Then who is?" said Bernie. "I'm not, and neither is . . ." Bernie looked at me. Hey! I was standing right by the silver bowl! And also it was empty. How the heck had that happened? ". . . Chet."

"So?"

"So who's left to be tense?" said Bernie. He rose. "We'll go, but before we do, I'll let you in on the count's theory."

"Theory about what?"

"The kidnapping, why we're here," Bernie said. "The count thinks that Princess was the real target."

"What sense does that make?"

"To someone angry about a backstage atrocity, maybe a lot," said Bernie.

"That's a disgusting accusation," said Mr. Ganz.

"But it's all we've got," said Bernie. "All I can pass on to Lieutenant Stine."

"Who's he?"

"The Valley detective in charge of the case."

"So I'm going to look bad to the police—is that the meaning of your threat?"

"Just the name," Bernie said.

"What name?"

"The eyewitness at Balmoral."

Babycakes was back to gazing into the distance. Now Mr. Ganz gazed into the distance, too. "Aldo Reni," he said.

"The count's secretary?"

"The maid will show you out," said Mr. Ganz.

"We can find our way."

We left, Bernie quiet and thoughtful, me licking my lips. In the front hall, Bernie paused at a table, picked up a magazine, leafed through. He went still for a moment, then slipped the magazine inside his shirt.

We got home late, Bernie tired, with dark circles around his eyes, me pretty peppy, having slept the whole way. The rumbling motion, roof down with the sky full of stars: I had some of my best sleeps on the open road. Normally Bernie would head right for bed at a time like this, flopping down clothes on, eyes closing in midair. But not tonight. Instead, he went into the office and opened the safe. He reached in and took out the glossy magazine photo of Princess on a satin pillow, the one Adelina had given us, where someone had drawn in a bull's-eye target over her fluffball head. Bernie sat at the desk, opened the magazine he'd taken from Mr. Ganz's house, riffled through the pages, stopped.

I went closer, saw that a page had been torn out, leaving a narrow ripped margin on one side, the side with those surprisingly sharp staples, as I knew from a chewing episode or two I'd had with magazines, back in my puppy days. He slid the glossy page with Princess's photo into place. It fit perfectly.

TEN

We were asleep, Bernie in the big bed, me at first at the foot of it, but in the night I'd moved to the front door and laid down with my back against it. Sometimes that happened, no idea why. A sliver of cool air—cool for the Valley, anyway—leaked in through the space under the door, and in a way that's hard to explain, I could sort of feel what was going on in the night, despite being off in dreamland. I had a lot of fun in dreamland. For example, I was now deep in the canyon, doing my quick trot—I can keep it up practically forever—on the scent of a fat javelina, when all of a sudden a crocodile came looming out of a cave, and I leaped a huge leap, right over its snapping jaws, but the moment I landed a huge bear—

Ring, ring. A phone tried to get into the dream, but then everything—bear, crocodile, the whole canyon—broke up in pieces that faded quickly away, and I was on my feet.

Ring, ring. Our phone, ringing in the middle of the night, the windows dark, the house all shadowy. I heard Bernie's sleepy voice, thick and scratchy. "Hello? Suzie?" A short silence, but by then I was in the bedroom, watching. Bernie was sitting up in bed, phone to his ear, rubbing his head with his other hand. "Clauson's Wells? The ghost town? What are you doing way out—" Bernie said. "Sure. You mean in the morning, or—" He went silent. I heard Suzie, speaking fast, her voice high, but I couldn't make out the words. "Now?" Bernie said. "Is someone with you? I thought—" I heard a click on the other end. The next second, Bernie was out of bed, pulling on his pants. "Chet?" he called. "Chet?" He was facing me, seemed to be looking right in my direction, but he didn't see me: I could never get used to how poor his night vision—and the night vision of all humans I'd ever known—was. How did they live like that? I went over to Bernie, wagging my tail.

"Where have you been hiding?" he said, giving me a quick pat. "Got to move, boy."

I ran to the front door, skidding to a stop on the wood floor, my claws making a nice skittery scratching sound. Something was up: I could feel it. I heard Bernie entering the office, spinning the dial on the safe. He came out, tucking the .38 Special in his belt. We were all set.

We drove fast under the night sky, at first the usual Valley night sky, dark and pink at the same time, with no stars, but after a while the pinkness faded away and the stars came out, and also the moon, just a thin silvery curve. I've spent a lot of time watching the moon, had many chances to see it change shapes, still had no idea what was going on. Did anybody? Probably not: I'd heard Bernie telling Charlie that the sun was just another star, but how could that be true? Look how big the sun is, and how hot, while stars are small and if they have any heat I've never felt it. Oh, Bernie. I took my eyes off the sky, looked sideways at him. He was hunched over the wheel, gripping it tight. Usually on nighttime drives we had some music, but not now. There was only the wind whipping by, flattening my ears. It made a funny feeling down my back. I shifted closer to Bernie.

We zigzagged up into some mountains, still zooming, Bernie shifting the gears real fast, the tires squealing on the turns. I loved that shifting. Suppose I managed to get my mouth on that leather knob, was it possible to—

"Chet!"

Interesting idea, but maybe not now. We were in a big hurry. Did I know why? Something about Suzie and ghost towns. Bernie was very interested in ghost towns and once we'd almost invested some money with a guy—kind of like the tin futures guy from the Dry Gulch Restaurant and Saloon, now that I thought about it—who wanted to buy up a whole ghost town and do something with it, can't remember what. In fact, maybe we had made that investment. Hadn't there been a visit to Mr. Singh soon after? Our finances had been a mess back then, and still were, but peeling up this mountain road I forgot about all that right away. Off in the distance a pair of narrow yellow eyes gleamed in the headlights. I barked and just like that they were gone.

"Chet? What's up, boy?"

I barked again, no real reason. We were on the job, out in the night, driving fast. Anything better than this? You tell me.

On the other side of the mountains the air turned cool and fresh, and the stars got brighter. We took a narrow paved road across flat desert, and Bernie floored it. Wow! The engine screamed and I would have, too, if I'd known how. Bernie's hair was blowing straight back. Hey! His forehead went much higher than I'd thought; but he still looked great. Faster, I was thinking, let's go faster, when all of a sudden the car made a funny little lurch.

"Uh-oh," said Bernie, slowing down. "What was that?"

I didn't know. This Porsche, brown with yellow doors, was very old, even older than our old mostly purple one, which went off a cliff back when we were working the Gulagov case. We had tools in the trunk, but nothing good ever happened when they came out, even though Bernie was always the smartest human in the room. Please, I thought, don't pull over.

Bernie pulled over. He got the tools, popped the hood. I trotted through the shadows, leaving my mark on a round cactus, a couple rocks, and a scrap of cardboard. By that time Bernie was bent over the engine, saying, "Probably something to do with the . . . Fuck!" Then came a clank-clank-clank as some tool fell deep inside all that machinery. I gazed at some distant hills, low rounded shapes, starless and darker than the sky, waiting for this to be over, and—what was that? A flash of light? Orange and yellow, there and gone in an instant, but: a muzzle flash. I'd seen muzzle flashes before, had no doubt.

"Chet! Stop that barking!"

But I couldn't. This was my job. I barked and barked until finally Bernie got his head out from under the hood, and gazed in the direction I was pointed at, toward those dark hills. "Chet? What is it? What's going on?"

A muzzle flash, Bernie! A muzzle flash in the night. I kept barking, hoping there'd be another, but there wasn't.

Bernie found a can of something and poured it into the engine. "Should hold 'er for now," he said, and closed the hood. We got in and Bernie fired the engine. "What's up, boy? Easy, there, easy."

We took off, not as fast as before, the engine sounding fine. I barked a few more times, but not loud. We were kind of headed in the right direction, if not to the exact muzzle flash point, then at least to the low hills. Soon our headlights picked out a signpost in the night. Bernie slowed down: an old wooden signpost, crooked and weathered, the color of bones. He read the sign: "Clauson's Wells, three miles."

We turned off the paved road, onto a dirt track, headed now toward where I'd seen the muzzle flash. We bumped along, taking it slow, which was fine with me—we've had car problems on desert tracks like this, one or two ending in long walks. "Drove cattle through Clauson's Wells at one time," Bernie said. "Last water for two hundred miles." He went quiet, then added, "If there's any left." Poor Bernie. He was so worried about water—would probably be talking about the aquifer any moment now—but whenever he turned on the tap, there it was, water out the yingyang. How could there be a prob— "Only one aquifer for the whole goddamn state, why can't anybody—" Bernie's voice faded again, but I knew he was talking to himself inside. I was pretty sure that humans did a lot of that, had trouble shutting down their minds. Not me, amigo: I can shut down my mind at the drop of a hat, whatever that means.

The low hills drew closer. Human things started showing up in our headlight beams: beer cans, a hubcap, strips of toilet paper stuck on spiny plants, another wooden sign, this one on the ground and pocked with little round holes. "They say Wild Bill Hickok rode through here, shot the town up pretty good," Bernie said. Hickok again? Was he the perp? Kidnapper of Princess and Adelina? And whoa. He'd shot up Clauson's Wells? What about that muzzle flash? Had to mean the dude was back, shooting it up again. Perps had a hard time going straight, almost never did. That was something you learned in this business.

"Chet! Easy, boy. What's got into you?"

I tried to keep my mouth shut, not easy. I knew we were getting close. Did Bernie? I gazed at him, hunched over the wheel, knuckles showing green in the light from the dash. Yeah, he knew. We were partners, me and Bernie. Just to be sure, on account of how you don't bring a spoon to a knife fight, I checked Bernie's belt, saw our .38 Special firmly in place, all ready for action. I was in the mood for Bernie to start taking potshots at something right this second. We were good to go.

The track suddenly broadened into a hard-packed street with dark wooden buildings on both sides, some lopsided, some worse than that, almost falling down. A big ball of tumbleweed rolled through our headlight beams and bounced out of sight. I'd had fun chasing tumbleweed in the past, once even—

A car was parked in front of one of the buildings, a building with swinging doors. I recognized those kind of doors from all the Westerns Bernie and I had watched. They meant saloon, and saloons meant fistfights and busted-up furniture. I also recognized the car, the yellow Beetle that always had treats inside: Suzie's car. Bernie pulled in behind it and cut the engine. He took the flashlight from the glove box and turned to me, finger over his lips. I knew what that meant. We hopped out, silent, like shadows. The wind made a high whining sound, not loud. Uh-oh. Was Bernie limping? Yes, just a bit. That sometimes happened after a long drive, on account of his wound. I slowed down and walked beside him.

We went over to Suzie's car. The windows were open. Bernie peered inside, keeping the flashlight off. I smelled treats. And also Suzie's smell—a very nice smell, soap, lemons, and something else that was just Suzie. The scent came in tiny waves through the driver's side window, but wait a minute: was it also coming—

Bernie made a quiet clicking sound in his mouth. That meant we were moving on. We stepped up onto a kind of sidewalk made of wooden planks, heading toward the saloon doors, but those wooden planks creaked under Bernie's very first step. He stopped dead, listened for a moment. I listened, too, heard nothing but the wind. We backed down onto the street, walked to a narrow alley that led along the side of the saloon. Very dark in the alley, with lots of strange shadows, some of which could have been men, but from the lack of human smell, except for Bernie's, I knew they weren't. We walked along, real quiet. We liked the night, me and Bernie.

At the end of the alley lay a flat stretch of desert and then the low hills, not as low as they'd looked from a distance. We approached the saloon from the back. The door was missing, and most of the wall as well. Inside I could make out a long, narrow room with a bar along one side and a cracked mirror behind it, the mirror lighter than everything else, almost glowing to my eyes. And in the glow, it was easy for me to see a man sitting on a stool facing those swinging doors, his back to us, a cowboy hat on his head, a rifle across his knees. Could Bernie see him, too?

Yes: he was pulling the .38 Special from his belt. Bernie took one more step, raised the gun, and spoke in a calm clear voice. "Rifle on the floor," he said. "Stand up, hands raised and open." The man didn't move. "I've got a gun on you," Bernie said. "Don't make me use it."

The man remained still. Then, from right behind us, came another voice, also calm and clear, but it made the hair on my neck rise up. "You're in the exact same situation, buddy boy. Drop it."

Bernie lowered the gun but didn't drop it. He turned; me, too. A man stood in the shadows, nothing clear but the gleam of his gun, pointed right at Bernie's head.

"Drop it or you're a dead man," he said. "You're under arrest."

"Arrest?" said Bernie.

"Sheriff's Department, Rio Loco County," said the man.

I heard quick footsteps. Bernie said, "Then we're on the same side. I'll need to see your—" And then the man in the cowboy hat was right behind him, rifle up high, like a baseball bat.

"Don't take to gettin' drawed down on," he said.

I leaped at him, not quite quick enough. The rifle butt cracked down on Bernie's head. Bernie fell. I hit the man in the cowboy hat hard in the chest, knocked him to the floor, got on top of him, lunged forward toward his neck, teeth bared. The man in the cowboy hat screamed in fear. *Scream away, buddy boy: no one does that to Bernie.* Then something hard cracked against my head, too, and the world went black.

ELEVEN

I came out of a deep deep darkness and opened my eyes. Bernie? Where was Bernie? I got up, stumbling a little, which took me by surprise, and felt a pain in my head, a kind of heavy, throbbing pain. It made me want to puke, so I did.

After that, I felt a bit better, although the pain didn't go away. I looked around. Just after dawn—I could tell from the silvery light, fresh and weak at the same time—and I was standing on a weathered and dirty wooden floor in a long, narrow room with a cracked mirror on one side. That cracked mirror brought everything back: the ghost town saloon and what had happened in the night.

Bernie? Where was Bernie?

I trotted back and forth across that dirty floor, picked up Bernie's scent right away, traced it to the falling-down back wall of the saloon where we'd come in, then turned and followed it the other way, toward those swinging doors at the front. I ducked under them and hurried onto the rough wood-plank sidewalk. His scent—the very best human scent I'd ever known, a lovely mix of apples, bourbon, salt and pepper—got stronger, mixed up with the nasty smells of two other men. I remembered those two other men, oh yeah. Out on the dirt-packed street lay two sets of footprints, the type made by cowboy boots, and between them ran a kind of smooth track, as though . . . as though what? Something bad, like they'd been dragging . . . I didn't want to think the thought.

All those markings, easy to track, and I tracked them past the alley Bernie and I had gone down the night before, and into a barn at the end of the street, a doorless barn, sagging and crooked. Light leaked through cracks in the walls, dust drifting through the rays. The markings, all of them—the two walkers and that smoothness between them—reached some tire tread tracks and came to an end. The tire tread tracks—grooves thick and deep, maybe some kind of truck—led toward the far wall, which was mostly missing, and outside. I followed them, nose to the ground.

They led me around a corner, onto the main drag of this horrible place, and stopped outside the saloon. There they got all confused with a bunch of other tire tracks. I trotted around in circles, hoping for—what? I wasn't sure. But Bernie! Where was he? And I was still trotting around like that, faster and faster, when the sun poked up over the low hills, and everything turned bright and golden. That made me pause and look up, and when I did I noticed that the Porsche was gone. Not long after, I realized that Suzie's car was gone, too.

I kept sniffing, hoping to pick up something: Bernie's smell, or Suzie's, or even the treats in her car. Those chew strips had an amazingly powerful smell, carried for huge distances. But no, nothing. Hold on: nothing but a very faint whiff of burned oil, a scent I knew very well. The Porsche. I stuck my nose right in the dirt. Yes, for absolute sure.

The burned-oil smell—by now I was into my trot, not the

real fast one, but not the real slow one either; this was the medium trot I can keep up forever—led me down the street to the desert track we'd driven in on. After a short way, the tread marks vanished in the hard stony ground, and a little later I caught one last whiff of burned oil, and then no more. I slowed to a walk, and then stopped. All of a sudden I felt sick, and puked again. This time not much came out, just some watery stuff. It pooled on the ground and some ants appeared out of nowhere. They stood on the edge of the sour-smelling pool I'd made, feeling at the liquid with their tiny feet. I was getting ready to step on them when I heard a tiny distant squeak.

At first I thought it might be the ants! Wasn't that crazy? Shows how I really wasn't quite myself at that moment. I moved away from the puke and ants, looked around. The movement made my head hurt, but I forgot about it right away. In one direction lay the low hills, with Clauson's Wells, the ghost town, at their base. In all the other directions, desert, as far as I could see, and maybe in the far distance, away from the sun, some mountains. So: my job was to—

That squeak. I heard it again. A kind of whimper, really, maybe the wind. And maybe not. Facts first, theories later, Bernie always said. Wasn't sure what he meant, but I loved when he talked like that. Bernie: always the smartest human in the room. I headed back to the ghost town.

The sun rose higher. We were past the real heat, but out here in the desert it was still plenty hot. My tongue felt hard and dry. What had Bernie said? "Last water for two hundred miles." So where was it? I sniffed the ground as I trotted down the main street, toward the saloon, smelled no water. Then I remembered Bernie also saying, "If there's any left." But there had to be. Bernie worried about water, but we always ended up having it out the ying—

The squeak, this time very near, coming, in fact, from inside the saloon; and not a squeak, but a whimper for sure. Bernie? Bernie would never whimper, no matter what. But what if—? The thought of something so awful it made Bernie whimper almost made me whimper. I squeezed under those swinging doors and went inside.

Bright sunlight shone into the saloon through the missing slats in the back wall. I noticed things I hadn't seen before: cobwebs everywhere, a rickety staircase leading up to another level, a few turds on the floor. I went over and smelled them: coyote. Not fresh. Didn't matter anyway—I wasn't afraid of coyotes; they were afraid of me. Sniffing at the coyote turds—interesting in their own right for reasons I couldn't explain—I heard the whimper again. It came from above.

Those stairs, all warped and slanted, didn't look good. Don't forget I'm a hundred-pounder, meaning pretty big. I started up. The stairs creaked under me with every step. After going real slow on the bottom ones, I couldn't stand the creaking and charged right up. One stair board came loose and fell through, landing with a clatter somewhere below, but by that time I was at the top, standing in a dusty corridor. I listened, heard nothing; and got the strange feeling that someone else was listening, too.

Most of the light in the corridor came from a window at the end. The window glass was gone, all except a narrow sharp-pointed shard sticking up from the bottom. The sight gave me a strange feeling down the middle of my chest and stomach. In my line of work, you had to jump out of windows from time to time. But not this window—important to remember that, boy, if the time came. Bernie sometimes called me that: *boy. C'mon, boy.* I could hear him saying it in my head. I liked the sound, listened to him say it a few more times.

Then I made my way down the corridor. Slow and quiet, boy. I knew how to do this, ears up, listening hard, paws coming down softly, all weight on the pads, claws hardly touching the floor. First came a room with an open door, in fact, no door at all. I looked in: completely empty, except for dust, grime, cobwebs. The next door was closed tight. The door after that, last one, stood open a little bit, not enough for me to squeeze through. I paused, listened, sniffed. Nothing to hear, but I caught a faint scent. It reminded me of someone. After a moment or two, I thought: Babycakes. But then I got another whiff. Not like Babycakes at all, much more peppery, for one thing, a pepperiness I liked. I put my shoulder to the door, gave it a soft push. It swung open a bit, and I could see into the room beyond.

An empty room, just like the first one, with only cobwebs, dirt, and—but no. Something else, in a shadowy corner: a tiny something with big dark eyes. Princess! I'd found her, me, Chet the Jet! Then I remembered I'd been looking for Bernie at the moment, not Princess, and I quieted down inside.

Princess lay on a pillow, not at all like her satin pillow; this one stained and filthy. I barked at her, a soft muffled bark I have, just saying hi. Princess didn't bark back, didn't make any sound at all, stayed right where she was on the pillow, gazing at me with those eyes. Hey. She was shaking, her whole body quivering as though cold, when in fact it was hot and stuffy in this room. I crossed over to her, wagged my tail just to show her—I wasn't exactly sure what.

But something friendly, anyway. Princess didn't seem to get the friendly part. She kept shaking, maybe even harder. I didn't know what to do. Had that ever happened to me before? Not that I could remember. I always did something. Staying in this room—what was that expression of Bernie's? A nonstarter. And leaving without Princess? That was a nonstarter, too. I had only one idea, and that was to give myself a good shake, so I did, the kind that begins at my nose, goes all the way to my tail and then back again. Whew. I felt great when that was over, and as a bonus my headache had vanished. A snack would be nice, and a long drink of cool—but what was this? Princess had shrunk away on the other side of the pillow, right against the wall, as far from me as she could get, and she was quivering even more. I got the crazy idea she was afraid of me. How was that possible? I was one of the good guys, here to help. I lowered my head and gave her a soft bump with my nose.

What the hell? Had that really happened? She'd bared her tiny teeth at me? Had I actually felt a nip at the end of my nose? Enough of this. I snatched her up by the scruff of the neck, none too gentle, and headed for the door. I suppose Princess thrashed around some, but I didn't feel it. She was so light, hardly weighed anything at all. How could anything so tiny even be? Then right away I remembered ants, probably from seeing them so recently, gathering around that pool of puke, and ants were certainly a lot smaller than Princess, and what about ticks, disgusting things I hated having on me and—I kind of lost the thread.

I carried Princess out the door, along the corridor, and down the stairs. She stopped thrashing on the staircase, went very still, especially when I had to step over the missing stair. Princess had no idea of what I could do. Just to show her, I leaped over the last few stairs, landing lightly on the saloon floor. Princess squealed, a funny little sound, part fear and part something else, maybe even plain excitement. A fun sound. I tried to think of something I could do that would make her squeal again, but nothing came to mind. So, failing that, as Bernie liked to say—not sure what he meant, but this was the kind of time he said it—I crossed the saloon, crouched under the front doors, and dropped Princess on the hard-packed street.

Don't know what I expected—often the case, to tell the truth—but Princess surprised me by bouncing right up and barking at me. A high-pitched, irritating sound even though it wasn't very loud, and angry, for sure. What did she have to be angry about? I barked back, one of my low rumbles. It had no effect on Princess. She kept up that high-pitched yammer, even darted forward like—could it be true?—she was thinking of biting my leg. I actually backed up a bit, as though that tiny fluffball, so far down there, could possibly do anything to a bruiser like me. Pretty embarrassing. I barked, real loud, mostly annoyed at myself. Maybe real real loud: Princess went quiet. She stood still, gazing up at me. I wagged my tail. Why not? Princess didn't wag back, not that she had much to wag with, just a little pom-pom thing. Instead her mouth opened and she started panting. I panted, too, no real reason at first, and then I remembered I was thirsty. Last water for two hundred miles, but where was it? I smelled no water.

So there we were, me and Princess, standing outside the saloon, all by ourselves on the main drag of this ghost town, panting. I got the feeling I should be doing something but couldn't think what. Then, with no warning, Princess suddenly turned and trotted away, her legs a blur. I walked along beside her, sometimes pausing to let her catch up. She didn't look at me, just kept going, maybe even increasing her speed. We went down the street, past the barn to the foot of the low hills. Princess turned sharply, trotting along the rocky face, came to a path, steep and narrow. She started up. I followed.

The path zigzagged up the slope, the ground stony, nothing green growing in it, not even the usual desert plants, like cactuses or thistles. But a different story when we came to the top: on the other side lay a small strip of grassy flatland, with a tree, and beside the tree a cabin. And in front of the cabin? A little pond, blue and sparkling.

The next thing I knew, I was up to my shoulders in the pond, drinking my fill. Ah, wonderful, cool water, with a clean rocky taste I loved. I glanced up, saw Princess approaching, still in her trot, legs going faster and faster. Desperate for water, I thought; but Princess surprised me again, hurrying right past the pond to the cabin door. She scratched at it, at the same time making a whining sound.

I got out of the pond, shook off the water, went over to Princess. She didn't seem to notice me, just kept scratching and whining. I pushed at the door with my shoulder. It stayed closed. But I noticed something: this wasn't one of those doors with a knob, impossible for me, even though I'd tried plenty of times. Instead it had a little round metal piece, for pressing down with the human thumb. We'd worked on this one, me and Bernie. I rose, came down on that thumb piece with one of my paws. Click: and the door opened.

I checked the insides: a small cabin with a single room; no furniture except a table and chair, and a cot against the far wall. I went closer. Someone lay in the cot, covered by a blanket, only some wisps of blond hair showing at the top. I barked. No response from under the blanket. I went to the cot, got a corner of the blanket between my teeth, and pulled.

Adelina Borghese. She lay on her back, eyes open. Before I knew it, Princess had somehow jumped right up onto the cot. She climbed onto Adelina's chest, started licking her face, whimpering at the same time. Maybe Princess didn't understand, but from my job I knew the meaning of the red round hole in the side of Adelina's head. And the smell: not yet strong, maybe just beginning, but there. I got Princess by the scruff of the neck again and carried her away. She didn't resist.

TWELVE

I didn't drop Princess this time, lowered her to the ground instead. She stood outside the cabin, shaking again. The cabin gave me a bad feeling. I moved away, glancing back at Princess, hoping to give her the idea, and after a moment or two, she followed. The lovely smell of water overwhelmed that other smell in my nose, from the cabin. I went to the pond and lapped up a little drink. Princess appeared beside me. She didn't have to dip her head to drink, already being right down on pond level. Out came her tongue, so tiny, and she started lapping. Lapping and lapping: it went on and on. How could all that water fit in her? At the same time I noticed how careful she was to keep her paws out of the pond. Why? I had no idea, but began to think that of all the members of the nation within the nation I'd come across in my career, there hadn't been any like Princess.

Other than that, I had no thoughts. We stood by the pond. The sun was higher in the sky now, and getting hotter, the air still and silent. It had a strange effect on me, making me still and silent, too. Then, at last, I had a thought and snapped out of it. The thought was: Bernie.

Where was he? I had no idea, didn't know where to begin thinking about it. My mind was blank. And in that state of blankness, I found myself moving—away from the pond, across the grassy flatland, toward the stony path leading down from the hill to the ghost town. I didn't realize why until I was practically on the path: Bernie would come for me, so I had to be easy to find. Then I realized something else: Princess wasn't with me. I looked back and there she was, still standing by the pond.

I paused, one front paw in the air. Princess seemed to be gazing in my direction. I barked. She must have heard me but showed no sign of it, remaining exactly where she was. I turned and went back for her. That was my job.

I walked around the pond, stood next to Princess. She looked up at me with those huge dark eyes. I gave her one of my low, rumbly barks, ready for anything, especially a sudden nip from those teeth, surprisingly big now that I thought about it. But Princess didn't bite. Instead she surprised me again, suddenly wagging that little pom-pom tail of hers. I retraced my steps to the stony path, Princess trotting beside me in her funny way, legs a blur, body advancing very slowly. Also—I noticed for the first time—she was holding her head tilted forward in a determined sort of way.

We climbed up the rocky slope, started zigzagging down the other side. Clauson's Wells spread out before us—the barn, main street, saloon. It didn't seem to be getting any closer: this was taking forever. Around a bend, a big boulder sat in the way, blocking our view of the ghost town. By the time we got past it, things had changed: a black-and-white sedan with blue lights on top was rolling down the main street. A black-and-white meant cops, and cops and us were on the same side, so right away I thought, Bernie, and picked up the pace, meaning I walked a bit faster. Princess gave me a quick upward glance, and picked up her pace, too, actually raising tiny dust clouds. The black-and-white stopped in front of the saloon and two men in cowboy hats got out, both carrying rifles. I stopped, too. I was pretty sure I knew those men.

A problem, right away: Princess didn't stop, kept scurrying, around the next bend and beyond. I bounded forward—one full bound and part of the next one—and caught her, snatching her up once more by the scruff of the neck, as gently as I could, but the point was it had to be done, gentle or not. For some reason, Princess didn't see it that way, and did the worst thing she could, which was to start in on her high-pitched barking.

The men spun around and looked our way. Could they spot us from way down there? I didn't know. All I knew was that Princess wouldn't shut up. I wheeled around and took off the other way, back up the slope, with the little bitch—the right word, Bernie said so—in my mouth. I heard the black-and-white's engine firing, down below, and ramped up to full speed, at the same time getting a funny feeling down my spine; I've been shot at before.

The engine noise got louder, but no way could they drive that thing up this hill. Or was there? Wouldn't they have to get out and follow on foot? Hard to tell. Humans and their machines: did it get any trickier than that? This was where Bernie came in. I gave up trying to figure it out, just ran my fastest. Cresting the top of the rise, I heard the engine cut out. The doors slammed. Then silence. The next sound would be a gunshot. I kept running, didn't look back.

We flew by the pond, the cabin, more grassy flatland, and then down a long winding trail through strange rock formations and onto flat desert floor. Princess had given up on the barking now, just whined from time to time. I got pretty tired of that, also tired of having to breathe through my nose. I like breathing through my mouth when I'm running, always have. But what choice was there? I ran and ran, finally realizing the strange feeling down my spine, the feeling of being aimed at, was gone.

Soon a tall saguaro appeared, rising up in the middle of nowhere. I slowed down, halted in its shade and turned back for the first time: nothing to see but the flat plain, and in the distance the high country we'd left, a bit wobbly in the heat waves. We'd come a long way. The important thing: no men with rifles. I let go of Princess. She tumbled to the ground, sprang up, and faced me—if you could say that, what with her way down there—and barked angrily. I barked back, angry, too. We barked at each other for a while. At last she shut up. I did, too, damn tired of barking, but I wasn't going to be first. Princess circled around the saguaro, squatted, and did her business, those dark eyes on me the whole time, why I couldn't say.

I glanced around. That was what Bernie would have done. He even had a word for it: rec, recoy, something like that. In a situation like this, the first thing you did was recoy the area, so I took a little walk, over to a spiny plant, which I marked, then on to a pile of stones that had golden glints in them, and a small round tumbleweed lying still. I marked the stones and the tumbleweed and a few other things, and was trying to remember what else was involved in a recoy—Bernie! Where was Bernie?—when I picked up a scent I didn't like: close to frog or toad except fishier, the fishy part sharper and more thinned out than the scent of an actual fish. I'm talking fresh fish, of course; rotten fish is another story. This particular smell—froggy, toady, fishy—meant one thing and one thing only: snake. Snakes scare the hell out of me. I'm not ashamed to admit it. But, and this might surprise you, I actually caught one once, fat and black, on a hike we took in high piney country somewhere. What got into me that day? The look on Bernie's face! I got a little lost in that memory, and when I came out of it, the snake smell was stronger.

I followed the scent. Hey! It was leading me back toward the saguaro, where Princess lay in the shade, watching me with those eyes of hers. And—oh, no!—behind her, a big snake was rising from its coil, mouth opening wide, fangs, so sharp, sticking out. Didn't Princess pick up the scent? What was wrong with her? But no time for any of those thoughts: I charged, barking my head off, aiming for the tail end, as far from those fangs as possible. The snake saw me coming—just those tiny slit eyes were plenty scary on their own—and whipped its head in my direction, so quick, and jabbed those fangs at me. That's their way—it's not an actual bite, as I knew from watching slo-mo on the Discovery Channel with Bernie. At the very last instant, but maybe too late, I launched myself in a tremendous leap, the highest in my life, and flew right over him. Something, possibly something sharp, just brushed the tips of the last hairs on my tail. I landed, skidded around, glimpsed Princess running—not trotting but actually running—away from the saguaro. The snake came toward me, slithering sideways, head up, eyes nasty. I booked, no second thoughts. You don't bring a spoon to a knife fight.

I ran in a wide circle, keeping plenty of distance between me and the snake, and caught up to Princess. She was still bounding crazily along, all her fluff streaming behind her. Underneath that coat, she was even smaller than I'd thought. I throttled down to my slowest trot and we kept going, side by side. Where were we headed? Away from men with rifles, away from snakes with fangs: all that mattered. As for what was going on in Princess's mind, I had no idea. She kept running, head forward in that determined way.

No one can run like that forever, and after quite a long time—the sun was at our backs now—Princess slowed to her fast trot, the one with the blurry legs. I walked beside her, keeping my eye out for snakes, seeing none. The only living creature other than us was a big black bird circling overhead. Not fond of birds, have I mentioned that already? Why are they so sour? Would I be sour if I could spend the day soaring through the blue sky? You tell me. And I was especially not fond of this bird in particular. I couldn't help wondering if it was following us from up there. Why would it be doing a thing like that?

Behind us, the sun sank lower. Our shadows got long in front of us, mine much longer than Princess's, of course. She was still in her fast trot, kind of amazing she could keep that up for so long. Maybe she didn't know how to go slower. I was puzzling over that when one of those strange buttes rose in the distance, towering over the desert floor. And what was that? A tiny glare at its base? The glare trembled, vanished, returned. A glare like that meant something shiny, and something shiny meant something human. Bernie was human. That was as far as my mind took me. I changed direction, headed for the butte. Without any prodding, Princess stayed with me.

The sun sank some more and the glare began to turn red. The glare got redder and redder, faded, and finally disappeared. By that time, there were shadows everywhere, the air cooling fast. The sky ran through all sorts of colors, and then went dark. Stars appeared, and the moon, not quite so thin as the night before. Princess was panting now, a small, whispery sound. We kept going, on and on. No idea what Princess was thinking; I was thinking: Bernie. The problem was that the butte didn't seem to be getting any closer. In fact, I realized after a while, I could no longer see it at all. And after that came some other realizations, having to do with hunger and thirst. My mind turned to a visit I'd made to the actual Rover and Company factory, where the best treats in the world got made, including these delicious—

With no warning, Princess came to a stop. I stopped, too. She just stood there, her head still forward, but not moving. We had to keep moving. I gave her a low bark. Princess didn't bark back, didn't whine, didn't do anything, just stood there. I stuck my head down and gave her an encouraging bump with my nose. Not hard at all, but what was this? She fell over sideways and lay still on the ground.

What was I supposed to do now? Her eyes were open, at least the one that I could see: the moon gleamed in it, a tiny curve of silver light. I waited for some idea, and one came to me pretty quick: why not pick her up again and carry her? No other ideas seemed to be out there, but I hesitated. Not that I was too tired for the job or anything like that; in fact, I felt strong and peppy, especially now that the air had cooled. There must have been some other reason. I was kicking around a few possibilities about what they could be, as Bernie liked to say, although in fact I had no possibilities in mind, so was actually kicking around nothing, and as for kicking, a ball, for example, I'd never done that except by accident . . . I lost the thread and a moment or so later saw that Princess was shivering.

I stood over her. The wind rose, sharp and cool, maybe even cold. Not cold to me, but to Princess, for sure. Her big dark eye, the one I could see, didn't seem to be looking at anything in particular. She didn't make a sound, just kept shivering. I lay on the ground and curled up around her.

The moon moved across the sky. Once a big bird—maybe that same bird that had tracked us during the day—flew across it. The moon, I'm talking about. A very strange sight, the way the bird shape appeared out of nowhere on the moon and then vanished. Princess wriggled closer against me. The shivering stopped. I could feel the beat of her tiny heart.

At dawn—and what a dawn, blazing up behind the butte, still so far away—we rose, stretched, gave ourselves a shake, did our business, and started walking. Correction, as Bernie sometimes said: I walked and Princess trotted, her fast trot with the blurry legs. She stayed right at my side, glancing up at me from time to time. I was boss. At least we'd cleared that up.

The sun rose higher, and with that came the heat, and also the bright glare, shining at the base of the butte. A glare like that meant something shiny. Shiny meant human. Bernie was human.

THIRTEEN

"Hey, get yer ass outside—you're not gonna believe this."

The next day, or maybe the day after. I was a bit confused, mostly on account of the dizziness. Also, and hard to believe, I was getting dragged down by the weight of Princess, dangling from my mouth. How was that possible? She weighed nothing at all. I myself was a hundred-pounder, Bernie, a two-hundred-pounder, sometimes more. That sometimes more part was always a problem. He would stand on the scale in the bathroom and say, "That can't be right." I got the biggest charge out of that for some reason. Once he'd picked me up to see if the two of us together could make the scale go past the end, or something, I wasn't sure what. Hate getting picked up, but of course I let Bernie.

"Whoa—is this for real?"

"Unless we're smokin' the same shit."

"But, dude, we are smokin' the same shit. We smoke the same shit every fuckin' day."

"So we're hallucinatin'? Haven't hallucinated—not a real good one—since 1969."

Hippies nearby? I knew just from how they talked. I looked

up and all of sudden the butte, which hadn't come any closer in so long, was right there; but unsteady, kind of wobbling. And at its base, also wobbling: an RV painted in rainbow colors, the sun glaring off its windshield; a tent with one open side; and two old guys, both bald except for long gray fringes all the way down to their shoulders. Hippies, no doubt about it.

"Will you look at that," said the one wearing a vest. "Wish we had a camera."

"We have a camera, dude," said the one with no vest.

"That right?"

"Yeah."

They passed a joint back and forth. I went right up to them and lowered Princess to the ground.

"Will you look at that. I thought it was a weasel or somethin', but it ain't."

"Course it ain't. No weasels in the desert."

"Sure are."

"Not."

The joint went back and forth. I stood there panting. Princess lay on the ground, eyes open.

"Point is, I thought it was a weasel he'd killed, like, the big dog, I'm talkin' about. But it's an itty bitty dog. The big one carried the little one. From outta nowhere, if you see what I mean."

"What do you mean?"

"Look out there. See anybody?"

"Nope."

"Then it's outta nowhere. How weird is that?"

"Huh?"

"Like, how often does it happen, two dogs from outta nowhere?"

"Beats the crap out of me."

I gazed up at these guys. The desert was full of old hippies—we'd run into them before, me and Bernie. Bernie didn't like them, not sure why, but I did, especially that hippie smell—sweat, leather, pot, toe jam—so interesting. I was smelling it now, maybe the all-time strongest.

"What do you think he's barkin' about?"

"Beats the crap out of me."

They took turns sucking at the stub end of the joint. "Could be he's thirsty."

"Can't think what else."

"Me neither."

Not too long after that, the hippie in the vest went inside the rainbow RV and returned with a bowl of water, which he lay on the ground.

"Get a load of them two goin' at that water."

"Like there's no tomorrow."

"Seize the day, man."

They bumped fists.

"Wonder if they're hungry."

"Sure as shit are thirsty."

"Go together sometimes, hungry and thirsty."

"We still got that pack of Slim Jims?"

"Slim Jims? Reckon dogs dig Slim Jims?"

Oh, brother. I liked hippies, but they had a tendency to be a little slow.

The hippie in the vest was called Disco; the other one was Crash. Crash produced some Slim Jims, tore one into little bits for Princess, tossed me a whole one, and soon another, and another, and maybe another after that. Night fell. Crash and Disco tried to build a fire but it went out. We all sat around where the fire would have been. Crash and Disco downed some beers, got going on another joint, a big fat one. The smoke drifted over to me and Princess in heavy clouds. Always enjoyed that smell. Princess stretched, lay down beside me, closed her eyes. I gazed at the stars and all sorts of thoughts went tumbling through my mind, way too fast to keep up, so I didn't even try. Except for missing Bernie, I felt pretty good. Soon I was just thinking about Bernie: his smell, how far he could throw the tennis ball when we played fetch, the slight limp from his wound when he got tired.

Later Crash switched on some music. They sang along, something about In-a-Gadda-Da-Vida, Baby. Nothing like Roy Eldridge and his trumpet, but not too bad. I sang along, too, doing my woo-woo kind of thing. Crash and Disco loved that, did some woo-wooing of their own.

"Maybe he's jonesin' for another Slim Jim," said Crash.

"Only one left," said Disco, "and I got the munchies."

So I didn't get a Slim Jim, which I suddenly wanted very badly. Maybe I had the munchies, too, whatever they were. But Crash and Disco were good guys, and they liked me. As my eyes closed and I sank into a lovely fuzziness, I heard them talking about how big and strong I was, and how much I might be worth.

I woke up in the morning, feeling tip-top. We'd slept in the tent with an open side, me and Princess, much warmer than out on bare ground, but she'd curled up against me just the same. I heard the sound of a car, far away, and thought: Bernie. But as it grew louder, I could tell it wasn't the Porsche. I rose anyway—Princess opened her eyes for a moment, then rolled over—and went outside.

From inside the rainbow RV came snoring sounds, one like honk-whee and the other more like honk-honk-HONK. They went together in a weird way, a bad kind of music. I snapped up a potato chip that happened to be lying by the RV—the ruffled kind, my favorite—and looked around. A dirty white pickup was approaching, trailing a long, low dust cloud. It dodged some spiny bushes, bumped across a gully and parked in front of the RV. A big guy with long hair and a bushy beard got out, banged on the side of the RV, and said, "Wakie wakie."

Sounds came from inside the RV—coughing, horking, and a few I couldn't identify. Then the door opened and Crash and Disco came out, both dressed as they'd been the day before, both blinking in the light.

"Hey," they said.

"Hey," said the bearded guy. "Where is he?"

Crash and Disco gazed around, saw me standing in the shadow of the butte, and pointed.

"Not a bad-lookin' animal," said the bearded guy.

"Not bad?" said Crash. "Check out the size of him."

"And the muscles," said Disco. "He'll do great up there."

"Maybe, maybe not," said the bearded guy. "Gonna hafta grow a thicker coat for one thing." He opened a door of the pickup, reached for something inside, then turned, sitting on the edge of the seat, his feet on the ground. "Here, fella," he said.

He was talking to me? This was all pretty confusing. I stayed put.

The bearded guy laughed, a nice laugh, not loud. "Smart, huh?" he said. "C'mon, I'm not gonna hurt you." And then he was holding up a biscuit, the real big kind, shaped like a bone. Hadn't had one of those in some time, but I remembered the taste: delish, and so crunchy, too. All of a sudden, my mouth was watering. The next thing I knew I was at the side of the pickup, standing by the bearded guy. He offered me the biscuit. At first, I didn't take it, but that smell: overpowering. "Don't care for biscuits?" he said. He started to withdraw it. I grabbed it, couldn't help myself. I did care for biscuits, cared a lot.

The bearded guy laughed again. I was aware of him watching me as I ate the biscuit. When I was done, he extended his hand as though to pat me. I let him. He was a good patter, patted my head, my shoulders, right down my back. "A hundred bucks," he said.

"Get outta here," said Crash.

"One fifty."

"Two," said Disco.

"One seventy-five," said the bearded guy. "Take it or leave it."

Crash and Disco moved off, muttering to each other. The bearded guy kept patting me, his eyes on them. He smelled okay, was a good patter, but one of those eyes did a tiny twitching thing I hadn't noticed before; it bothered me, hard to say why.

Crash and Disco returned. "Deal," they said.

The bearded guy took out his wallet, counted out some bills, handed them over. Crash and Disco bumped fists again.

"Beer for breakfast?" said Crash.

"Twisted my arm," said Disco.

"Some other time," said the bearded guy. He reached behind his back, held out another biscuit. I took it without hesitation this time: an excellent biscuit, and I hadn't had a decent meal in ages.

"What's your hurry?" said Crash, or maybe Disco; I wasn't really paying attention.

"A long way to go," the bearded guy said. He gave me another pat. But—what was this? In his other hand he had a—too late! A choke chain! I hated choke chains, and now this one was around my neck. I bolted; and was still in midair when those hard links dug deep on my neck and all my breath got cut off. I landed with a heavy thud. From behind came the sound of an even heavier one. I turned, saw the bearded guy stretched flat on the ground, still gripping his end of the chain, that twitch going strong now in one of his eyes.

I tried to run, surged forward with all my power.

"You believe that? He's draggin' you across the goddamn ground."

But no air, no air at all. I heard the bearded guy scramble to his feet, and the force on the other end got much stronger. Still I pulled and pulled, fighting for air, but I couldn't get any. A horrible wheezing noise started up, and the whole world went black at the edges. There was nothing to do but try to pull, try to move, try to stand. Then, from out of the black edges, came Princess, running full speed.

"What the hell is that?"

"We'll throw her in for nothin'."

"Midget like that in Alaska?" said the bearded guy. "She wouldn't even—ow!"

"Ha ha—you see that?"

"She bit his fuckin' ankle!"

Then a roar from the bearded guy, and the chain squeezed tighter, digging way in. The black edges grew thicker and thicker, leaving only a small circle of the normal world, and then all was black.

Bumpity-bump. Must have fallen asleep in the car, nothing unusual about that. I opened my eyes. Uh-oh. Everything stayed dark. And this was not the Porsche—I could tell by the sound, the smell, everything. Underneath me: a hard metal floor. I rose, my head hitting some kind of soft roof. I knew soft roofs like this: people snapped them onto the back parts of pickups. Memory returned, that twitchy eye most of all.

I felt a current of air, followed it, bumped into the side wall of the pickup bed. My nose found the tiny space between the soft roof and the side wall, where the air leaked in. I pushed into that space, and light leaked in, too. Just a sliver, but enough for me to see it was true: I was in the bed of a pickup with a snap-on roof; an empty bed, except for me. Also, I still had the choke chain around my neck. The free end glinted in the shaft of light, just lying there, attached to nothing.

I nosed into the tiny space, wriggled around, pushed and pushed. A soft roof, made of something that just wouldn't give. I got my front paws up on the side wall, drove up off my back legs. Pop! A snap let go, and all at once that tiny space was much bigger. I stuck my head through, looked out.

A desert track, like many I'd seen, but here was something strange: a barbed-wire fence running along beside it as far as I could see in either direction, signs hanging off the fence here and there. Beyond the fence stretched the desert, pretty much the same as on this side, no buildings, no humans. The only human in sight was the bearded guy: twisting toward the front, I could see his head in the back window of the cab. And at that very moment, he too twisted around—and saw me. That eye of his twitched, big-time.

Things happened fast. Must have lunged against that soft roof once more, and popped another snap open, because the next thing I knew I was airborne. Then came a hard landing and I was up and run—

Oh, no. The choke chain, squeezing tight around my neck, brought me up short. How had that happened? And then I saw: the free end hadn't come loose, was stuck inside, meaning I was getting dragged by the pickup. The bearded guy hit the brakes, hit them hard. The rear end skidded out wide, yanking me over the stony ground, the chain tightening fast and hard, blackness closing in again. Then all at once I shot free, just a short length of chain around my neck, the rest of it clanking against the side of the pickup.

I ran back up the track the way we'd come, the barbed wire fence on one side. The bearded guy shouted something, swung the pickup around. The engine revved hard behind me. I ran—ran my fastest, paws hardly touching the ground, ears flat back—but that engine noise got louder and louder, screaming in my ears. I didn't think, just found myself changing direction slightly and then leaping—up and over that barbed-wire fence. Not a real high fence, even kind of flimsy, only a few strands of wire, hanging loose, with lots of space between them, an easy fence for a pickup to plow right through. I raced ahead, down a long gradual slope, expecting to hear the scream of the engine any moment.

That didn't happen. After a while, I glanced back, saw the dirty white pickup parked on the other side of the fence, the bearded guy standing beside it, watching me. I kept going.

For a long time, I was alone. Then I had company: another one of those big black birds not far above. My tongue hung out, thick and dry, too big for my mouth. What had Bernie said about finding water in the desert, some trick of the Indians? I came close to remembering.

Later on, the sun at my back now, very hot, I came over a rise and saw something strange on the desert floor: a huge piece of plastic with circles on it. Red in the center, then yellow, then blue, although I can't be trusted when it comes to colors. But: a bull's-eye target, for sure. I went closer, at the same time aware that the big black bird no longer hovered above me, but was now streaking away, shrinking smaller and smaller.

Everything got quiet. I felt kind of funny, and paused, one

paw raised. The next moment a howl came down on me, out of nowhere, the loudest sound I'd ever heard, as though the whole sky was in a rage. Something shiny flashed over my head, moving almost too fast to see, and right after that—KA-BOOM! An enormous explosion, very near, knocked me down, and a huge fireball rose from the place where the target had been. Heat rolled over me in waves. The earth shook. I lay there, all curled up. A plane roared overhead, so close to ground level that I could see the picture on its nose—a woman in a bikini. Then everything got quiet again. I found a hole between some rocks and burrowed inside, lying still, not making a sound.

FOURTEEN

A Jeep bobbed up over a ridge not too far away, turned in my direction. I stayed where I was, deep in my hole, silent and still, harsh smells from the explosion still in the air. The Jeep stopped where the bull's-eye target had been and the driver got out. She wore cammies—Bernie owned cammies, too, way back in his closet, from the war—and had binoculars around her neck. I didn't like binoculars. When humans put them up to their eyes they seemed even more like machines than usual. That was what the driver did now: she raised the binoculars and swept them back and forth across the slope where I lay. All at once, she froze, the binoculars pointed right at me. No way she could see me, not with how I was hiding in the rocks. Then I noticed for the first time that the end of what was left of the choke chain lay outside the rocks, out in the open, glinting in the sun.

The driver lowered the binoculars, made her way up the slope, coming right toward me for sure. When she got close, just beyond my hidey-hole, she stopped and squatted down, peering inside. "Oh my God," she said. "Are you all right?" She had a nice voice and a nice face, but I didn't move or make a sound.

Lots of things dangled from the driver's belt. One was some kind of radio. She spoke into it. "Delta three," she said. "Affirmative on that dog. Not a coyote. Repeat, dog. I'll bring him in." She clicked off. "C'mon out, big guy. Must've been quite a scare, huh? Everything's all right now. I'm not going to hurt you."

I'd heard that before. I didn't move.

"Thirsty?" she said. "You look a little thirsty." She walked down to the Jeep, returned with a metal dish, poured water from a canteen—oh, the smell—and laid the dish near me.

I didn't move, not for the longest time. She squatted out there in the hot sun, patient, kind of like Bernie. The smell of that water, so cool and fresh: who could resist it forever? Not me. I crept forward and slurped up all the water in the dish, keeping my eyes on her the whole time.

"Knew you were thirsty," she said, refilling the dish. I drank the refill, and then another, and some more after that. "Been through the mill, haven't you?" she said. I didn't get that. I lay by the dish, most of my body outside the hole, chin on the ground, eyes on the driver. She had a nice voice and a nice face; was patient like Bernie. "Okay if I look at your tag?"

I didn't stop her. She reached out, examined the tag. "Chet, huh? That's a nice name." She took a notebook from her pocket. "I'll just copy down this number."

I'd never been in a plane, had no desire to, but pilots! They turned out to be great. At least these pilots were. They had a cool lounge beside the runway, with a grill out front. And what was cooking on the grill? Burgers, burgers by the ton! Not sure what by the ton meant, exactly, but anytime it had to do with food, good things happened.

"A burger lover, aren't you, Chet?" said the driver, who maybe was a pilot, too, possibly even the boss; everyone called her Major.

And, yes, I was a burger lover, no denying it. "Room for one more?" she said.

What a question.

I had one more, plus part of another I split with the major. After that, someone found a rubber ball and we had a game of fetch. One of the guys, Colonel Bob—who may in fact have been the top boss, hard to tell, what with the whole pilot world being brand new to me—was a pretty good thrower, his arm almost as strong as Bernie's.

"Got a set of wheels on you, huh, Chet?" said Colonel Bob.

Wheels? What was he talking about? But I liked Colonel Bob, especially his big red face and short gray hair, cut flat on top. He gave me a nice pat. So did the major. And some of the others. After some more fetch, I got tired—not like me at all, getting tired in the middle of fetch—and lay down in a shady spot overlooking a strange black plane on the runway, scary just to look at. My eyes closed.

"He'd be fun to have around," someone said.

"Who could afford to feed him?" said someone else.

I had a bad dream that ended with ants crawling on Adelina's face and Bernie saying, "Where is he?" I opened my eyes—and there, following the major out of the lounge, was Bernie! Not a dream, but the real Bernie, hurrying toward me, a big smile spreading across his face. I was up and running. I had no intention of knocking him down, just wanted to give him a nice greeting. Down on the ground, I licked his face, half aware of pilots coming out, laughing in a nice way. Then I heard Colonel Bob say, "Bernard? Is that you?"

Of course not: it was Bernie. Bernie! And I was so happy to see him I'd never be able to sit still again. But then came a surprise: Bernie rose—I could tell he wanted to so I let him out from under—and looked over at Colonel Bob.

"Where does it say I have to see your sorry face again?" he said.

"Right back at ya," said Colonel Bob. He strode up to Bernie. Was a fight about to break out? Colonel Bob was a big guy, bigger than Bernie. I got ready. But instead of a fight the two of them shook hands, and then Colonel Bob pulled Bernie close and they started slapping each other's backs real hard. Colonel Bob turned to the other pilots and said, "Gonna need that bottle of JD from my office. Weren't for this asshole, you wouldn't have to be putting up with my bullshit."

"Why is that, Colonel?" said one of the pilots.

"Son of a bitch saved my goddamn life, is why," said Colonel Bob. "Say hi to Bernard Little."

Bernie's name was Bernard? I was just finding that out now? What the hell was going on?

We sat in the lounge drinking JD, except for me. I had water and a biscuit or two Bernie had brought, the best kind, from Rover and Company. I'd tasted JD once, a story for some other time. The pilots crowded around, and Colonel Bob brought out a bunch of maps, said things like "Basra's here, we were thereabouts and the bastards came from thisaway." But Bernie—I was on the floor, right beside him—got all uncomfortable, shifting around, clearing his throat, mumbling his answers, so whatever had happened in some long-ago time between Bernie and Colonel Bob remained a mystery to me.

Another bottle of JD appeared. The major came in, handed what was left of the choke chain to Bernie. He ran it through his fingers. "He was wearing this?"

The major nodded. "Is it yours?"

"Chet's never had a choke chain on him in his life."

Not exactly true: there'd been that bad time with Mr. Gulagov, and maybe long before, back in my puppy days in that horrible crack house—had there been a choke chain then? I wasn't sure. While I was thinking about all that, more maps had come out, and Bernie no longer seemed uncomfortable.

"It's a kidnapping case," he was saying, "at this point involving a woman—possibly two women—and a dog."

"Chet?" said the major.

Bernie shook his head. "A show dog named Princess." He took out a picture: Princess on her satin pillow. "Don't suppose you saw her, too?"

"Uh-uh," said the major.

"No reason she'd be anywhere around here," Bernie said. "On the other hand, no reason Chet should be either." He pointed to the map. "Last time I saw him was at Clauson's Wells."

"Way down there? Did he run away?"

Me? Run away? I paused over the last of my biscuit.

"Chet?" said Bernie. "Never. The fact is, we had a little trouble with the county sheriff. Maybe a misunderstanding—I'm still trying to sort that out. Meanwhile, Chet and I got separated."

"Who's your client?" said Colonel Bob.

Bernie smiled. Have I mentioned what a great smile Bernie has? "You haven't changed," he said. "The client is the husband of one of the missing women, Adelina Borghese. They own the dog."

Adelina: in my mind I saw her with ants on her face and didn't feel like the biscuit anymore.

"And the other woman?" said Colonel Bob.

"Suzie Sanchez. She's a reporter for the *Valley Tribune*. We were in Clauson's Wells on a tip from her."

"Got pictures of the women?" said the colonel.

Bernie did. I caught a glimpse as he handed them over: Adelina holding Princess; and Suzie and Bernie in our backyard at home. Colonel Bob studied that one the longest. "You married?"

"Not anymore," said Bernie.

"This the ex?"

"No."

"Any kids?"

"One."

"Boy or girl?"

"Boy."

"Two girls here—twins. The mom got custody."

"Uh-huh," said Bernie. Silence. Bernie drained his glass and rose. "We better hit the road. I owe you guys."

"Hell you do," said Colonel Bob.

I rose, too.

"What a smart dog," said the major. I liked the major; one of those humans with a feel for me and my guys.

"We'll keep an eye out for these women," said Colonel Bob. "And the pooch. But I wouldn't mind a quick swing over to Clauson's Wells, if you've got time. Shouldn't take more than twenty minutes."

Twenty minutes? I didn't know what that was exactly; but not long, right? And I'd come so far, although the details of the journey were getting a little hazy in my mind. But far, that was the point. So how was this going to be possible?

I only started to get it when we were actually up in the chopper, Bernie and me kind of close together in the back, Colonel Bob at the controls up front. Were we zooming or what? The ground down below blew right by. Wow. So this was how the birds felt. The pukey part, too, I wondered? The truth was I preferred the Porsche, riding shotgun.

Bernie and Colonel Bob wore headsets, plus flying in a chopper turned out to be noisy, so I couldn't pick up much when they talked, but soon we swooped down in a long curve that made me dig my paws into the floor, and Bernie said something like, "Didn't see that before."

And the Colonel asked some question about a pond.

"Yeah," said Bernie.

"Let's put 'er down," said the colonel.

We landed and got out; so good to feel the ground under me. I looked around and saw where we were: on that grassy flatland above Clauson's Wells. There was the pond where Princess and I had drunk, and beyond it, the cabin where—

"What got into him?" said Colonel Bob.

But Bernie understood. He was hurrying after me. I pelted toward the cabin door, rose up, came down with my paw on the thumb piece. This time the door didn't open.

The colonel ran up. "He knows how to open doors?"

"Some," said Bernie.

"Where did you find him?"

"A long story," said Bernie. I wanted to hear it, but Bernie went silent. He put his thumb on the thumb thing and pressed down. Didn't open of course. I could have told him that . . . except I couldn't. I got a bit confused, and in that moment of confusion, Bernie raised his foot and kicked in the door. That splintering sound—I loved it! Kick it again, Bernie.

"Is this legal?" said Colonel Bob.

"Under ghost town law," Bernie said. Colonel Bob laughed. He liked Bernie a lot: I could tell from that laugh. I could also tell that Colonel Bob didn't mind a little rough stuff. Neither did we, me and Bernie. Bernie kicked the door again. It sagged off its hinges and swung open.

We went in, Bernie first, me almost squeezing in ahead of him. Everything looked the same as before—table, chairs, cot—except for one thing: the cot was empty. No Adelina. I went over to the cot, sniffed around, picked up the bad smell, but just barely.

I barked, a deep low bark that sometimes comes out all by itself.

"What's going on?" said Colonel Bob.

"Don't touch anything," said Bernie, taking surgical gloves from his back pocket and snapping them on.

FIFTEEN

Bernie searched the cabin, went over it on his hands and knees. Something about Bernie—or any human—on hands and knees always got me going so I had to wait outside with Colonel Bob. We walked around the pond. The sun was hot on my back. I paused for a drink.

"Taste good?" said Colonel Bob.

It did. We walked some more. "This PI gig pay at all?" the colonel said. "That car of his looks pretty beat up." Huh? He was talking about our car, the Porsche? I glanced up at him, saw the faraway look in his eyes. Sometimes humans got that look when they were talking to themselves inside; I was pretty sure of that. And if no other humans were around, sometimes bits of that talk leaked out. Like now, when he stopped and said, "Saved my goddamn life." He took out a pack of cigarettes and lit up. I loved the smell of cigarette smoke, but Bernie was trying to quit so I didn't get to enjoy it as much as I'd want. Colonel Bob tossed the match into the pond. "Hell on earth," the colonel said. The match sizzled. What a sound! The things it did to my ears! Do it again, Colonel Bob!

But he didn't, just stood by the pond with that inward look, taking deep drags off the cigarette, and soon Bernie came out of the cabin, tucking away the surgical gloves.

"Find anything?" said Colonel Bob.

"Just the spotlessness," Bernie said.

"Meaning?"

"Don't know yet," said Bernie. He glanced at me. "But something not good."

Colonel Bob held out the cigarette pack like he knew Bernie would take one, and Bernie did. The colonel flipped him the matches. Bernie lit up. I got ready for another sizzle, but it didn't happen. Instead Bernie blew out the match, shook it a bit, then put it in his pocket.

"Pack in, pack out?" said the colonel.

Bernie shrugged.

"It's the way to go," the colonel said. "Wish I had your discipline."

"Me?" said Bernie. "Discipline?" Was that a new word to Bernie? Sure was to me.

"Yeah," said Colonel Bob. "You."

Bernie was silent. They smoked by the side of the pond.

"How's the leg?" said the colonel.

"Perfect," said Bernie.

"No ill effects?"

"I was lucky."

"Sure looked bad that night," the colonel said. Bernie stayed silent again. "That stupid night," said the colonel.

"Yeah," Bernie said.

"Think about it much?"

"Nope," said Bernie. And then: "Some."

There was a long silence. The smoke from their cigarettes rose in the still air and slowly mingled. The colonel said, "Life is pretty good."

"Yeah," said Bernie.

Pretty good? Life was great! How could anyone miss that? It was right out there every day.

"We done here?" said the colonel.

"For now," said Bernie.

"Want to fly us back?"

Huh? Bernie could fly the chopper? He looked at the colonel, a funny expression on his face, and started laughing. The colonel laughed, too. They laughed and laughed, doubled over, laughed till tears came.

"Hey, Chet, down boy. Easy."

That laughing till tears came thing: always too much for me, but I tried my hardest to stay down.

Back in the Porsche, on the open road—in this case, empty two-lane blacktop—me in the shotgun seat: anything better than this? The truth was it could have been a little better if we'd had music, or if Bernie's hands had been more relaxed on the wheel. He was thinking: I could feel it, like some actual wave pressing against me. These thought sessions usually turned out pretty well for us. I watched the passing scenery, feeling tip-top, my mind a complete blank.

We came over a ridge, stopped at an overlook, and got out. Loved pit stops. I marked a boulder, a twig, and a spot on the ground where I smelled some creature I hadn't smelled before. That was always interesting. There were so many creatures I'd seen on the Discovery Channel but never smelled. Baboons, for example: wouldn't mind getting a whiff of them. I glanced over at Bernie, saw he was watching me. "Got a feeling you know a lot more about this than I do, boy. What's going on?"

I ran over to him, wagging my tail. What did I know? So much: me and Princess, that snake, the hippies and the bearded pickup guy, and what else? Adelina. Adelina and the ants. My tail went still. Bernie gave me a pat. "Let's go have some fun with a couple of morons," he said.

Sounded good to me.

Not long after that, we began to see traffic. Then came some roadside trailers, a gas station, a diner—I could always spot a diner from the shape, the smell arriving as we blew by—and we entered a town.

"Welcome to Nowhereville," Bernie said.

Hadn't heard of it, but I always liked going someplace new.

We parked in front of a low brick building with a gold star on the door and went inside. A man in a brown uniform stood behind a counter, tall and lean, with a crooked nose; once Bernie had made this perp's nose even more crooked than that. The uniformed man had a gold star on his chest, a cowboy hat on his head, and a bandage on his neck, maybe from a shaving cut. Bernie got shaving cuts all the time, but never so low down. The man saw us and stopped what he'd been doing, which was nothing.

"You again?" he said. Something familiar about him, but it wouldn't quite come to me.

"Nice to see you, too, deputy," Bernie said. "This here's Chet."

The man gazed down at me. I picked up his smell and began to remember. His hand went to that neck bandage and I remembered more. "So?" he said.

"Jog your memory at all?" said Bernie. "Seeing Chet?" He put his hand on my head, rested it there. That growling: was it me? I stopped.

"Nothin' wrong with my memory," the deputy said. "Too bad about that little misunderstanding over in Clauson's Wells, but we didn't see no dog, end of story."

"That's funny," said Bernie. "He saw you."

"Huh?" said the deputy.

"All you had to do was tell me," Bernie said. "A simple thing."

"Tell you what?"

"That you'd seen him, maybe followed him around a bit."

"Followed him around?"

Another man came in through a door at the back, tall and lean like the deputy, but with a straight nose. I recognized his smell, too. He gave Bernie a look, not friendly, and said, "He's back."

"But he's not making much sense, sheriff," the deputy said.

"Happens sometimes when you get your bell rung," said the sheriff. "An accident on our part, and we're truly regretful, but how were we supposed to know you were a PI in good standing?"

It's easy to tell when humans get angry: their faces flush, their voices rise, they start throwing punches. Bernie's different. When he gets angry—and it doesn't happen often—not much changes; sometimes all you see is this muscle in his jaw, getting hard and lumpy. I was seeing it now.

"An easy mistake to make," Bernie said, his voice not rising, growing quieter, if anything. "But why compound it?"

"Compound?" said the deputy. All humans have eyes too close together, in my opinion, but some, like the deputy, are worse than others.

"I think we're bein' threatened," the sheriff said. His eyes weren't that close together, but they were so pale they didn't seem to have any color, just two black spots in the middle of white. This was confusing. Wasn't a sheriff some kind of lawman, a cop? Normally I liked cops.

"No threat," said Bernie. "More of an opportunity."

"How so?" the sheriff said.

"In fact," said Bernie, "the kind of opportunity that doesn't come along very often—a do-over, no questions asked."

"Lost me," said the sheriff.

Me, too, and some time ago, but that didn't matter. Bernie was doing what he did best, being the smartest human in the room. I got the feeling I'd be grabbing these guys by the pant leg sometime soon, kind of crazy since they were lawmen.

"Your original story doesn't fit certain facts I've established since," Bernie said.

"Tough titty," said the deputy. The sheriff watched Bernie closely and didn't say anything. I got the feeling he was listening hard. Not me: this was way too complicated.

"What facts?" said the sheriff at last.

"Here's just one. You both denied seeing Chet here down in Clauson's Wells. But it's clear that's not the case."

"How?" said the sheriff.

Bernie turned to the deputy. "What happened to your neck?" he said.

The deputy's mouth opened, closed, opened again. "Boil," he said. "Infected boil."

"That's not the way they've got it written on your chart," Bernie said.

"Chart?"

"You know—medical records," Bernie said. "At that nice clinic just down the street."

"What the hell?" said the deputy. The sheriff made a gesture, maybe to hush him, but the deputy kept going. "They showed you my chart?"

"Would that be ethical?" Bernie said. "Just happened to be where I could see it, nobody's fault. But the point is they've got you down for a dog bite. More of a scratch, really, since the skin wasn't penetrated. Nothing about a boil, infected or otherwise."

Silence. The feeling in the room changed in a way I liked.

"Have to get that corrected, won't you, Les?" said the sheriff.

"Right away," the deputy said.

"No rush," Bernie said. "I made a copy of the original."

The sheriff held out his hand. "Mind if we take a look?"

"Not a hard copy," Bernie said. "Sorry—should have mentioned that. I scanned the relevant page and emailed it to my office." He took out his cell phone. "Amazing what these things can do."

More silence. The deputy's hand moved down to the butt of his gun. "Sounds like a possible felony to me," the sheriff said.

"Let's call in the FBI," Bernie said. "If they're not involved already."

"What's that supposed to mean?" said the sheriff.

"Nothin'," said the deputy. "Why are we even listenin'? He's just a bullshitter."

"Les?" said the sheriff. "Shut up."

I was with the sheriff on that. I'd seen bulls, and what they could leave behind, amazing, but I didn't get the connection to Bernie.

"And because of possible FBI involvement, you've got to be prepared for all the facts of your stakeout at the saloon in Clauson's Wells coming out."

"What facts?" said the sheriff.

"That's the question," Bernie said. "Let's start with what you were doing there in the first place."

"Tole him that already," said the deputy.

"The on-the-lookout for vandals tale?" Bernie said.

"Wouldn't put it that way," said the sheriff.

"How would you put it?" Bernie said.

"We were pursuing a long-running investigation."

"About vandalism?"

"Correct."

"And you had a tip that night."

"Correct again."

"Who from?"

"Don't know how things run in the big city," the sheriff said, "but here in the sticks we protect our informants."

"From the FBI?"

"Say again?"

"Simple question," Bernie said. "Are you going to protect your informant from the FBI?"

"Christ Almighty," said the deputy. "Why's he keep bringing up the FBI?"

"It's this case I'm working on," Bernie said.

"Already told you," the sheriff said. "We don't know nothin' about that."

"Diddley," said the deputy.

Diddley? Bo Diddley was back in the picture? I tried to sort the case out in my mind, got nowhere, had a nice big yawn. The deputy noticed and backed up a step or two.

"That's not going to help you," Bernie said. "This is one of those expanding cases, expanding fast, and you'll get swept up in it whether you like it or not. We have the kidnapping of Adelina Borghese and her dog Prin—"

"We already—"

"—cess, and that has international implications, which is what'll be bringing the FBI in. Now we've got this missing reporter Suzie Sanchez—"

"Didn't see her neither," the sheriff said. "Told you that, too."

"It's possible you didn't see her," Bernie said. "But not possible you didn't see her car—it was parked right outside the saloon." Bernie took out a photo: Suzie's car and Suzie standing beside it.

The sheriff glanced at the photo, shook his head. The deputy shook his head, too. For some reason two humans doing that at the same time is a thing I like to watch; I lost track of what was going on and missed part of the next bit.

". . . what we didn't discuss before," Bernie was saying, "namely that cabin on the ridge above the town. Who owns it?"

"Cabin?" said the sheriff.

"What cabin?" said the deputy.

Bernie smiled, no idea why; and it looked kind of strange, with that anger muscle still showing in his jaw. "Did I mention Suzie Sanchez's job? She's a reporter for the *Valley Tribune*. No one knows where she is right now, but she was working on the Borghese kidnap story and the last call she made came from Clauson's Wells. See what this means?" The sheriff and his deputy remained silent. "The spotlight's going to be shining down on your little county," Bernie said, "and soon."

"What spotlight?" said the deputy. "We shoulda taken this guy and—"

The sheriff held up his hand. "It's just his approach—maybe could use some improvement."

"Who are we talking about?" said Bernie, still smiling.

"There you go," the sheriff said. "Probably why we end up in these misunderstandings. But I'd never want anyone thinking this office isn't behind any legitimate investigation."

"He's a fuckin' PI," said the deputy. "Nothing le—"

The sheriff raised his hand again, this time adding, "Les?" The deputy cut himself off. "Now this cabin you mention is a total unknown to us, like it or not. But maybe it's owned by the same guy who owns the ghost town."

"Someone owns Clauson's Wells?" Bernie said.

"Sure does," said the sheriff. "There's all these plans to make it a tourist attraction."

"Name of the owner?" said Bernie.

"Have to look that up," the sheriff said. "Some investor from Vegas."

Bernie stopped smiling. "Sherman Ganz?" he said.

"Yeah," said the sheriff, his eyebrows rising; a good sign for us, and one I always spotted. "If you know the answer, why ask?"

SIXTEEN

"Don't know exactly what game they're playing, that sheriff and his deputy," Bernie said, back in the car, zooming out of Nowhereville, "but one thing's for sure—they stink."

No doubt about that, but it's not putting Bernie down—something I would never do!—to say the sense of smell isn't usually his strength. Bernie was full of surprises. And what was better than this? In the Porsche, on the job, two-lane blacktop stretching as far as I could see, big blue sky above. A little tasty nibble and everything would have been perfect. When had I last eaten? Couldn't remember. My mind wandered a bit, mostly going over the smells of different foods I liked. Steak, for example, especially with A.1. sauce, burgers, especially bacon burgers, and just plain bacon, too, all by itself. In fact, the smell of just plain bacon sizzling over a flame was one of the most amazing things in life. You may not know this, your sense of smell perhaps more like Bernie's, but there are two kinds of smells—smells you have to find and smells that find you. Bacon smell finds me, every time. Bernie likes his bacon crisp, but he always takes mine out of the pan first, because I prefer the juicy kind of bacon, with lots of those thick, white fatty parts, so delicious, and to tell the truth totally uncooked bacon wasn't at all bad either, something I knew from this one time when somehow completely by accident I'd gotten hold of a whole family-size package of gourmet fresh-from-the-farm—

"Chet? You hungry? How does a picnic sound? I could go for a little picnic my—easy, boy."

Bernie pulled off the road, bumped up to the top of a rise, and parked. I love picnics, and Bernie always makes sure we have a nice view. He popped the trunk, took out our gas burner and the cooler, soon had sausages cooking over the open flame. We gazed out on the desert and gobbled up those sausages—loved sausages, too, almost as good as bacon—glistening with lovely grease, just perfect; turned out we were both famished, me and Bernie. After that, Bernie started in on a shiny apple. Apples are something we usually share. He took a few bites then reared back and threw the core as far as he could, and that's far. I was already on the move when he had his arm back, of course, and the apple core was still tumbling on the stony ground when I scooped it up and trotted back to Bernie, fetch with an apple being a little different from fetch with a ball, since there was nothing left to drop at his feet. So I just stood beside him, feeling good for no reason. He gave me a pat, the soft pat-pat-pat kind, a bit too quick, meaning his mind was somewhere else.

"I just don't know, Chet," he said, gazing down the two-lane blacktop. "What's the logical next step? Vegas." He pointed. "Thataway. But I don't feel it." He tapped his chest. Same here: in my own chest I felt nothing but the slow and steady boom-boom-boom that was always there.

Bernie packed up our picnic stuff. I heard an engine sound, far off, coming from thataway; a bike, not a car. Then I spotted a glare on the blacktop, at the distant line where the ground touched the sky. We hopped in the car. Bernie, turning the key, paused and said. "Hear something?" Oh, Bernie. He peered down the road. Hey. Suddenly the motorcycle was much closer, the dark shape of the rider bent low.

"Looks like fun, huh?" Bernie said. And almost before he'd even finished saying it, the bike flashed by. Bernie's head whipped around in the direction it had gone. "Was that Nance?" I didn't know, in fact hadn't seen much, getting caught up in the roar of the engine and the smell of the exhaust. Bernie floored it and we fishtailed onto the road, headed in pursuit.

I love pursuit, especially in the Porsche. No one gets away from us, baby. Not quite true: there'd been that time in the high mountains, chasing after one of Gulagov's men. He'd gotten away, all right, but not for long, and only because the Porsche had ended up shooting off the cliff. But that was the old Porsche, maybe not as old as this one, but not as good either, Bernie said so; something about compression ratios, I couldn't remember what, just had enjoyed watching Bernie and our garage guy, Nixon Panero, working on the engine, black liquid splashing everywhere.

And now we were flying, closing the distance between us and the bike real fast, the wind blowing me back against the seat. The whistling of the wind in my ears, the howl of the engine, and . . . ? Was that me howling, too? Nothing like a good chase to get me going; I was conscious of that beat inside my chest, now speeding up, going boom-boom-BOOM, boom-boom-BOOM, practically shaking the whole car. Were we going to catch that biker or what? And when we did, well . . . I actually wasn't sure about that part, since Nance was on our side, right? But I'd worry about that when the time came, as humans liked to say, or never, which was my approach. I glanced down at Bernie's pedal foot: to the metal!

And sideways the whole desert was just a blur, whizzing by so fast I couldn't even—

What was that? A funny little lurch?

"Uh-oh," said Bernie. "Did you feel a little—?" Then came a clunk, and another clunk, followed by a whole bunch of them, plus more lurching. The Porsche went all jerky, kind of stumbling to the side of the road like a human who'd had way too many.

We sat there, the engine going pop-pop, pop-pop. The bike grew smaller and smaller and finally vanished. It got very quiet, except for the pop-pop. Bernie's hand curled into a fist; he had big strong fists and plenty of perps, gangbangers, and bad guys had seen what they could do. He raised his fist as though to punch the steering wheel, something I'd seen guys—good and bad ones—do plenty of times; but then Bernie paused, his hand relaxing, and no punch came. That was one of the very best things about Bernie.

Out came the tools, and not long after that the manual, too. Nothing good ever happened when Bernie had his head deep in the engine. The wind fluttered the pages of the open manual, Bernie trying to still them with an oil-stained elbow, a tool in each hand. After a while, I couldn't bear to watch, and took a little—what was Bernie's word?—recon, that was it. I took a recon around the area, smelled the scent—froggy, toady, fishy—of a snake, but very faint. I followed the scent, lost it, circled around, and picked it up again, and there, in the shadow of a big rock, I found—what? I wasn't sure; some kind of strange snake, very pale, with no eyes at all, just nasty holes where eyes should have been.

"Chet! What the hell's going on?"

I realized I was barking my head off and stopped. But then I caught sight of that eyeless head again, and maybe more barking started up. "Chet? What is it?" Bernie's voice changed, stopped being irritated, not that he ever got irritated with me. "Find something?" He came over, saw the snake, and laughed. Then—oh, no—before I could stop him, he reached down and picked it up. Snakes bite! Didn't Bernie know about those fangs?

But this snake didn't bite, just dangled in a limp sort of way from Bernie's hand. "Only a skin, Chet," he said. "Nothing to be afraid of—the snake got too big and shed it, that's all." For some reason I thought that was plenty to be afraid of and hurried back to the car. I even considered lying underneath it, but then I heard something dripping from the engine.

Sometime later, Bernie turned the key, listened hard, and said, "Voilà," a brand-new word to me. Maybe it meant "pulling a U-ee," because that was what we did, not following that bike, but headed in the other direction, thataway.

"Vegas," Bernie said. He took a deep breath. "I can't think straight when it comes to Vegas." Bernie not think straight? Ridiculous. I shifted closer to him. Soon we had music—Billie Holiday, in one of her sad moods. I preferred her in her happy moods, with Roy Eldridge blowing that trumpet, so I was kind of glad when the cell phone rang and Bernie switched her off.

"What's up?" Bernie said.

I could hear the voice on the other end: Lieutenant Stine. "Nothing good," he said, and some more I didn't catch and then Bernie touched a button and Lieutenant Stine's voice came through our speakers. ". . . and Suzie Sanchez still hasn't shown up at work and no one there's heard from her. Sure these cases are related?"

"Not sure of anything right now," Bernie said. "But she was working on the Borghese story and Clauson's Wells is an hour or so from their ranch."

"This is in Rio Loco County?"

"Right. Know anything about the sheriff?"

"No," said Lieutenant Stine. "Why?"

"Bad vibe."

"That's it? Bad vibe? We talked about holding back on this case, didn't we, Bernie, and how that's not going to happen?"

"Bad vibe is all we've got," Bernie said. He'd left out the smell, but there was nothing I could do about that.

Long silence. "I'll look into him," said the lieutenant.

"And the deputy, Les somebody," Bernie said. "Did you check Suzie's apartment?"

"Telling me how to do my job? Course I sent somebody out."

"And?"

Papers rustled in the background. "Guy there said he'd just arrived and hadn't seen her."

"Guy?" said Bernie. "What guy?"

"Friend from out of town, it says here."

"What friend?"

More rustling. "McKnight," said Lieutenant Stine. "Dylan McKnight."

Bernie slammed on the brakes. I thought I was going to get thrown out of my seat, but the car spun around so fast, taking off the other way, that I ended up hardly moving at all. Bernie could drive, no doubt about that. The squeal of burning rubber, the smell that went with it: so exciting I was almost beside myself, whatever that meant. Some foggy idea about another one of me almost took shape at the edge of my mind, and while that was happening I missed a bit of the conversation.

". . . didn't run him through the system?" Bernie was saying.

"Not according to this," said Lieutenant Stine. "Any reason we should have?"

"He did time at Northern State, for Christ's sake."

"What charge?"

"Drugs."

"Dealing?"

"Yeah."

"Dealing what?"

"Pot."

"Pot, huh? That still a crime in this jurisdiction?"

"What the hell?"

"Just a joke, Bernie. Look, this guy—what's his name? McKnight?—didn't arouse any suspicion, but I'll send someone out again if you want."

"Forget it," Bernie said. "We're almost there." He clicked off.

I looked around. We were almost where? What was going on? All I knew was that Bernie and the lieutenant weren't getting along. Weren't they friends? I shifted around a bit, found a comfortable position. A very comfortable position, in fact, and I loved comfortable positions.

When I woke up, we were still in the desert but I could see the tops of the downtown towers. They seemed to be floating in the sky, with nothing holding them up. For a moment I thought I was still dreaming.

I'd been to Suzie's place before. She lived in a garden apartment not far from Max's Memphis Ribs, the best restaurant in the whole Valley, in my opinion, and not just because the owner, Cleon Maxwell, was a friend of ours and gave us two-for-one coupons, but mostly because of those ribs: the juicy meat and then when you're done with that—the bone! Back to Suzie's apartment. There were lots of garden apartments in the Valley, but Bernie didn't like any of them, on account of those little lawns and plants always being the wrong kind, bad for the aquifer.

We got out of the car and walked to Suzie's door. Bernie didn't say anything about the aquifer, didn't seem to even notice the lawn or the plants. Other times at Suzie's door, Bernie would knock softly, with a look on his face that reminded me of Charlie. Not now. He banged on the door and his face was hard.

The door opened and there stood Dylan McKnight, pretty boy, barefoot and barechested. He looked like an actor from the kind of movie Bernie hated. His eyes went to Bernie, then to me, back to Bernie. Dylan McKnight actually had a nice smell; and mixed with it, I picked up the scent of a woman, not Suzie.

"Oh," said Dylan McKnight, "it's you."

"Where is she?" said Bernie.

"Who?"

The next thing I knew we were inside the house and Bernie had Dylan against the wall.

"Suzie?" Dylan said, his voice getting squeaky. "You mean Suzie? I don't know where she is. I already told the cops. She was gone when—"

Bernie lifted Dylan right off the floor. "We don't have time for this," he said.

"But I swear, I—"

"Honey?" A voice—a woman's voice, not Suzie's—came from down the hall. We all turned to look. A naked woman appeared. "Oops," she said. A naked human was an interesting sight, but in my opinion they always look better with their clothes on, no offense. She backed up a step, tried to cover herself with her hands, but her hands were small and there was a lot to cover.

"My fiancée, Vanessa," said Dylan.

Vanessa raised one of her hands for a quick finger wave. Bernie lowered Dylan to the ground, let go of him.

"Fiancée?" said Bernie.

"Means we're getting married," said Dylan. "I wanted Vanessa to meet Suzie."

"She sounds so fabulous," said Vanessa.

"How did you get in?" Bernie said.

His eyes were on Vanessa, but he must have been talking to Dylan because Dylan replied, "Still have a key. I told her I'd give it back so she wouldn't have to worry about loose keys floating around."

"She knew you were coming?"

"Oh, yeah, sure. She said we'd go out to dinner, like the two couples."

"What two couples?"

"Me and Vanessa, you and Suzie." Dylan gave Bernie a funny look. "She's nuts about you, man. Don't you know that?"

"This is Bernie?" Vanessa said. "Hi, Bernie." Another quick finger wave. "And what a nice doggie."

"Get dressed," Dylan said.

Vanessa giggled, started backing away, trying to cover herself, at the same time shrugging her shoulders and raising her eyebrows, a human look that meant, Hey, what can I do? At that moment Bernie must have finally realized his mouth was open. It slowly closed.

Doggie? I closed my mouth, too.

SEVENTEEN

We went home. I loved home and hadn't been there in way too long. While Bernie got the mail out of the box and flipped through it—lines appearing on his forehead, meaning lots of bills—I ran around the lawn sniffing for trespassers. And did we have them, in spades. Spades are a kind of shovel, which I know on account of this perp who once swung one at Bernie and was now wearing an orange jumpsuit at Central State, somewhere in all that being the connection between spades and trespassers, but why worry where exactly? Instead I followed the scents: squirrel, bird, the mailman, toad, and several of my guys, including—Iggy? Was it possible Iggy had been out? I hadn't smelled Iggy in a long time, couldn't be sure. I glanced over at Iggy's place and at that very moment he ran up to the window and saw me. He started barking that yip-yip-yip, got his front paws up against the glass, lost his balance, and tumbled out of sight.

"C'mon, Chet."

I followed Bernie inside. Ah. I stretched, a really good long stretch, butt up, head down, a little squeak coming out of my mouth for some reason, didn't even sound like me, me with my deep growly bark, so I barked a few deep growly barks just to hear them and hadn't quite finished when I noticed a rubber chew toy—one of my favorites, shaped like a doughnut—lying in a corner of the front hall. I'd forgotten all about it! I bounded over and got to work. Meanwhile, the message light was blinking. Bernie pressed the button.

"Hey, this is Janie." Janie, the groomer; hadn't been groomed in a while, could probably use it. "Got your message, guess we're playing phone tag. It's just about that Post-it note. How's Chet doing? I'll be out of reach till the eighteenth, hiking up in the Blood Mountains—please give me a call then."

"Post-it note?" Bernie said. "What's she talking about?"

I paused in mid-chew, came pretty close to remembering.

Beep. "Chuck Eckel here. You're kind of hard to reach, buddy. If I don't hear from you real soon we're gonna have to close out your position."

"What the hell?" Bernie stabbed at the number pad. "Hey," he said. "Bernie Little."

"Bernie, my man, where you been?" I recognized the voice of the Hawaiian shirt guy from the Dry Gulch bar, at the same time realizing it was one of those human voices I didn't like, very friendly on the outside but nasty way deep down.

"Working," Bernie said.

"Forgotten what you do," said Chuck Eckel.

"I'm a private investigator."

"A private dick, huh?"

Bernie hated that expression; his whole body tensed up. "Does all your information come from crappy novels?" he said.

"Say what?"

"Never mind," Bernie said. "What's up?"

"Whoa," said Chuck Eckel. "Back up a sec. What was that crack about crappy novels? I don't read any goddamn novels."

"You win," said Bernie.

Silence on the other end. When Eckel spoke again, the friendly covering of his voice was all gone. "Enough pleasantries," he said. "You've got two hours to cover your position."

"What are you talking about?"

"Your tin play, what else?"

"But I already covered my position—that three grand, remember?"

"It's deteriorated since then—all this shit in La Paz."

"Lost me," said Bernie.

"Don't you read the papers—the miners are all on strike, they're rioting in the streets."

"But . . . but shouldn't that raise the price?" Bernie said.

"Through the roof," said Eckel. "But that wasn't your play. You went short. I need a check for five grand—you've got two hours." Click.

Bernie just stood there, like . . . like he didn't know what to do. That was impossible. Plus Bernie wasn't the tallest man I'd ever seen—that would be Cedric Booker, the Valley DA—but no way could you call him short. I went over and stood beside him. He glanced down at me, smiled a little smile.

"Feel like another visit to Mr. Singh?"

Sure. Always had time for Mr. Singh, but a visit now? Didn't he already have the watch?

"It'll have to be the ukulele," Bernie said.

The ukulele? Oh, no.

* * *

"What a beautiful instrument," said Mr. Singh. He turned it over in his hands. "Genuine Hawaiian koa, highly flamed, Sitka spruce top braces, bone nut. Do you play?"

"A bit."

A bit? Bernie was a master!

"Would a brief selection be possible? Anything at all."

Of course, it was possible. How about "Waltz Across Texas"? "Parachute Woman"? "Ghost Riders in the Sky"? And there was always "Surfin' USA," guaranteed to get them up and dancing. Suddenly I was in the mood to see Mr. Singh dance. I don't exactly dance, myself, but when dancing starts up I'm no wallflower either, kind of confusing, the wallflower part, because I've often seen flowers—even flowers growing by a wall—dancing in the breeze.

But no brief selection came. Bernie just shook his head and said, "Maybe another time."

We left with some money, drove in silence to an office building, not one of the downtown towers, but a crummy old place across from a strip mall. A security guard with a toothpick sticking out of his mouth said, "No dogs." I had to wait in the car. That happened sometimes and I was cool with it. While Bernie was gone I thought about how good it would be to jump up and snatch the toothpick right out of that security guard's mouth and then just stand there, letting him think he could catch me.

"Tin futures, never again," said Bernie as we drove away. "Even if you have to tie me down." Tie Bernie down? Couldn't and wouldn't. As for tin futures, I had no clue. And neither, it looked like, did Bernie. That meant no one had a clue, so there was no point even thinking about it. I'm the type who can stop thinking about something in a flash, so I did.

* * *

Back home, we went into our own office and Bernie got busy on the whiteboard. I lay on the floor and listened to the marker going squeak squeak, also got involved with its smell, a real head-clearer.

"Over here," Bernie said, drawing a box and writing something inside it, "we've got the Borgheses—the count and Adelina. Passaic? What the hell was that about? Info came from Suzie, and of course that's part of the . . . Then"—squeak squeak—"we've got Aldo, the secretary, Italian name but his English is perfect. Nance, the trainer, supposed kneecapper of Babycakes. And don't forget Princess."

Forget Princess? Never. She'd attacked that big bearded guy!

"Hey, Chet, what got into you?"

That growling—was it me? I put a stop to it. Bernie turned back to the board. "Babycakes over here, with Sherman Ganz." Squeak squeak. "Lives in Vegas but owns Clauson's Wells, according to the Rio Loco sheriff, who gets his own box down here. And maybe a map would help. Rio Loco Ranch, county seat, weapons test center, Vegas, and what about . . ." The marker moved faster and faster, the whiteboard got blacker and blacker, Bernie's voice started going fuzzy, the marker smell lost its head-clearing power. ". . . motorcycle . . . scope . . . cabin . . . Suzie . . ." A deep sigh: that was me.

Ring ring. The phone. I opened my eyes: in the office, Bernie at the desk, head down, his own eyes closed. They cracked open blearily as he reached for the phone and knocked it off the desk.

"Bernie?" A voice came from underneath, where the phone had fallen, an irritated voice I knew well: Leda. Bernie bent down, groped around. "Are you there?" she said. "Is this one of your juvenile—"

"Um," said Bernie scrambling up from under the desk. "Uh, hi."

"What's going on? You sound weird."

"Phone is maybe um . . . bad connection."

"I can hear you fine."

By this time, Bernie was in his chair at the desk, phone in place; he waited, back straight, alert.

"Were you asleep?" Leda said.

"At—" Bernie checked his watch. "—one thirty in the afternoon? Of course not."

"Listen, something's—"

"I'm listening."

"Please don't interrupt, Bernie. I barely have time to explain this."

"Explain what?" said Bernie, leaning forward, phone tight to his ear.

"Bernie, please."

"Please what?"

"Please stop interrupting."

"I'm not interrupting."

"You just did."

"I did not."

"Bernie, for the last time."

Bernie's mouth opened and closed.

"The point is," Leda said, "Malcolm's out of town on business and a major account is suddenly blowing up so I've got to stay till it's sorted out, plus it's the maid's day off and—"

"You want me to pick Charlie up from school?"

"There you go ag—" Leda cut herself off. "Yes," she said, lowering her voice a bit. "And keep him for the night if possible."

A big smile lit up Bernie's face.

* * *

Charlie went to a private school—meaning you have to pay money to go there even if you live two blocks from the best public school in the Valley, where you don't have to pay a dime—a big, long thing I'd heard Bernie say more than once, in fact every time he cut the check. He saw us and came running across the school's beautiful broad lawn, mowed like a putting green—for some reason, whenever I get on a putting green, and it hasn't happened often, the urge to run around hits me, crazy running with lots of sharp back-and-forthing—and gave Bernie a big hug. Then a big hug for me, and soon after that I was taking him for a ride on my back. Hey! He'd grown a bit, but still nothing for me; I could have carried him all day.

"Is that your dog?" said a kid.

"His name's Chet," said Charlie. "I call him Chet the Jet 'cause he's so fast."

"Can I pat him?"

"Sure."

Kids patted me. Were we having fun or what? It was a nice school, worth every penny.

Back home, Charlie was hungry, so we had a little snack: milk and cookies for Charlie, a biscuit for me, and then another, since I turned out to be hungry, too, and a beer and some pretzels for Bernie, me helping out by finishing off what was left in the pack.

After snack time, Bernie said, "Got any homework?"

"Nope," said Charlie.

"Then how come your backpack's so heavy?"

"It's a mystery," Charlie said.

Bernie laughed.

"That's what you do, right?" Charlie said. "Solve mysteries?"

"Sometimes," Bernie said.

"How many bad guys have you killed?"

Bernie was silent for a moment. "What makes you think I've killed any?"

"Mom says so."

Bernie nodded, took a deep breath. "In this job, solving mysteries, we've sent some bad guys to jail, Chet and I, but I've never killed anybody."

"But Mom—"

Bernie held up his hand and Charlie went quiet right away. "In the war, that's another story."

"You killed bad guys in the war?"

"Yes."

"How many?"

Bernie licked his lips. I'd seen plenty of humans do that, including just about every single one Bernie'd ever interviewed, but I'd never seen him do it himself till now. "I don't know, exactly."

"Two?"

"More than two."

"Nine?"

"Less than nine."

"Somewhere in between?"

"Yes."

There was a silence. Then Charlie said, "That's not too many, Dad."

Bernie looked away, out the window. Charlie drained the last of his milk, leaving a white mustache behind. I loved those!

"What was the war about?" he said.

"I'm not sure," Bernie said. "I don't think anyone is."

"But it happened anyway?"

"Some wars are like that—the real reasons come later," Bernie said. "How about we go outside and play catch?"

"Teach me how to throw the curve ball," said Charlie.

"You're too young to throw the curve ball."

"But I need an off-speed pitch."

"I'll teach you the cutter."

"Like Rivera?"

"Just like Rivera."

Or something like that: I couldn't hear too well on account of I was already at the front door, waiting as patiently as I could.

EIGHTEEN

"Brush your teeth?" said Bernie the next morning.

"Yeah," said Charlie.

"Didn't hear any spitting," Bernie said. So what? Bernie didn't hear a lot of things; but I hadn't heard any spitting either. Hey! Charlie was tricky.

He laughed.

"Go brush your teeth," said Bernie.

Charlie went into the bathroom. I followed Bernie into the office. He took down the Niagara Falls picture, opened the safe, and removed an envelope.

"What's in there?" said Charlie from the doorway.

"That was quick," Bernie said. "How many teeth did you do?"

"All of them, Dad. Wanna smell my breath?"

"No, thanks."

Why not? Sounded like a great idea to me. I sidled over to Charlie.

"What's in the envelope?" he said.

Bernie gazed down at Charlie for a moment, then handed him the envelope. Charlie opened the flap and took out two things:

a magazine and the glossy photo of Princess with the bull's-eye target drawn over her. That reminded me of the huge bull's-eye target out in the desert and the plane that came screaming out of the sky and I missed a bit of what came next. When I tuned back in, Charlie had the magazine open and was placing the Princess photo against the narrow ripped margin inside.

"It fits," he said.

"Sure looks like it," said Bernie.

"Is it a clue?"

"I think so."

"About what, Dad? Is that little dog in trouble?"

"Probably," Bernie said.

"What are you gonna do?"

"Find her."

"Can I come?"

Bernie smiled. "What about school?"

"I could do a report on it."

"Nice try."

We dropped Charlie off at school, then swung by Nixon Panero's. Nixon Panero was one of our best sources, kind of strange because we'd put him away for a year or two. He had an auto body shop and garage at the end of a long line of car places in a bad part of town. My old buddy Spike was lying by a stack of tires. He saw us and came charging over—not really charging, now that Spike was getting on a little, his angry face turning white—and stood in front of the car, hair on end, barking and barking. Spike was still one scary-looking dude, part Rottweiler, part pit bull, part unknown. We got out and Bernie went into the office. Spike had no interest in Bernie. He came right for me, showing his teeth, gone all yellow and brown, and lunged for my neck, still surprisingly quick.

But not quick enough, not quick like—this! And in a flash it was old Spike who got taken by the neck. His fur tasted horrible, like motor oil. I let him go. He retreated a step or two and growled. I growled back. He growled. I growled. He turned, walked over to the stack of tires and lay down, his eyes on me. I moved toward the bays where the mechanics worked, glancing back once. Yes, one of my best buddies, but Spike couldn't be trusted.

The Porsche was already up on a lift and Bernie and Nixon were standing under it, peering up.

"Say that again?" Bernie said.

"Gonna cost you," said Nixon.

"I caught that," Bernie said. "I meant the part about what's wrong."

Nixon told Bernie what was wrong, but I missed most of it, partly because of all the strange words, mostly because Nixon was hard to understand anyway, on account of him always chewing on a big plug of dip.

"But I thought you'd checked all of this out while it was still on the lot," Bernie said. "Before money changed hands, if you see what I mean."

"Course I did," Nixon said. He spat out a nasty glob. "But like I told you, can't make no promises with these antiques. They're tempermental—like them old-time Hollywood stars."

"Didn't know you were a movie buff."

"The biggest," Nixon said. "I got every movie Bette Davis ever made, bar fuckin' none." He tapped with his wrench at the underside of the car. "Want me to get started on this or not?"

Bernie was gazing at Nixon, mouth open. He closed it, opened it again, and said, "Yeah."

I went over and sniffed at the nasty glob. Wow. My stomach lurched and I backed away. Believe it or not, I'd actually seen

Spike lick up a glob just like this, maybe bigger. Had to admire the big guy, no doubt about it.

The sun was high in the sky when we drove out of there and hit the freeway. The car sounded lovely to my ears, strong and purring, almost like some powerful animal, except its smells were all machine.

"Bette Davis," Bernie said after a while. A new name to me and I waited for more. But no more came. Much later, Vegas rising in the distance, Bernie said, "Suzie would sure get a kick out of . . ." He went silent again.

We tracked down Sherman Ganz at his tennis club. Been on plenty of golf courses—especially a while back when Bernie took up running on them in the evening to get in shape. Love golf courses, the water hazards especially. But this was my first time at a tennis club, although I've had a lot of experience with tennis balls, of course. All kinds of balls, really: tennis balls, baseballs, rubber balls, lacrosse balls—my favorite actually, the way those suckers bounce, and just wonderful for chewing, can't begin to tell you the feelings that zing up and down my teeth—and even footballs, which you have to grab by the end. Soccer balls and basketballs are impossible unless—and it took me forever to figure this out—you gnaw a hole or two in them, and then they shrink down to a manageable size. The problem with that, as I found out one time when Bernie was playing in a Police Athletic League game and the ball suddenly came bouncing to where I happened to—but maybe we'll get to that another time. At the moment, Bernie and I were walking down a lovely path, flowers growing all around—oh, the smells, I can't even begin—to a tennis court, thwack thwack sounds rising toward us.

On one side of the net stood a tall blond guy with a bucket of balls at his feet; on the other side, an older guy, small, with a gray beard: Sherman Ganz. I always notice beards. A strange human thing: only some men have them, and women never. What was that about?

The tall blond guy took a ball from the bucket and hit it to Ganz. Ganz wore white shorts, had skinny legs like sticks. He swung his racquet and hit the ball back. The tall guy let it go by, took out another ball. "Brush up, Shermie, brush up. Spin on the ball, always spin on the ball." He hit the ball over the net. Ganz swung, this time missing the ball completely. "Brush up but through, up but through, up but through," said the tall guy, sending over another ball. Brush? I knew brushes, saw none around. Maybe tennis was tougher than it looked, but I didn't worry about that because a ball came bouncing over in our direction—we were now beside the court—and I snatched it out of the air, and who wouldn't have, the ball being right there practically saying, "Catch me." And then—this part was a bit harder to understand—I was on the court, racing toward the net. Up and over: not much of a challenge, tennis nets turning out not to be very high, but still it felt so great, being airborne and all, that I kind of twisted around still up there, if you see what I mean, and landed facing back at the net, and the next thing I knew I was jumping over it again, from the other direction, and, yes! doing the spin move once more, and when I landed this time, somehow with two balls in my mouth now—how had that happened?—I—

"Chet!"

We sat on a patio overlooking the court, Sherman Ganz and Bernie facing each other across a table, me at Bernie's feet, still and silent. The tall guy was feeding balls to a woman now, saying, "Racquet back, firm wrist, relax your hand, brush, brush." A very tough game: balls were spraying all over the place. I ignored them completely.

"What's so important," said Ganz, "that you show up at my lesson with no appointment?"

"We ended up with something of yours from our last visit," Bernie said, "wanted to return it."

"I don't recall giving you anything," said Ganz.

"True," Bernie said. "This was more in the borrowing line."

"Borrowing?"

Bernie laid the magazine on the table.

Ganz glanced at it. "You borrowed a copy of *Show Dog World*?"

"I confess."

"But why?" said Ganz. "I would have lent it to you, no problem. Why didn't you ask?"

"How's Babycakes?" Bernie said.

"Fine," said Ganz. "You didn't answer my question."

"There are so many questions in this investigation—that's the problem."

"You're talking about Adelina?"

"And Princess," Bernie said.

Ganz gave Bernie a long look. He had cold eyes. "And Princess, goes without saying."

"It's even more complicated than that," Bernie said. "Do you know a *Valley Tribune* reporter named Suzie Sanchez?"

"I don't think so."

"You don't think so?"

"In my work I get interviewed a lot," Ganz said. "I can't keep track of every two-bit reporter."

Now Bernie's eyes got cold, too, as though some light had turned off inside. I never liked seeing that. And maybe neither did Sherman Ganz. Under the table, one of his legs started twitching. That I always liked seeing: it meant we were getting somewhere. Where, I didn't know, and another problem: grabbing Ganz by the pant leg wasn't going to happen because he was wearing shorts; had that ever come up before? I tried to think.

"I wouldn't characterize Ms. Sanchez that way," Bernie said.

Ganz shrugged. The wind rose and fluttered the pages of the magazine. Bernie laid his hand on it. He had beautiful hands; I never got tired of looking at them.

"You mentioned your work," Bernie said. "What is it, exactly?"

"I'm an investor."

A new one on me. I was familiar with lots of human jobs—cop, perp, gangbanger, correction officer, biker, sharpshooter, bodyguard, vet, groomer, and of course PI, just to name a few—but not investor. Oh, and developer. From the look on Bernie's face, I decided investor was something like that.

"Investor in what?" Bernie said.

"Nothing esoteric," said Ganz. Didn't know esoteric, but it sounded bad. And I didn't believe him: with that pointy gray beard and those skinny legs, the color of bone, Ganz was capable of esoteric and probably worse. "Brick and mortar," he went on, losing me completely. "Hotels, shopping malls, apartments."

"Anything down in Rio Loco County?"

Under the table, the twitchy leg got twitchier. "Not that I recall," Ganz said. "I don't carry the whole portfolio around in my head."

"You look like the type that would," Bernie said.

I came very close to getting this, on account of a show we'd once seen on the Discovery Channel with women carrying big loads on their heads; although those women didn't look at all like Ganz, so maybe Bernie was on the wrong track.

"What are you driving at?" Ganz said.

"Here's a hint," Bernie said. "Clauson's Wells."

That twitchy leg, and how bonelike it looked: I got a funny feeling at the roots of my teeth, like they wanted lots of pressure real bad, the kind a lacrosse ball could provide, if one happened to be around, which was not the case.

Ganz stopped meeting Bernie's gaze. "I might have some interests there, now that you mention it."

"Such as ownership of the whole town?" Bernie said.

"Perhaps," said Ganz. "We're not talking much of an investment. It's more of a public service."

"Oh?"

"The plan is to fix it up, show people what the Old West was like," Ganz said. "Schoolkids, church groups, tourists."

"Do you do a lot of public service?"

"Ten percent of our profits go to the ASPCA, not that it's any of your concern."

"Good for you," Bernie said. "How about law enforcement organizations? Do you give to them, too? Or maybe just the odd lawman?"

"You're not making much sense."

"The Rio Loco county sheriff, for example? Or his deputy?"

"I don't know them," Ganz said. "Never actually been to Clauson's Wells. I have people for that."

"Did one of your people call the sheriff, tip him off?"

"Tip him off about what?"

"That we'd be showing up in Clauson's Wells, give him plenty of time to set up in the saloon."

"I have no idea what you're talking about. In fact, I have no idea what you're doing here. And I don't appreciate your tone."

From his pocket, Bernie took out the bull's-eye photo. He unfolded it, opened the magazine, slid the photo into place.

The twitchy leg went still. Bernie said nothing. He just waited. I waited, too, for what I wasn't sure, but the whole world had gone still, a weird thing that happened sometimes, and it always had a big effect on me. Then, from down on the court, came the voice of the tall guy: "Brush up. Up and through. Spin, spin."

Ganz winced, something humans do when they feel a sudden pain—I knew that from Leda's migraines. "I sent this," he said. "But I had nothing to do with Princess disappearing, or Adelina, whatever's going on now."

"Can you prove it?"

Ganz took a cell phone from his pocket, the big kind, and pressed buttons. "I was in meetings in LA the day of the kidnapping. The governor was there, now that I think of it—he can vouch for me."

"Maybe you just made the arrangements."

Ganz started to rise from his chair, and his voice rose, too. I got my legs under me. "I'm not a violent man. I abhor violence."

"You think defacing that photo and sending it to the Borgheses wasn't a violent act?"

Ganz sank back down. "I'm ashamed of that," he said. "But it was symbolic—I would never ever harm a dog. I was just so incensed about what happened at Balmoral. It obsessed me."

"Obsessed people can do uncharacteristic things," Bernie said.

"And I did," said Ganz. "I confess—I sent the photo. But that's all." He gazed at Bernie's face, which showed nothing, not even to me.

"You told us you admire Adelina," Bernie said.

"Exactly. I could never harm Adelina either."

"What's admirable about her?"

"Everything—her devotion to the show world, her generosity, her stoicism."

"What does she have to be stoic about?"

"You've met her husband."

"Do they have problems?"

"Nothing that I know of."

"This admiration of yours—how far does it go?"

"That's a nonstarter if you're suggesting what I think you're suggesting," Ganz said. "I have no interest in women. You can't be much of a detective if you didn't twig to that."

Words were flowing back and forth over me, not unpleasant though I'd pretty much stopped paying close attention. But what was this? Bernie not a good detective? He was the best! And something about a twig? I glanced around, spotted a twig immediately, and snatched it up. A tasty twig; I gnawed on it, went back to being all peaceful until I heard Bernie say: "What do you know about the cabin above Clauson's Wells?"

That brought the memory of Adelina and the ants, and I let go of the twig.

"Nothing," Ganz said. "I didn't know there was a cabin. Why is it important?"

"It may not be," Bernie said.

But it was. Did I make some sound, one of those low barks? Maybe, because all at once Bernie tapped his foot against my side, soft and gentle. Then he rose. I rose, too.

Ganz eyed the magazine. "You said you were returning it."

"Maybe someday."

"Meaning you don't believe me," Ganz said. Bernie didn't

answer. "I want Adelina found," Ganz said. "I'll pay you to find her."

"We already have a client." Bernie turned. Me, too. We started up the flower-lined path, but after a few steps Bernie turned back. "Nance used to work for you?"

"Correct."

"Why did she leave?"

"I assume she got a better offer."

Down on the court, the tall guy got excited. "Yes!" he said. "Spin, always spin. Spin controls the ball."

I thought about that all the way back to the car, couldn't quite make it work for me.

NINETEEN

Motive, means, opportunity," Bernie said as we drove away from Sherman Ganz's tennis club, Bernie at the wheel, me riding shotgun, a nice fresh tennis ball in my mouth. "Three strikes and you're out. And he sent the threatening photo that started it all. So why don't I get the sense that . . ." He went silent. I could feel him thinking, like pressure in the air. I was thinking, too: didn't three strikes and you're out come from baseball, not tennis? Any way Bernie could be confused? I wasn't buying that, not for a second, whatever a second happened to be. But something about time, not a whole lot of it, maybe—

"A red herring?" Bernie said. Uh-oh. We'd run into red herrings before, very bothersome, although the truth was I'd never actually laid eyes on one, hadn't smelled the faintest hint of fish at the tennis club. Also I'm not a seafood fan. Once at a cookout I'd gotten hold of piece of salmon—very small, nothing that anyone would miss—but to my complete surprise there'd been this bone that ended up getting caught in my—

"And if so, then this whole trip was a wild goose chase," Bernie said. "Should have followed that bike."

Whoa. Wild goose chase? Not the first time that had come up, but we still hadn't gone on one and, oh, did I ever want to, real bad. I glanced around, saw no geese, no birds of any kind.

Bernie sighed. "Just won't click into place," he said. "Adelina and Ganz having an affair—that would've been a different story." Adelina. And Princess, with her blurry-legged run. Princess: Where was she? I lay down on my seat, curled up. Bernie gave me a pat. "Tired, Chet?" he said. "Grab a little shut-eye." The fact was, I hadn't been feeling at all tired, but now I was, just like that. I grabbed some shut-eye.

And woke up feeling tip-top. Where was I? In the shotgun seat, my favorite place on earth. I sat up straight, gave my mouth a nice big stretch.

"Hey," said Bernie, "feeling better?"

Feeling better? Feeling best! Sun shining up above, warm breeze blowing by, and what was this? We were pulling into Donut Heaven, and just at the very moment it hit me that I was famished. Was life good or what? Ravenous one moment, crullers the next.

Lieutenant Stine was waiting in a cruiser. We parked cop-style, driver's window to driver's window. The lieutenant didn't say hi, just nodded. No smile either—not that he was the smiling type, although he usually had a smile for me—and there were dark patches under his eyes.

"In case you thought it couldn't get any worse," he said, "they're out of crullers." He handed Bernie a cup of coffee. Love the smell of coffee—have I mentioned that already?—but the drink itself does nothing for me.

"How's that possible?" said Bernie.

"Hell if I know," the lieutenant said. "Sometimes everything bottoms out at once—you ever think about that?"

"Too much," said Bernie.

"*The Power of Positive Thinking*—ever read that?"

"No."

"Don't bother—it's complete crap." The lieutenant sipped his coffee. "Thought you were a reader, Bernie."

"When I get the chance."

"What do you read?"

"Sea stories, mostly."

"But you're one of those desert aficionados."

"Go figure."

Lieutenant Stine raised a paper bag. "No crullers," he said, "but they had some bear claws. Chet care for bear claws?"

Whoa. Care for bear claws? Was that what he said? Had the lieutenant ever watched the Discovery Channel, seen what bears could do with those claws?

"My guess would be yes," Bernie said. It would? He reached into the bag and pulled out . . . something that didn't smell like any animal at all—in fact, smelled a lot like crullers—and had no sharp or dangerous parts, not that I could see. Bernie held it out for me. I sniffed but didn't take it. No rash moves for me, amigo. Bernie laughed and dropped it on the floor in front of my seat. I leaned down, did some more sniffing, finally tried a lick or two.

Well, well, well. Not unpromising. I took the tiniest bite out of one corner. A lot like a cruller, but—was this even possible—even tastier? I tried a bit more, and then some more after that, and then it was all gone. Yes, even tastier than a cruller. Bear claws: what a world!

Bernie and the lieutenant ate bear claws, too, wiped their mouths with little paper napkins. I licked my lips and then again, kept licking them until I couldn't pick up the slightest taste of bear claw, even took a few more licks after that.

Lieutenant Stine produced a pack of cigarettes, offered it to Bernie.

"Thought you'd quit," Bernie said.

"Likewise."

They lit up. A plume of smoke drifted in my direction. Ah. I'll admit something here and now: if I could smoke I would.

"You look up that guy McKnight?" the lieutenant said.

"He's clean."

"What else?"

"Zip."

"So you're nowhere?"

Bernie nodded.

"Holding back on me, old buddy?" said the lieutenant.

"Why would I do that?"

"Give me a tough one," Lieutenant Stine said. "You don't trust me. You don't trust the department. You don't trust anyone."

"That's not true."

"Which part?" said the lieutenant, glancing past Bernie, at me.

"I'm not holding back," Bernie said. "You'll just have to take my word for it." They looked at each other, both squinting a little through the smoke.

"For now," said Lieutenant Stine.

"Fair enough," said Bernie. "Anything on the green pickup sighting?"

"The witness turned out to be legally blind."

"Check on the Rio Loco sheriff?"

"Earl Ford," said the lieutenant. "He's clean, too. Backwater loser, but clean. The deputy, on the other hand, maybe less so." He took a notebook from his shirt pocket, leafed through. "Lester Ford."

"They're brothers?"

"Cousins," said Lieutenant Stine. He flipped a page. "Lester's got a dishonorable discharge from the army, even though he was in the marksmanship unit at Fort Benning. Been deputy sheriff of Rio Loco County for eight years, during which time he beat two charges of accepting bribes, was also involved in a resisting-arrest death of some dealer, or possibly an immigrant smuggler, records aren't clear about that. But the deceased was seventy-two years old." The lieutenant put his notebook away. "Not prosecuted," he said.

"Does Lester ride motorcycles?" Bernie said.

"No information on that," said the lieutenant.

"How does he get a badge with a dishonorable discharge on his record?"

"Out in the sticks like that?" said the lieutenant. "Jack the Ripper could get a badge." He took one last drag and dropped his cigarette out the window. Bernie did the same. I sniffed up the last of the smoke, felt my mind sharpening. I stood up tall and straight on my seat. Jack the Ripper: a new one on me, but I was ready. We'd taken down a lot of perps, me and Bernie, were afraid of nobody. Okay, bears maybe, and snakes, but except for them, nobody. Bernie reached for the key.

"Almost forgot," said the lieutenant. He tossed over a small gadget, maybe a cell phone.

Bernie caught it. "What's this?"

"Suzie Sanchez's digital recorder. Her boss found it in her desk. No sign of her laptop or any notebooks—must've had them on her."

"Why are you giving it to me?"

"I checked—nothing on it," said the lieutenant. He gave Bernie a funny look. "Nothing useful."

Lieutenant Stine drove off. I thought we'd be driving off, too, but I was wrong. Instead Bernie examined Suzie's recorder, turning it over in his hand, then pressed a button on its side.

"Milk." Hey! Suzie's voice, very clear. Some humans have much nicer voices than others, full of all sorts of different sounds, like music. Suzie was one of those; not as nice a voice as Bernie's, of course, but close. "Eggs, fruit, cheese, um, uh . . . bourbon? In case a certain someone comes shambling over?" She laughed. "Shambling—he'll never forgive me. Um. And dog treats—don't forget them."

Never. That made total sense to me. I could listen to Suzie all day.

Bernie did some clicking on the buttons. After that came a little silence, and then: "cheese, um, uh . . . bourbon? In case a certain someone comes shambling—" Click click. "Uh . . . bourbon? In case a—" Click click. Bernie listened to that bit a few more times. Did he have a hankering for bourbon? That was worrisome—still pretty early in the day, no? And us on the job.

Click click and more Suzie. "Count—what is that, exactly? Conte. Contessa. Christ, what a world. Contessa Suzie Sanchez to see you." She laughed again. "Villa in Umbria—villas have names, maybe? Get name. Manhattan co-op—purchase price? Passaic Realty?" In the background a phone started to ring. "Hello?" Suzie said. "Yes, this is she. Who are—" And after that, nothing.

We sat in the car, Bernie gazing at the little gadget, me gazing first at nothing and then at a cat that appeared in the window of a building across the street. The cat saw me, too—I could just tell—and opened its mouth in a big yawn. Yawning in my face, just to infuriate me, no doubt about it. Care to come outside and try that again?

"Chet? You all right?"

Uh-oh. I was halfway out of the car; I eased myself back inside. Every single thing cats do infuriates me, if you want the truth.

"What's on your mind, boy?" Nothing at all. But cats were just so . . . so . . . Bernie gave me a pat.

"How about we swing by the professor's?"

The professor? I got a grip. Loved the professor. I would have wagged my tail, but somehow it was stuck down in the space between my seat and the door.

We drove to the college. We had experts for this and that, me and Bernie, Otis DeWayne, for example, for weapons. The professor—he had a long, complicated name that I'd never gotten clear, but it didn't matter since Bernie just called him Prof—was our expert for money. Not making money—humans with lots of money have a certain way about them, hard to describe, and Prof didn't have it—but everything else about money, which was what, exactly? What was important about money except making it? Couldn't tell you.

The college was close to downtown but didn't look like downtown, which was all towers and nobody on the streets. It had old buildings with tile roofs and lots of trees and grass, and humans, most of them young, all over the place, walking, sitting, just lying around or even—hey!—playing Frisbee!

"Wow. See what that dog just did?"

"Chet? Can you give the Frisbee back, please?"

"Is that your dog?"

"We're more of a team."

"I can't believe he jumped that high. He should be on TV."

"Don't give him ideas. Chet? The Frisbee, please?"

I gave back the Frisbee, except for the tiniest little piece that seemed to have been chewed off. Couldn't beat our place on Mesquite Road, but if we ever had to live someplace else, me and Bernie, here at the college would be nice. College kids were the greatest.

Prof had a couch in his office. He was lying on it when we came in, his hands folded over his big round stomach. "Hi, guys," he said. "Just contemplating a little aperçu of Marx's."

Prof was brilliant—did I mention that? I caught the "hi, guys" part and that was it.

"Which is?" said Bernie.

"'The production of too many useful things results in too many useless people.'"

Prof: impossible to understand, but, big surprise, I came so close to getting that.

"Like it?" Prof said.

"Yes," said Bernie.

"Wouldn't it be funny if Marx turned out to be right after all?" Prof went on. "About everything, that is? I'm not saying tomorrow or the next day, but later, two or three hundred years from now."

"My sense of humor doesn't stretch that far," Bernie said.

Prof laughed. "Working on anything interesting?"

"Kidnapping," Bernie said.

"Ah," said Prof, "the life of action." That I got completely. The life of action: what could be better? "How can I help?" Prof said.

Bernie went over, handed him a sheet of paper. Prof had his glasses up on his forehead. He lowered them, squinted at the sheet. "Passaic Realty Group? You want their financials?"

"Anything about them," Bernie said. "Also whatever you can find about Count Lorenzo di Borghese and his wife Adelina."

"Entering rarefied circles now, Bernie?"

"Sir Bernie," Bernie said.

Prof laughed again, his stomach jiggling, a sight I liked a lot. He rose from the couch, not easily, and went to his computer. Bernie looked over his shoulder. Tap-tap-tap. "She's the one missing, I see," Prof murmured. Tap-tap-tap. I moved to the window and gazed out at the kids playing Frisbee. After a while Bernie came over and watched with me.

And sometime after that, Prof turned from the computer. "Well, Sir Bernie, here's the story," he said. "Adelina Borghese, née Simkins, is the sole owner of the Passaic Realty Group, a company started by her father, now deceased, and inherited one hundred percent by her. Passaic owns a villa in Umbria, purchased three years ago for four point five million euros, a co-op on the Upper East Side of Manhattan assessed last year for six million and change, a ski house in Sun Valley that I can't find much about—probably a software glitch; have to get one of my students to fix it—but which judging from comps has a value in the one point five neighborhood, plus a ranch in Rio Loco County paid for with three million in cash last March. Other than that, Passaic's assets appear to be in tax-free Treasuries amounting to thirty million dollars, give or take."

"They're loaded," Bernie said.

"She is, anyway," said Prof.

"What do you mean?"

"Passaic is in her sole name, as I mentioned. And Italian counts—counts of any kind—aren't necessarily rich. How much is the ransom demand?"

"There is no ransom demand."

"No? Why else kidnap a wealthy person?"

"It's possible she wasn't the real target."

"Who was?"

"A show dog champion named Princess."

"Hmmm," said Prof. He put his hand to his chin. I got the feeling he was going to figure it all out, right there and then. "A statistical study of the role of the accidental in crime—wonder if anyone's done that?" he said.

"No idea," said Bernie.

Meaning Prof had figured it out or not?

Prof thought some more. We waited. "Marx had a dog named Toddy," he said at last.

"Didn't know that," said Bernie.

"He liked dogs," Prof said. "Speaking of which, I happen to have a rawhide bone somewhere around here. Think Chet would be interested?"

TWENTY

This guy Marx was all right in my book—I'd actually had a book once, a leather-bound book that smelled very interesting, not really mine, but the property of an antiques dealer who'd hired us for something, not sure what. A long story, kind of crazy, since while Bernie and the antiques dealer were busy in the front of the store, I'd taken the leather-bound book out back and buried it in the yard. Why, I can't say at this late date, just hope we return there someday so I can dig the thing up and put it back where I found it. Where was I? Right, Marx. A good guy I looked forward to meeting someday, and Toddy, too, of course.

I thought about all that while I finished off Prof's rawhide bone, a big thick one with a lovely smoky smell. Meanwhile, we were stuck in traffic, sun glaring off rear windows as far as I could see. Getting stuck in traffic was one of those things that made Bernie's hands go tense on the wheel, but not today. In fact, he had only one hand on the wheel; the other held Suzie's recorder. Click. ". . . a certain someone comes shambling—" Click click. "Conte. Contessa. Christ, what a—" Click click. "Hello? Yes, this is she? Who are—" Click click. "Who are—" Bernie kept doing that, kind of driving me crazy a bit, although I knew he had his reasons—hey, we're talking about Bernie here—so I stayed quiet, except for just the slightest picking at the armrest with one of my paws, my other paws remaining absolutely still. But I was relieved when the phone rang and Bernie put the recorder aside. "Hello?" he said.

Aside, and actually in reach of my—but, no: at the last instant—I was already on the move!—he picked up the recorder and slipped it into his shirt pocket.

"Hello?" A voice I knew came over the speakers. "Count di Borghese speaking."

"Hi, Lorenzo," Bernie said. Silence on the other end. "You said to call you Lorenzo, right?"

"Certainly—this is America, after all," said Borghese. "I await your report."

"Nothing to report yet," Bernie said.

"What does that mean?"

"We haven't established any leads, not the kind worth reporting."

"Should not the client be the judge of what is worth reporting?" Borghese said.

"That's not the way we work," said Bernie.

Another silence, longer than the one before. What was this conversation about? Was it going well? No idea on both counts, but I spent no time on the problem because at that moment in a car stuck beside us I spotted a very annoying sight: a fat white cat perched on the driver's shoulder. On the driver's shoulder, and a cat—that really bothered me. I shifted closer to Bernie, but somehow climbing or hopping up on his shoulder? Big shoulders on Bernie? Yes. Big enough for me, a hundred-pounder?

No way. The cat swiveled its head, looked right at me. And, yes, again, for the second time in one day, a cat yawned right in my face.

"Lorenzo? Going to put you on hold for a second."

Uh-oh. Bernie was looking at me in a way I hardly ever saw from him, maybe never. I stopped what I was doing, whatever that happened to be, and gave myself a shake, not a complete one on account of being in the car: for a real good shake I need the wide open spaces.

"Lorenzo? I'm back. You were saying?"

I glanced out the window. Traffic was moving now, the cat no longer in sight. But can you believe it? A cat on the driver's shoulder. What was next? Cats at the wheel? I stuck my head out the window and panted until my mind cleared. It happened real quick.

"I was saying—trying to say—before all that uproar," said the count, "that your way of doing business is not satisfactory."

"In what way?"

"I need more information."

"I told you there wasn't any."

"An accounting of your activities, then."

"My activities?"

The count's voice sharpened. "To take one example—did you follow up on my suggestion?"

"The Babycakes lead?" Bernie said. "A dead end."

"Dead end? Did you interrogate Ganz?"

"We talked."

"And?"

"We ruled him out."

"Ruled him out? This means?"

"That he didn't do it."

Hey! That was what it meant? I'd heard the expression a lot, had never quite grasped it. Good thing the count asked. He had a funny way of talking, hard to understand, plus his breath had smelled of fish and he had a mustache and mustaches always bother me, but still, I started to like him. I liked most humans I'd come across, except for bad guys, perps, and gangbangers, and even some of them—take this one dude, for example, who'd got his ear caught in a—

But maybe a story for another time, because at that moment the count, even though I was starting to like him, sounded annoyed.

"How can you be ruling him out? Ganz is ruthless, capable of anything."

"Don't think so."

"What are you saying?"

"That he's not the type who's capable of anything."

"Then you have misunderstood the man, and badly," said the count. "I am paying for results."

The count was paying? Had I known that already? Now I liked him even more.

"I'm aware of that," Bernie said. "But we're in for the duration, money or no money."

Uh-oh.

"Your business plan is unusual, no?" said the count. He had that right.

"It works for us." Oh, Bernie. "How well do you know Earl Ford?" he said, losing me completely.

And maybe the count, too. After a slight pause, he said, "This name again?"

"Earl Ford."

"Never heard of him."

"He's the sheriff of Rio Loco County," Bernie said. "His office is about twenty miles from your ranch."

"There are still sheriffs here? Like the Wild West? What a country!"

The count had that right, too!

"How about his deputy, Lester Ford?" Bernie said.

"Is he of the Detroit Fords?" said the count. "I dined with several on the Costa Smeralda."

"These aren't the Detroit Fords," Bernie said.

"Then I don't know them," said the count. "Why do you ask?"

"I'm surprised they haven't interviewed you," Bernie said.

"Why would they?"

"The kidnapping happened in their jurisdiction."

"I have talked only with Lieutenant Stine and the state police. Your system is very complicated."

"So is this case," Bernie said.

"How troubling to hear that," said the count. "I'm boarding a plane right now, but I expect to be informed of your progress from now on."

"All right," Bernie said. "Just one more thing—what were the circumstances of Nancy Malone coming to work for you?"

"How can that possibly concern you?"

"Is it true she used to work for Ganz?"

"What lies has he been telling you?"

"We're trying to separate truth from lies. That's a big part of our job." It was? First I'd heard about it. Our job was to track down perps and grab them by the pant leg. But Bernie had his reasons, whatever that meant, and I had my own ways, which was why we were such a good team, except for our finances. ". . . backstage at Balmoral," Bernie was saying, "and so the Nancy Malone question may be relevant."

"Ah," said the count, "now we get to the famous kneecapping."

"Did it happen?"

"Of course not."

"Did you see it?"

"See something that didn't happen? What kind of detective are you?"

I wasn't exactly sure what this conversation was all about, but one thing I did know at that moment: I'd stopped liking the count.

"Someone saw it happen," Bernie said.

"That's a lie," said the count. "Ganz *claims* to have seen it—even you are aware of the difference, no? Poor Nance hardly even touched that foul creature."

Fowl? A kind of chicken, right? I'd had some fun with chickens in my time, but where did they fit in?

"Not only an accident," the count was saying, "but Babycakes wasn't even hurt, could have competed."

"Why didn't she?"

"Because of Ganz."

"Why wouldn't he want her to compete if she could?"

"He is—what is your expression?—a drama queen. Have you not spotted such an obvious fact?"

"But if Nance—"

The count's voice rose. "This has nothing to do with Nance."

"Is it true she worked for Ganz?"

"Did you not hear me?" the count said, his voice rising some more. "Do what I'm paying you to do—find Princess."

"And Adelina?"

"Yes, yes, of course. Did I say Princess? This is the stress. My meaning was Adelina. Find her. And Princess, too."

"It would help if—"

Click.

After that, Bernie was quiet for a long time. Once or twice he spoke, saying things like, "Business fucking plan" and "Costa fucking Smeralda," and somehow I knew things were okay. We drove through the Valley, past malls and big box stores and rows and rows of houses rising into the canyons as far as I could see—and somewhere in those canyons was our canyon with our house and Iggy right next door, my best buddy, who'd once, before the electric fence, caught a bird, I'll try to get to that later, snatched the little bugger right out of the air!—plus golf courses with fountains of spray shooting up over the putting greens—have I mentioned putting greens yet, my very favorite running surface, the feeling under my paws indescribable?—fountains of spray often topped with rainbows. Was there a better place to live? Hard to imagine.

But we weren't headed home. I knew that because we didn't take the ramp just before the longhorn bull billboard, this huge bull raising a frothy mug of beer, one of my favorite sights in the whole Valley. Instead we kept going, in traffic that thinned out as we rose through the hills and came down into the desert on the other side.

"Before we head back to work," Bernie said, "kind of just for fun, let's see if the count really did get on a plane."

Did that sound like fun to me? Not really, and besides, work was fun—I had the best job going—but Bernie deserved some fun, too. Once, on a night when Suzie had stayed for a sleepover, I'd woken up and heard her through the door, saying to Bernie, "All work and no play makes Jack a dull boy." Did that have anything to do with anything? Hard to tell. All I knew was that no boy named Jack ever appeared, and I missed Suzie.

"Where the hell is she?" Bernie said at that exact same moment. We were partners, me and Bernie. "How do you hide a yellow Beetle?" Good question. For the rest of the ride I kept my eyes on the traffic, saw all kind of cars, trucks, buses, motorcycles, RVs, and even a whole house on a trailer—would it be great to live like that or what?—but no yellow Beetles.

We drove through the gate at Rio Loco Ranch—I remembered that overhead sign, and something about a perp named Hickok—and went past the corral, empty today, no white horse prancing around, but I could smell him, not far away, so passing the barn I let out a quick, loud bark, just to see if anything happened, and what was that? One of those weird whinnies that horses make? Yes, and scared out of his freakin' mind, no doubt about it. A good feeling came over me, like we were making progress on the case.

The road swung around the barn, led to a huge house with the kind of tile roof I like, lots of trees and gardens, all very nice.

"Call this a ranch house?" Bernie said as we hopped out. I had another quick scan of the house, found nothing not to like.

Bernie knocked on the door, a real big one. I always enjoyed this moment—on the trail of some perp, waiting for a door to open. My tail was up high, stiff; all set for anything. Once, at a moment just like this in Sunshine City, a whole hive of—

The door opened and there stood a big dude with a ponytail, taller than Bernie and just as broad. I remembered him from before, cleaning a rifle in the barn. He looked at Bernie, then at me, back to Bernie: I loved when they did that!

"Hi, Aldo," Bernie said, "we're looking for the count."

"Do you have an appointment?"

"It's about the case—he'll want to see us."

Aldo's forehead wrinkled up and his eyebrows got closer together, always a sign of something, what, I wasn't sure of, but something good for us. "He's not here."

"Where is he?"

"I'm not, uh, authorized."

"Requires an object," Bernie said.

"Huh?" said Aldo, which was my thought, too.

"Not authorized to do what?" Bernie said.

"Tell you his whereabouts. But it wouldn't matter anyway because you couldn't reach him."

"He's in jail?" Bernie said.

"Jail? Why do you say that?"

"No reason," Bernie said. When he's really enjoying himself, Bernie sometimes gets this crinkly look around his eyes; he had it now. "Central State or the Federal Pen down south?"

"For God's sake," said Aldo. "The count's not in prison—he's on a plane."

"Where to?"

"New Yo—I'm not authorized."

"Understood," Bernie said. "He's on a plane to parts unknown." He sniffed the air and said, "Do I smell coffee?" I almost fell over. For one thing, I'd never seen Bernie sniff the air. But mostly: I myself didn't smell coffee, not the faintest whiff.

"Coffee?" said Aldo. "There's none made."

Whew.

"Then how about brewing up a quick pot?" Bernie said. "Nice to drink coffee while we talk."

"We're talking?"

"Why not? Your English isn't so bad."

"Huh?" said Aldo.

"For a foreigner, I mean," Bernie said.

"Foreigner?" said Aldo. "I'm from New Jersey, born and raised."

"Passaic?"

"Yeah, Passaic. How'd you know?"

"That's why we have to talk," Bernie said.

"'Cause I'm from Passaic?"

"And other reasons."

"What other reasons?" Aldo said.

By that time, Bernie and I were already in the house.

"Sherman Ganz let us in on a little secret," Bernie said. We were in the kitchen, a huge room with two tiny silver bowls in one corner, Bernie sitting at the counter, drinking coffee, Aldo standing. I went over and sniffed the bowls—both empty—caught a faint peppery whiff: Princess.

"Oh?" said Aldo.

"You were his source on the Babycakes kneecapping incident," Bernie said.

Aldo sat down. I stayed on my feet, eyes on his pant leg. "Why would he do that?"

"Is it true?" Bernie said.

Aldo's face lost some of its color. A big guy, Aldo, bigger than Bernie, but not as strong, not nearly. A force came from Bernie when you were near him; I didn't feel that from Aldo.

"Are you going to tell the count?" Aldo said.

"For what reason?"

"You're working for him."

"I don't think Ganz has anything to do with this," Bernie said. "So your involvement isn't relevant. But I wouldn't mind hearing why you did it. Simply love of fair play?"

"Not really," Aldo said. "Babycakes doesn't play fair either."

When he gets real interested in something, Bernie's eyes light right up—you can see it from across the room, which was where I happened to be, headed for the narrow space behind the stove, often a good place for finding scraps.

"You know they've gone head-to-head a bunch of times," Aldo said.

"Princess and Babycakes?" said Bernie.

"And Babycakes always won, except at Balmoral."

"What's the unfair part?"

"Babycakes is good, no question about it, but Princess is great, one of the greatest competitors I've ever seen."

"You know something about the show world?"

Aldo gazed into his coffee cup. "I used to." Behind the stove: nothing, not even a spiderweb or a dust ball.

"And the unfair part?" Bernie said.

"This move she taught Babycakes. It's got nothing to do with any of what's in the book—you know, the criteria—but it gets them every time."

"The judges?"

"Exactly. Just before they parade the dogs around, Babycakes has this move where she raises up one paw"— Aldo held up his hand. —"like she can't wait to get going but is too well trained to jump the gun."

"Sounds pretty cute," said Bernie.

Aldo smacked the counter, so hard his coffee cup fell and smashed on the floor. A big surprise to me, and to Bernie, too: I could tell by the way his eyebrows went up. "But it's worth zero points—I just told you," Aldo said. "She taught Babycakes to cheat."

"She?"

"Nance, of course. She worked for Ganz. Didn't you know that?"

"I never got the full story."

"The story is the count got tired of losing and hired her to come teach Princess some even better trick," Aldo said. "But guess what."

"Princess refused?"

"Goddamn right. She's way too proud."

"You like her."

"Princess? She's great—the best dog I ever worked with, by far."

"You worked with Princess?"

"They canned me when Nance came over. I was her trainer from the beginning."

"I thought you were the secretary."

"That's what they call me now. They're just keeping me on the payroll till I find something else—Adelina's doing, of course. If the count had his way, I'd be out in the street."

"Did you know Adelina in Passaic?"

"Sure. Her dad had show dogs going way back, and my mom was the trainer."

"And she taught you?"

Aldo nodded. "When Adelina and the count got into the show world, she offered me the job."

Bernie reached for a roll of paper towel, tore some off, and cleaned up the coffee spill and all the broken pieces. Aldo watched him the whole time, but Bernie never looked at him until it was all cleaned up. Then he said: "The kneecapping—it happened the way you said?"

"Yes."

"No chance it was an accident?"

"No."

"And you told Ganz because you wanted to get Nance fired?"

"Anything wrong with that?"

"It's a little indirect," Bernie said. "In my experience indirect methods tend to go wrong."

Aldo snorted. Always interesting when humans do that. I can snort, too, but it happens by itself and means nothing. Human snorts mean something, but I don't know what. "You're right about that. The count bought the accident story and threatened to sue Ganz."

"What did Adelina think?" Bernie said.

"Adelina believes whatever the count tells her. She's crazy about him."

"Yeah?" said Bernie. "I was about to ask whether there's anything between you and Adelina."

Aldo's eyes closed to slits. "Trying to pin something on me? For a moment there I thought you were straight up."

"Only trying to solve the case," Bernie said.

"The usual bullshit," Aldo said. That again? I smelled none. "But to satisfy your sick curiosity, there's nothing going on between me and Adelina, never was. We knew each other as kids."

"How come she let you get fired?"

"She fought him on that."

"But Borghese's the boss?"

"Wouldn't say that. But he's the love of her life, like I said."

"How did they get together?"

"She went to Italy after college, studied art for a year."

"And he owned some famous paintings?"

"The count? He owned shit. One day she took a riding lesson and he was the instructor."

Bernie rose, dumped the wadded-up paper towel in the trash. "You a good shot, Aldo?" he said.

"Why do you ask that?"

"Saw you cleaning that thirty-ought-six in the barn the other day."

"Not a particularly good shot, no," Aldo said. "And the gun's not mine."

"Whose is it?"

"Adelina's."

"Don't tell me she's a hunter."

"An animal lover like Adelina? Never. But there's sometimes target shooting when guests stay here, Coke bottles on a fence rail."

Shooting bottles off a fence rail: I loved that. Would it be happening soon? Some action would be nice.

"Is she a good shot?" Bernie was saying.

"Adelina? About like me."

"And the count?"

"Worse." Somewhere above in the house a phone rang a few times, then stopped. Aldo looked up. "Where do you think she is? What happened?"

"Don't know," Bernie said.

They talked some more, but I stopped listening, caught up in seeing Adelina's face again, with the ants. I went over and lay down by Princess's tiny silver bowls.

TWENTY-ONE

Back on the road, Bernie said, "Reminds me of Shakespeare."

Shakespeare? I didn't recall the case. We've cleared a lot of cases, me and Bernie, and who could be expected to remember every one? "All that intrigue, like at some royal court, I'm talking about," he added sometime later. The truth is, I don't know much about court, have been in a courtroom only once. I was Exhibit A. Not sure what that is, exactly, but it meant I had to walk across the room—with some uniformed guy, not Bernie—and on a leash. The leash is something I can do if I really, really have to, and afterward Bernie gave me a Polish sausage. Never had one before or since, but it did look like a pole, except much shorter, and tasted great. Exhibit B was a .44 Magnum I dug up out of some perp's flower bed. He's probably still wearing an orange jumpsuit at Central State.

A lovely day for driving: blue skies, clean air, Elmore James coming through the speakers. The trumpet is my favorite instrument but right behind comes the slide guitar. The feeling that goes from deep in my ears and down my neck all the way to my tail—and then sometimes back up the other way, meeting the next feeling already zooming down!—hard to describe. Bernie sang along—"The Sky Is Crying," "Mean Mistreatin' Mama," "It Hurts Me, Too"—but kind of softly, and he didn't do his usual air guitar thing on the steering wheel, which actually made for a safer trip. "I got a bad feeling," he and Elmore James sang. Bernie has a real nice voice—have I mentioned that already?—but Elmore James has a voice a lot like the slide guitar, a voice that could do things to me inside.

"The blues, Chet," Bernie said. "Nothing like the blues."

No doubt about that, at least not in my listening experience. But what with Elmore James's voice and the slide guitar both doing shivery things inside me at once, there was only so much of the blues I could take, and I was kind of glad when Bernie switched it off. Not long after that, we were on a desert track I remembered, the lopsided buildings of Clauson's Wells rising in the distance.

"Square one," Bernie said, as we hit the hard-packed main street of the ghost town. I'd heard him use that expression—square one—before. It meant we weren't doing well. The town was quiet, no one in sight. The wind rose, blew a plastic scrap across the street. We parked in front of the saloon and went through the swinging doors.

Bernie looked around: the long bar, the cracked mirror, the stool lying on the dirty floor. And what was this? Among all those stale and dried-out coyote turds, a single fresh one. I sniffed around the room, picked up a scent, followed it to the big hole in the back wall—coyote, been and gone—and returned to Bernie.

He was setting the stool upright. "Lester Ford sits here," he said. "Earl comes up from the corner in the back. Set up real nice, Chet. Question is, then what happened? I woke up the next morning in a cell." He gave me a pat. "How about you? What's your story?"

All of a sudden I was up on my back legs, front claws kind of pawing at Bernie, a total no-no.

"Hey, what is it, boy? What's wrong?" Bernie gave me a hug and I felt better, whatever it was that had gotten into me now under control. I went over and sniffed at the rickety stairs leading up to the floor above.

Bernie followed me. "Want to go up?" he said. "Doesn't look safe." I started up the stairs. Bernie laid a hand on my back. "Hold it," he said. I stopped. He moved around me. "I'll go first." Bernie go first? No way. He was a pretty big guy. What if something bad happened? I pushed past him. "Chet!" But Bernie wasn't going up first and that was that. I charged ahead, flew over the missing stair, one more big lunge and I was at the top, spinning around to watch Bernie. He came to the missing stair, stepped over it, but not easily, in fact landing heavily, and a look of pain crossed his face, there and gone in a flash, but I caught it—his wound from the war—and then came splintering sounds and the whole staircase collapsed in a slow-motion kind of way, with Bernie scrambling up at the same time in slightly faster slow motion. He fell beside me, safe.

"Chet, get off, for God's sake."

I got off. Bernie rose, looked down over the edge, dust rising from below.

"Guess we're stuck here forever," he said.

Oh, no. What would we eat?

Bernie peered down the corridor, light from the broken window at the end shining on his face. There were lines on his skin I didn't remember ever seeing. "Been up here before?" he said.

We moved along the corridor, side by side. First came the doorless room, all cobwebby, then the closed door. Bernie opened it. "Sometimes there is a God," he said. I looked inside, saw nothing but a ladder. I don't claim to understand every single thing he says.

We came to the next door, the one partly open. I smelled that peppery smell, very, very faint, and went right in. And there in a shadowy corner, just like before, lay Princess's pillow, not her satin pillow, but the stained and filthy one. I sniffed it to make absolute sure. No doubt. I stood up straight and barked.

Bernie came over, crouched down beside the pillow and sniffed at it. "Don't smell a thing," he said. It had taken me a long time to reach this point, but I believed him. He picked up the pillow, looked underneath; nothing underneath to see. Bernie turned the pillow over and gave it a shake. A few long silver-tipped white hairs floated loose, drifted to the floor. Bernie picked one up, held it to the light. "Princess?" he said. "Princess was here? Here the whole time?" He took out a baggie and put the silver-tipped white hairs inside. "You went up and found her, didn't you, boy?" A strong breeze sprang up in the room, and not too long after that I realized it came from my wagging tail.

Bernie rose. "But you got separated. First question—how did that happen? Second question—" He went to a closet at the other side of the room, yanked open the door real quick, like he was trying to surprise something inside: but empty, except for a single wooden hanger on a rail. "—was Adelina here, too?" The breeze at my back died away.

We left the room, walked down the hall to the broken window. Bernie gazed at the pointed shard sticking up from the bottom, raised one foot, and kicked it out. Smash! Crash! And a tinkling sound from down below. I loved when Bernie did things like that, loved smashing and crashing in general.

He bent down and stuck his head out the window. I stuck my head out, too. Hey! I could see pretty far. Straight ahead rose those low hills with the cabin and the pool of water, the roof of the cabin just visible. To one side, beyond the sagging barn where I'd found all the tire tracks, lay a wide stretch of desert, marked by tall saguaros. On the other side, more desert, but greener, with lots of low plants, and cutting through them a dirt track, dust rising from a big boxy vehicle, kind of like . . . kind of like an RV. And not just any old RV, but an RV with a rainbow paint job, an RV I knew.

"Chet? What's up, boy? See something?"

I kept barking.

"You want to go up that hill again, take another look at the cabin?"

Was I pointed at the cabin? No. I was pointed at the rainbow RV, now on the move, getting smaller and smaller. I leaned way out the window—felt Bernie's hand on my collar—and barked my head off, lined up from the tip of my tail to the tip of my nose on the RV.

"The RV?" Bernie said. "Something about the RV?" I barked, but just once more, not loud. "The RV it is," he said.

Not long after that, Bernie was lowering the ladder out the window. "Next comes the tricky part," he said. But we got down no problem, except for a bit of a tumble at the end, followed by landing together in a pile. I popped up right away, shook off the dust; and so did Bernie. Bernie shaking off the dust was a sight to see. We could handle the tricky parts, me and Bernie.

"That's the Old Trading Post Highway they're on," Bernie said, in the Porsche, fishtailing away from the saloon. "We'll have to double back all the way to . . . but wait a minute—isn't there a shortcut by the . . ." He went silent, at the same time spinning the wheel. We shot down an alley between some crooked buildings and came to a stony flatland. Bernie slowed down, steering around rocks and bushes, bumping along until we reached a shallow gully. We drove beside it for a while, then came to a grade, not steep, that led right down inside. Bernie headed into the gully, kept going. "Dry wash," he said. "But guess what."

I had no idea.

"When Coronado came through here, this wash was a river, running twelve months a year."

Coronado again. His name came up now and then—Bernie didn't like him, not one little bit—but we hadn't run across him yet. I sat straight in the shotgun seat, still and silent, ready in case Coronado was lurking somewhere up the line.

The sandy bottom of the dry wash was hard and smooth, and we went pretty fast. From time to time Bernie spoke: "Imagine what it must've been like," and "If there was a time machine, I'd be . . ." And other things I didn't understand. All I knew was how great things were here and now. The sun, the breeze, a few real trees growing alongside the wash, and what was that flashing by? One of those pincushion plants? Painful, I knew, but their skinny red fruits tasted great, if only you could get at them, which I'd tried to do plenty of times, only tasting one once, when Bernie picked it for me. But right now, way more important: poking around the pincushion plant what was that? Javelina? Yes, a big fat one. I twisted around and—

"Chet?"

Not too long after that, another shallow grade appeared off to one side, and we followed it up and out of the wash. Almost right away, we came to a hard-packed track with lots of tread marks on it. Bernie stopped the car. "Old Trading Post Highway," he said. "Via shortcut, courtesy of your latter-day Kit Carson." Kit

Carson: another dude who'd come up before. Was he in cahoots with Coronado? No clue. But Bernie looked pretty pleased about something, so I felt pleased, too. "Now we wait."

We waited, for what, I didn't know. Bernie stuck a cigarette in his mouth, then dug around under his seat for matches, and guess what he found. Matches, yes, but also a big biscuit from Rover and Company. I'd been smelling that biscuit for ages, had done some digging for it myself, unsuccessful. When it comes to biscuits from Rover and Company, old ones taste as good as new ones, maybe even better. We had a nice time waiting, Bernie smoking, one arm resting, relaxed, on the top of the door frame, me working on the biscuit, and hoping Bernie would blow some smoke rings. Loved watching smoke rings, but he didn't blow any.

Still, nothing wrong with watching smoke drifting away, even not in rings, and I was happily doing that when I heard a distant motor. I gulped down the rest of my biscuit, stood up on my seat, head turned toward the sound.

"Good boy," Bernie said. He tossed his cigarette butt away, started the car, and revved the engine. Vroom vroom: I could listen to that all day.

A dust cloud rose way down the Old Trading Post Highway and soon I spotted the rainbow RV down under that cloud. The rainbow RV came closer and closer, got noisier and noisier, and slowed down as it went by, the two guys in front turning to look at us, and at that moment I got a real good look at them: Crash and Disco! I barked. Did they see me? Couldn't have, because they kept going—even speeding up—instead of stopping for a get-together. Bernie gunned it. We swerved onto the track and took off after the rainbow RV.

After a only few moments, we'd caught up, were right on their tail—just a way of talking we have in the PI business, since of course there was no real tail around except for mine—but then the RV sped up some more and opened a bit of a gap. Bernie laughed. "Planning to lose us in that rattletrap?" Hey! Was this a chase? Loved chases. Bernie stepped on the gas and then we were right behind them again. The RV went faster, jerking and shaking now. A bicycle came loose and fell off the side, and then a propane tank. It hit the track and bounced right over us, not missing by much.

"Enough," said Bernie. He swung out, shot past the RV, held up his hand, and pointed sideways. The RV slowed and pulled over. Bernie circled back, parked in front of it, nose to nose. Crash and Disco stared down at us from the cab; my buddies—they'd given me water and Slim Jims—but they didn't look happy to see me.

"Hippies?" Bernie said, gazing up at them. His hand moved toward the glove box, like he was going for the .38 Special, but he hesitated, ended up leaving the glove box unopened. "Desert's crawling with hippies," he said. "Why is that?" He lost me there—were we going to get Crash and Disco to crawl around on the ground? Sounded like a fun idea. I hopped right out. Bernie got out, too, and we closed in on the RV, Bernie on one side, me on the other, the way we'd practiced so many times. Practice was great—it almost always ended with a treat—but I'll have to go into that later.

TWENTY-TWO

The side windows of the cab rolled down. Right away I smelled sweat, leather, pot, toe jam. Disco, wearing a bandanna covered with stars, looked down at me—no, not friendly at all, what was up with that?—and turned away. Disco, who'd given me Slim Jims, and what else had we done together? Couldn't remember at the moment. I stood up, front paws on the RV door so I could look through the open window; hated not seeing what was going on. My buddy Disco shrank away from me.

"Mind switching that off?" Bernie said.

"You referrin' to Iron Butterfly?" said Crash, behind the wheel.

"Got it on the first try," said Bernie.

"He wants us to lose the music?" Disco said.

"Seems like it," said Crash.

"How come, bud?" said Disco. "You don't dig 'In-A-Gadda-Da-Vida'?"

"I'm crazy about it," Bernie said. "But we'll have a better talk without the distraction. And probably best if you guys step outside."

"You a cop or somethin'?" Crash said.

Bernie flashed his badge. "Cooperating with them," he said, his usual answer, beyond me—and I kind of think beyond most of the humans who'd ever been on the receiving end. But I loved when the badge came out. Bernie was a deputy—honorary, whatever that meant, but something good, better than a normal deputy—in a little town down across the Mexican border where we'd helped clear a case involving stolen tequila. Bernie's hangover the next day: let's say my head ached just looking at him and leave it at that. But they'd sent two badges, so I was an honorary deputy, too, even if my badge had gotten a bit chewed up somewhere along the line.

Bernie tucked the badge away.

"What do you want with us?" Crash said.

"We weren't botherin' nobody," said Disco.

"Who said you were?" said Bernie. "Just a couple quick questions and you can be on your way."

"What questions?" Crash said.

"Yeah," said Disco. "What questions?"

"Concerning an investigation," Bernie said. "Hop out and we'll clear it all up."

Crash and Disco glanced at each other.

"Uh," said Disco.

"We're in kind of a hurry," said Crash.

"Big hurry," Disco said.

"Yeah?" said Bernie. "Where you headed?"

"No place," said Disco.

"No place *in particular*," Crash added.

"Then time's not really a factor, is it?" said Bernie.

"Um," said Disco.

"And just to head off any misunderstanding," Bernie said, "this investigation has nothing to do with weed."

"No?" said Crash.

"Or any other substance, legal or not."

"In that case . . ." Crash opened his door and climbed out.

Disco turned toward the handle of his door, saw me, up close and personal. "How am I sposta get out with the fuckin' dog leanin' in like this?"

"Language," said Bernie.

"Huh?"

"His name's Chet," Bernie said.

"Huh?"

"Say—how am I sposta get out with Chet leanin' in like this."

"Huh?"

"Say it," Bernie said, his voice pleasant, the look he was giving Disco anything but. "No sense in getting off on the wrong foot."

Disco said it the way Bernie wanted.

"See how easy that was?" said Bernie. "Chet?" he said. "If you please."

I dropped down on all fours, backed away from the door. "'If you please'?" said Disco. "Like, to a dog?" He opened the door and stepped out.

"Probably as good a place to start as any," Bernie said. "With Chet, here." He motioned for Disco, and Disco walked around to the other side of the RV. I followed. We stood on the Old Trading Post Highway, me and Bernie facing Crash and Disco. "How come you know him?" Bernie said.

"Know who?" said Disco.

"Believe he's talkin' about the dog," Crash said.

"This dog right here? Never seen him before."

"Me neither."

"That's funny," Bernie said. "He knows you."

"What do you mean, he knows us?" Crash said. "You can read his mind or somethin'?"

Disco laughed and slapped his thigh. "That's a good one."

"Not only that," said Bernie, "but he likes you."

Disco and Crash looked at me. I wagged my tail; not a lot: I was starting not to like them so much, no idea why.

"See?" said Bernie. "So let's not spoil it."

"Maybe he likes us—" Crash began.

"Dogs always like us," Disco said. "Hell, all animals do—remember that mule down at Arrowhead Junction?"

"—but that don't mean we know him," Crash said. "'Cause we don't."

Bernie gazed at them for a long moment. "Happened to notice a couple Slim Jims on the console in your rig." He had? And I'd missed them? How was that possible? "I'm going to take a wild guess that you guys shared a Slim Jim or two with Chet."

"You'd be wrong," Crash said.

"Yeah," said Disco. "So how much you wanna bet?"

"Wouldn't have taken you for a betting man," Bernie said.

"That an insult?" said Disco.

Bernie smiled. "Let's bet."

"Yeah? Like what?" said Crash.

"If you win," Bernie said, "we go away and stop bothering you."

"Sounds good," Crash said.

"If you lose, we get the Slim Jims," Bernie said. "And you have to destroy the Iron Butterfly CD."

"No way," Disco said.

"Then just the Slim Jims," Bernie said.

"You're on," said Disco.

"So hit the road," Crash said. "You lose. We ain't never seen this dog before."

"Have to prove that," Bernie said.

"Prove?" said Crash. "No one said anything about prove."

"How are we gonna do that?" Disco said.

"The difficulty of proving a negative?" Bernie said. "You've got a point."

"Damn straight I do."

"So we'll have to work on this together," Bernie said. Disco and Crash both had their mouths hanging open, kind of loose, always a good sign for us, although apart from that and the promise of Slim Jims coming soon, I wasn't too sure what was going on. But I did notice one interesting thing: way in the back part of their mouths, Crash and Disco were both missing teeth, lots of them. For some reason that made my own mouth feel weird for a moment or two. Life could be strange.

"Work on this together?" said Crash.

"What the hell does that even mean?" said Disco.

"Let's start with Clauson's Wells," Bernie said.

"The ghost town?" said Disco. "What's that got to do with the price of eggs?"

Eggs? What was on Disco's mind? Some combination of eggs and Slim Jims? That would sure taste great. I loved eggs, had one every day, mixed in with my morning kibble. For my coat, Bernie said, but no matter how hungry I might be I'm a pretty careful eater, never slobber anything on my coat, so I'd never really understood the whole egg and coat thing.

"Clauson's Wells was where Chet and I got separated," Bernie said.

"So?" said Disco.

"So it would be interesting to know the last time you guys were there."

"Never," said Disco. "Never in our goddamn lives."

"What's the closest you've come?"

"To Clauson's Wells?" said Crash.

Bernie nodded.

Disco scrunched up his eyes, something certain humans did when they were trying to think really hard. "Asides from right here, Red Butte, I guess."

Crash elbowed him in the ribs. "What the hell are you talkin' about?"

"Ooof," said Disco. And then, straightening up, "Red Butte, for Chrissake, where we park the goddamn—" Disco saw that Crash was glaring at him and cut himself off, clamping his mouth shut.

"Red Butte?" Bernie said. "Think I've seen it on the map."

"Don't know about no maps," said Crash. Disco, lips pressed tight together, shook his head.

"One of those isolated buttes," Bernie said, "sticking up all by itself." Yes: I could see it, all red in the sunset, with the little red glare at the bottom. "My memory makes it thirty or forty miles northeast of Clauson's Wells."

"Whatever," said Crash.

"Thirty or forty miles," Bernie said, turning to Disco. "That's doable for Chet."

Disco shrugged.

Bernie took a step toward him. "What's the matter?" he said. "Cat got your tongue?"

Say what? Cats? Bernie? He'd never mentioned cats before, not once. Everything had been going along so smoothly and now this. I curled my own tongue deep inside my mouth, safe from the short but sharp and nasty teeth I'd learned about on a cat-chasing adventure or two that hadn't ended well.

"No problem," Bernie said. "I've got a good map in the car. We'll figure this out in no—"

He turned, looked down the Old Trading Post Highway. A car—no, a pickup—was coming, shimmering the way things sometimes shimmered in the desert, engine noise already loud and clear. And somehow Bernie had noticed first! Cats did bad things to me.

We all watched the pickup. It drew closer: a dirty white pickup moving fast, then slower, finally stopping right beside us, dust swirling around. That pickup looked familiar. The door opened and a big guy with long hair and a bushy beard got out. I knew him, too. The big guy was all red in the face, looked mad about something. He strode over to Crash and Disco—didn't seem to notice me and Bernie at all—and said, "Where the fuck have you assholes been? I want my money back. A hundred and seventy-five bucks, right now." He held out his hand.

Disco began shaking his head very fast.

"No?" said the big guy. "You're telling me no?" He was wearing a T-shirt; the muscles in his arms—huge ones—started twitching. One of his eyes twitched, too. I remembered that from before.

"Easy now, Thurman," Crash said. "We got company." Crash's eyes slid in the direction of me and Bernie.

Thurman turned toward us, his glance passing quickly over Bernie, settling on me. His face got even redder. "The fuckin' dog," he said.

Talking to Crash and Disco, Bernie had been smiling quite a bit, but now he wasn't. He turned to Thurman. "His name's Chet."

"Huh?" Thurman said. "They're tryna sell him to you now? What a scam."

"Chill, Thurman," said Crash. "You're gonna screw up the whole—"

"No one tells me to chill," Thurman said. And all at once he took a big roundhouse swing at Crash. I wouldn't have thought Crash capable of moving real fast, but he was. He ducked, just like that, almost quicker than I could see. I've only had one encounter with a duck, and it didn't duck at all, attacked me, in fact, so I don't get the ducking thing; but that's another story. Thurman swung. Crash ducked. And Thurman's huge fist caught Disco square on the chin. He toppled over and lay still.

Thurman moved on Crash. Crash backed away, ending up against the RV, no place to go. "A hundred and seventy-five bucks or you're next," he said.

"Don't have that kind of bread right now," Crash said. "And this is a real bad time for you to—"

"Then I'm takin' the dog," Thurman said. He wheeled around toward me. I growled. I hated the choke chain and never forgot things like that.

"Not an option," Bernie said.

Thurman faced Bernie. "You stay out of this," he said. "The dog's bought and paid for."

Bernie moved slightly, stepping between me and Thurman. "When did this happen?" he said.

"None of your business. Take my word for it."

"And where?"

"Don't hear too good, do you, pal?" said Thurman.

"Anywhere near Red Butte, by any chance?" Bernie said.

"You lookin' for trouble?" Thurman's eye twitch got going.

"Trouble's already here," Bernie said. "Now the only question is how it gets handled."

Down on the ground, Disco moaned and began to stir.

"You'll get handled, you don't get out of my way," said Thurman.

Bernie didn't budge. "And I hear just fine, by the way," he said. Huh? Bernie really thought that? "Sharp enough to pick up the sound of a loser."

Thurman's mouth opened. All that black hairy beard and then a very red tongue in the middle: it had a strange effect on me, made me feel like scrapping. At the same time, I noticed Crash sidling toward the cab of the RV. I sidled over with him. He looked at me and mouthed some word. Mouthed, like with no sound. What was I supposed to make of that? I had enough trouble with ordinary sounded-out words; if you weren't careful, you could get impatient with humans sometimes. I showed Crash my teeth, didn't know what else to do. He stopped sidling.

"You callin' me a loser?" Thurman said.

"Just picking up on what's being advertised," said Bernie.

"Don't like the way you talk," Thurman said. How was that possible? I could listen to Bernie talk forever. "I'm thinkin' maybe you're a faggot."

"Thinking or hoping?" Bernie said.

"Oh, Christ," said Crash. At the same moment, Thurman lunged forward and unleashed another of those roundhouse crushers, this time at Bernie.

Bernie knows a lot about boxing, and fighting in general—have I mentioned that already? He did some boxing back when he was in high school, plus we have a big DVD collection of old boxing matches. Bernie's favorite boxer is Sugar Ray Robinson.

He presses the slo-mo button to see exactly what Sugar Ray is doing, and says things like "wow" and "can you believe it?" Then he presses the button for normal speed and the other guy is falling down and Sugar Ray is raising his arms to the sky.

One of Sugar Ray's slo-mo moves is this little head shift, just as a punch is coming. "See him slip that punch?" Bernie would say. That was what Bernie did now, slipping Thurman's big roundhouse—I could hear the whoosh of air—and stepping inside, his own fists jabbing thump thump. Thurman went down, rolled over in the dirt, and sat up, blood dripping from his nose. Then: a surprise. Thurman reached in his pocket, pulled out a narrow little flat-sided gun.

And our own gun, the .38 Special? In the glove box. But I didn't think about that, didn't think about anything. The next thing I knew I was in midair. Thurman saw me and the gun shifted in my direction. Then Bernie was in midair, too. Thud, smash, and BOOM. We landed on Thurman, me and Bernie, and the gun went off. I heard a loud ricochet, very near, then sank my teeth deep into a wrist—Thurman's, I hoped. Yes, Thurman's: had to be his cry of pain, Bernie would never make a sound like that. Then came another cry of pain as Bernie did something to him and Thurman screamed, "Stop, stop, I give up."

Bernie had some violence in him deep down—me, too—as more than one perp had discovered. He rose, the gun in his hand. "C'mon, Chet. Back off."

I backed off, licked my lips. Human blood: there were times when I thought it could become a habit.

Bernie looked around. Thurman lay on his back, bleeding from nose, mouth, and wrist. Nearby, Disco was on all fours, puking. And Crash was over at the RV, door open, already climbing into the driver's seat. Were we having fun or what?

Bernie said, "Freeze." He didn't bother aiming at him, kept the gun pointed to the ground. Crash froze. "Hands up." Crash raised his hands. "Step on out of there." Crash started to step out of the cab. At that moment, a sound came from inside the back of the RV, a single high-pitched yip.

"What was that?" Bernie said.

I knew.

TWENTY-THREE

Gun loose in his hand, still pointed toward the ground, Bernie walked over to the RV. No one else moved. Except for me, of course: I went with Bernie. He opened the side door of the RV.

At first nothing happened. I glimpsed a really messy place, with dirty dishes, piles of clothes, lots of empty bottles. Then out came Princess, bursting out, in fact. She flew through the air, missed her landing, somersaulted a few times, bounced up, looked around frantically, and saw me. Princess ran right over, wagging that pom-pom tail. My tail was wagging, too; I could hardly keep my back paws steady on the ground—that's how forceful my tail can get. I lowered my head, gave her a little bump. That sent her somersaulting again. She found her feet, started racing around me in a crazy way. That got me racing, too. We charged around the RV, the Porsche, the pickup, then charged around them again, and a few more times, finally coming to a stop at Bernie's feet.

"Good boy," he said. "Real, real good." I felt great, my very best. Bernie leaned into the RV. "Adelina?" he called. "Adelina? It's me, Bernie Little. You can come out. It's safe."

Adelina didn't come out. I thought of her face, and those ants. But the ants hadn't been on her face, had they? They'd been circling my puddle of puke. I got a little confused.

"Suzie?" Bernie said. "Are *you* in there?"

Suzie didn't come out either.

"Suzie? Suzie?"

"Hey," said Crash, watching from beside the cab, "ain't no one in there."

Bernie turned to him. "If I find anything bad, say your prayers."

"Like what kind of bad?" said Crash. "Gonna shoot me 'cause of dishes in the sink?"

Bernie moved toward Crash, raising the gun. For a moment, I thought Bernie was going to crack him across the face with it, even though I'd never seen Bernie do such a thing, not like this, to a skinny old hippie. And Bernie didn't. "Facedown," he said.

"Huh?"

Bernie pointed the gun at a spot on the road. "Facedown," he said. He motioned with the gun at the others: Disco, now on his feet, rocking back and forth, and Thurman, sitting up, nose still bleeding. "All of you," Bernie said. "And not a word. Not a sound."

They all lay down on the road. "Farther apart," Bernie said. They shifted farther apart. "Chet," Bernie said. I went over and stood behind them. Princess stood beside me. I could hear the drip drip of Thurman's blood in the dust. Then, from behind, came the creaking sound of the RV taking Bernie's weight, and after that his soft footsteps as he moved around inside.

Thurman raised his head, turned toward Crash, and said in a low voice, "I want that fuckin' money." I went closer to him and growled. He lowered his head. Princess followed me. She made a funny high-pitched noise, a sort of bleep. Was that meant to be a growl? I glanced at her; she had her head up in that determined way.

Bernie came out of the RV, stood on the highway, looking down on the three men. Thurman was a bad guy, no doubt about that, but Disco and Crash, too? They'd given me water when I was thirsty, and don't forget the Slim Jims. I watched Bernie. He gave Disco a little kick in the ribs, not hard at all, more of a poke to get his attention.

"Don't hurt me, man," said Disco. "I ain't done nothin'."

"Where's Adelina?" Bernie said.

"Who?" said Disco.

"Adelina Borghese, Princess's owner."

"Princess? Don't know her neither."

Bernie knelt, held out his hand. "Hey, Princess," he said. Princess approached him, pom-pom waving. Bernie gave her a pat. Her pom-pom wagged faster. "Where're your tags, Princess?" he said. She rolled over. Bernie scratched her stomach. Her paws made funny little movements. Bernie: enough.

Bernie rose. He gazed down at the three men again, again toed Disco in the ribs. "Where're her tags?" he said.

"Tags?"

"Her ID."

"Dunno," said Disco. "Hey, Crash, she ever even have 'em?"

"Shut up," said Crash.

"Huh?"

"Exercise your goddamn right."

"What right?"

"The right to shut up in front of a cop."

"He's no cop," Thurman said.

"Got a badge," said Disco.

"And some kind of bullshit story to go along with it," said Crash.

"What story?" said Thurman.

"Thurman?" Bernie said. "I want you to exercise your right." He turned to Crash. "You—got a name?"

"Crash."

"Real name."

"Real name, man? Depends on what's reality. And we all got a different reality."

"Where's your ID?"

Crash didn't answer.

Bernie moved on to Disco. "Name," he said.

"I'm exercising my right," Disco said.

Bernie backed toward the cab, opened the door. The moment he turned to climb in, Thurman was up and running. He was a pretty fast runner for a human, especially such a big one, and he almost reached the pickup before I brought him down. We rolled around in the dirt for a bit, and he cried out a few times, but it couldn't have been from pain because I really wasn't doing that much to him. Some humans have a real deep fear of me and my kind—even some kids!—a complete mystery to me.

"Lie still," Bernie called from the cab of the RV. Didn't even come running: Bernie trusted me.

Thurman lay still. I backed off. And just as I was backing off, Princess ran up in her blurry-legged way and started barking furiously in Thurman's face.

"Doesn't like you much," Bernie said, getting out of the cab. He had another gun in his hand now, and a couple driver's licenses. "Why is that?"

Thurman said nothing, just lay on the ground.

"Here, Princess," Bernie said, and Princess ran over, stood beside him. I stayed where I was, guarding Thurman. Bernie approached Crash and Disco, squatted between them. "Whose .44 Mag?" he said.

No answer.

"Got a witness who says a big gun like this was used to pistol whip the driver," Bernie said.

"What driver?" Disco said.

"Zip it," said Crash.

"The driver in the kidnapping," Bernie said.

"Kidnapping?" said Disco. "You talkin' about the dog? Can't kidnap a dog."

Bernie dropped the licenses on the ground, one in front of Crash: "Herman T. Crandall—looks like you on a real good day"; the other in front of Disco: "Making you Wardell Krebs. Seen a lot of guys like you, Wardell, in a lot of situations like this—we're talking about a major fork in the road, right here, right now—and they almost always make the wrong choice."

"What's the choice?" Disco said.

"Shut your mouth," Crash said.

"Letting your buddy here do the thinking is a common mistake," Bernie said. "His reality is life in the pen. What's yours going to be?"

"Life in the pen?" Disco said.

"Might be some chance of parole," Bernie said. "Especially if you've got no record. Got a record? Any of you?"

Silence from the guys on the ground.

"On the other hand, the victim is a prominent citizen," Bernie said.

"Victim?"

"Shut up."

"But it's a dog. A dog can't be a citizen."

Why not, whatever a citizen was?

"Not talking about Princess," Bernie said. "Any information you've got on the whereabouts of Adelina Borghese or Suzie Sanchez, now's the time to come across."

"Never heard of these fuckin' people," Disco said.

Bernie rose. "You're done," he said.

Bernie got plastic cuffs from our glove box, cuffed Thurman, then Crash, then Disco. After that, he got on the phone. We waited. While we waited we shared the two Slim Jims Bernie found in the RV. "Won 'em fair and square," Bernie said, tearing off Slim Jim bits for Princess. Thurman, Crash, and Disco lay silent on the Old Trading Post Highway.

Not long after the Slim Jims were gone, we started getting company. First came some state troopers we didn't know, then Lieutenant Stine and some of his uniformed guys, finally Sheriff Earl Ford and his deputy, Lester. A lot of talk started up, back and forth, voices raised and lowered, sometimes just about everyone talking at once. That was always too much for me. Humans aren't at their best in big groups, no offense. A big group of my guys—something I'd never actually seen, not a real big group, no idea why—now wouldn't that be something? I wandered over to the Porsche, lay in its shade. Princess lay down beside me. For a moment our gazes met. Then she closed those big dark eyes, wriggled a bit closer to me.

I kept my own eyes peeled, if that meant keeping them open. The eyes peeling thing sounded horrible—once I'd seen Bernie have a little slip-up with the potato peeler. Right now he was standing at the edge of the crowd, still and watchful. After a while, people began to leave: first the state police, followed by Lieutenant Stine and his men, taking Thurman and Crash with them, then two wreckers removing the pickup and the RV, raising lots of dust on the road. When it cleared, there was no one left except Disco, cuffed in the back of the sheriff's car, Sheriff Earl Ford, Deputy Lester Ford, Princess, and us. Earl and Lester moved closer to Bernie, their tall shadows falling over him, eyes hidden under the rims of their cowboy hats. I moved closer to him, too.

"Guess we should be saying congratulations," the sheriff said.

"No need for that," said Bernie. "And the case is far from solved. Unless someone already found them and forgot to tell me."

"Them?" said the sheriff.

"Adelina Borghese and Suzie Sanchez," Bernie said. "The missing humans in the case. Got them stashed away somewhere?"

"What's that supposed to mean?" said the deputy.

"He's just bein' funny," said the sheriff. "Startin' to get to know him, Les. Even gettin' to like him, yes, sir. Bernie here don't mean no harm—he's one of them funnymen, is all."

"Don't get the joke," said the deputy.

The sheriff nodded. "That's the problem with humor, isn't it, Bernie. Gets in the way of communication sometimes."

"That's true," Bernie said.

"And communication's kind of been our problem with you," the sheriff said, "right from the get-go."

"One way of looking at it," Bernie said. "So starting at the get-go, who tipped you that I'd be in Clauson's Wells?"

"See, here we go again," said the sheriff. "No one tipped us about you, told you already. We were following up on a vandalism report and you just happened to be there."

"Hard luck," said the deputy.

"But we felt bad about it, didn't we, Les?"

"Real bad," said the deputy.

"And now we're feeling bad again, which is what we'd like to talk about," the sheriff said. "Kind of left out, if you want the truth."

"That's what I want," Bernie said.

"Then we're all on the same page," said the sheriff. "Which is why we're—how would you put it?—"

"Pissed," said Lester.

"Not pissed," Earl said. "More like miffed. We're a mite miffed you didn't call us out here first, before all those others—didn't call us at all, in fact—when we were the closest."

"And it's our goddamn county," said the deputy.

"I'll remember that next time," Bernie said.

"Next time?" the sheriff said. "Thinkin' of comin' back?"

"We've still got two missing women," Bernie said. "Unless you know something I don't."

"Second time you made that suggestion," Earl said. "Any reason?"

The sheriff and his deputy gazed at Bernie; I couldn't see their eyes on account of the shadows cast by the cowboy hats. Bernie gazed right back. It was very quiet. I got the feeling of something about to happen.

"Sheriff here asked you a question," Lester said.

"I don't see how a yellow Beetle just vanishes," Bernie said.

"No?" said the sheriff. "You from back east or somewheres?"

"Born and raised in the Valley," Bernie said.

"Then you should know," said the sheriff, making a big gesture with his hand. "These here are the wide-open spaces. Everything vanishes."

"Yeah," said Lester. "Some quicker than others." The wind rose up and blew a big tumbleweed ball across the road.

"Way quicker," the sheriff said. He and Lester got in the cruiser and drove off, taking Disco away. Bernie watched till they were out of sight; me, too. Princess curled up on the ground and licked her coat.

The count and Nance were waiting in front of the big house at Rio Loco Ranch when we drove up. They came running to the car. The count reached in and picked up Princess, squeezed onto the shotgun seat beside me. "Mia piccola" something or other, he said, a whole lot of words flying through the air, completely missed by me. The count gave Princess lots of kisses and Nance patted her back, patted the count's back, too. Princess wriggled and squirmed.

"She's filthy," Nance said.

"Yes, yes," said the count, "my filthy little champion." He laughed and gave Princess a few more kisses. Then he handed her to Nance and turned to Bernie. "Excellent work," he said. "Please send me your final accounting. In the meanwhile, here is an interim payment."

He gave Bernie a check. Bernie looked at it and said, "This should be good for the whole thing. But there's no final accounting till we find Adelina."

"Surely with these arrests," said the count, "the search is now fully in the hands of the police."

"We signed on to do a job," Bernie said. "It's not finished."

The count gave Bernie a long look. "As you wish," he said. Nance was watching Bernie, too, maybe not paying attention to Princess. Princess leaped out of her arms and ran to the front door. She sniffed at it and whimpered.

"Isn't that something?" said Nance. "She trying to tell us how homesick she was."

"Poor baby," the count said, and some more that I missed because at that moment Bernie turned the key, using a lot more force than usual, and revved the engine, vroom vroom, over the count's voice. We took off.

TWENTY-FOUR

Back home, Bernie was restless. He checked the messages, made some calls, worked on the computer, paced around; smoked a cigarette and then another. I don't like it when Bernie gets restless. It makes me restless, too, and when I get restless weird things seem to happen without me really being aware of them, like for example, right about then while Bernie was taking a deep drag, a distant look in his eyes, should I have been gnawing on this shoe? A loafer, I think it's called, a present from Leda, with little . . . what was the word? Tassels, yes; little tassels, now gone, and kind of tasty, on the front. Bernie never wore the tassel loafers, but even so. I was thinking about trying to make myself stop when I heard a car parking in front of the house.

I was at the door before anyone knocked; and was pretty sure who this person was, from the sound of his walk. Bernie, cigarette hanging from his mouth, squinting against the smoke, opened up. Yes, Lieutenant Stine.

"You look like something the cat dragged in," he said.

Whoa. Run that by me again? Bernie and a cat? Never. And how could a cat drag Bernie? I'd probably have trouble dragging him myself. I gave Bernie a careful look, tempted to give it a try on the spot.

"Came all this way just to say that?" said Bernie.

The lieutenant shook his head. "Came to say congratulations, but now I won't bother."

"Congratulations for what?"

"Cracking the case."

"You found Adelina and Suzie?"

"Neither one, yet," said the lieutenant. "But we're closing in."

"On what leads?" Bernie said.

"Nothing you'd call an actual lead," the lieutenant said. Old man Heydrich, our neighbor on the other side from Iggy's place, was on the sidewalk, gazing down at a little something left by one of my guys, then staring right at us. Actually, right at me. He was accusing me? No way. I tried to remember the last time I'd done something like that on the sidewalk, and flat out couldn't, just about for sure. I yawned at old man Heydrich in a friendly way. His normally angry face, skin all pinched between the eyes, got angrier than ever. Bernie, looking past Lieutenant Stine, noticed old man Heydrich and invited the lieutenant inside.

"Thought you'd never ask. Anything drinkable in the cupboard over the sink?"

Turned out there was. Bernie dropped ice cubes in a couple of glasses, tossed an ice cube to me. A special treat, at first crunchy, like a cold biscuit, and then all of a sudden lovely cool water trickling down my throat. I took the ice cube to the corner by the fridge and curled up.

Bernie and the lieutenant clinked glasses. "They're down in central lockup," the lieutenant said. "We booked the two of them on kidnapping and theft, plus some minor stuff. Same charges for the third one, up in Rio Loco."

"Theft?"

"That would be the dog," said Lieutenant Stine. "Can't kidnap a dog, by definition."

Can't do what? I was pretty busy with what was left of the ice cube, hadn't quite got that. But whatever it was hadn't sounded right.

"Any of them got a record?" Bernie said.

"Oh, yeah." The lieutenant unfolded some sheets of paper. "All of 'em—the two hippies mostly for dope dealing, but there's auto theft, too, plus an armed robbery."

"Armed robbery? They don't look like the type."

The lieutenant put on glasses, always interesting when that happened. "Did three years for a casino heist in New Mexico."

"Those two guys knocked over a casino?"

Lieutenant Stine's eyes moved back and forth behind his glasses. "Wouldn't say knocked over, not successfully. And the casino maybe was more of a convenience store on tribal land with a couple of slots in the back, one of which they attempted to boost when no one was looking."

"Sounds more like them," Bernie said.

"Not that simple," the lieutenant said. "The one they call Crash got off a few shots."

"Anybody hurt?"

"Blew out a few windows is all—still puts them on another level in my book. The third guy, Thurman Barger, has a long record—multiple assaults, burglary, kidnapping."

"Kidnapping?"

"Took a teller at gunpoint, bank job gone wrong. Did seven years up in Colorado." The lieutenant drank some bourbon. "These are the guys, Bernie." Bernie was swirling his own bourbon in the glass, staring at it going round and round, something

I'd seen him do before. "You're thinking what's the motive," Lieutenant Stine said. Bernie nodded. "They're still clammed up," the lieutenant said, "but the hippies'll crack eventually."

"Surprised they haven't already," Bernie said.

"Probably just holding out for a better deal," said the lieutenant. "We're going to offer our guy short time in return for his testimony, assume the same thing'll happen in Rio Loco. Hold-up right now is a disagreement in the DA's office about how short."

"Christ," Bernie said. "Two people are missing."

Lieutenant Stine drained his glass and stood up. "I'll keep you posted."

Bernie was staring at the swirling bourbon again, didn't respond.

"Can't just sit around the house," Bernie said, after we'd been sitting around the house for some time. Not really sitting: more like pacing from room to room, with stops in the office for lots of writing and erasing on the whiteboard. "Gotta do something." Fine with me. I beat Bernie to the door. He opened it, but just as we stepped outside the phone rang.

A voice came over the machine. "Bern? Chuck Eckel here. Give me a call, ASAP." Beep.

"Haven't even cashed the goddamn check yet," Bernie said, "and it's already gone." He slammed the door real hard, shaking the whole house. Iggy must have heard the sound: from somewhere in his place came a yip-yip-yip. I checked his window and didn't see him.

We took a long drive, out of the Valley, into the desert. Night fell and it got cool; I could smell Bernie, a very nice smell for a human, actually a bit doglike in some ways. We went from two-lane blacktop and lots of cars to a hard-packed track and none.

"Tin futures," Bernie said. "What was I thinking?"

I shifted a little closer to him.

After a while the moon appeared and I saw all sorts of things: a tall saguaro that seemed to be moving; a pair of eyes that seemed to be on fire; and in the distance, the huge flat-topped butte where Princess and I had first met Crash and Disco. It looked pink in the moonlight, although I can't be trusted about colors, according to Bernie. But I loved the sight of the butte at night, pink or not. Some creatures, including humans—humans especially, in my experience—were afraid of the night, but not me.

"Red Butte," Bernie said, as we parked in its shadow. He gazed up at it. "There's an Indian legend, something about this being the first step on a stairway to the stars." We got out of the car. "And then a human offended the gods—the usual story—and all the other stairs came tumbling down."

Huh? Then where were they? I looked around, saw nothing but flat moonlit desert.

Bernie took the flashlight from the glove box. "Or is that some other butte, up in Utah? Maybe this one has no story." He slung the evidence bag over his shoulder and tucked the .38 Special in his belt. "Be nice to have a real education."

Didn't know what Bernie was talking about, thought maybe it had something to do with Suzie. Suzie was missing and Adelina . . . Adelina. Adelina and those ants, back in the cabin near the ghost town.

"Chet? What is it? Down, boy."

What was this? I'd stood up, pawed at Bernie. Very bad. I dropped right down, tail curling between my legs.

Bernie knelt down in front of me, took my head in his hands. "What's on your mind? What's wrong?"

I have this sound I can make—the truth is the sound just comes out on it own sometimes—a rumbling deep in my throat, not a growl or a bark, more like . . . I don't really know. Whatever you'd call the rumbling sound, I was making it at that moment, down under Red Butte.

Bernie stroked my head. "Wish I spoke that language," he said. He rose and we got going. I gave myself a shake and felt better. We were on the job.

"Clockwise or counterclockwise?" Bernie said. "The earth revolves around the sun counterclockwise, so let's go the other way." I didn't move. Would you have? "To turn back the clock, push time the other way, which is kind of what we do anyway, right, boy?" I stayed where I was, looking at nothing, just waiting. These moods of Bernie's always passed, and everything returned to normal. "Solving crimes, I mean—isn't it a bit like time travel?" I breathed in, breathed out. The night air was fresh, cool, delightful. Bernie peered up at the butte. High above hung the moon and stars. "This could be any time," he said. "Before the Spanish, before the Indians, any time at all." He tapped his head. "Only this says no, screws everything up."

Whoa. Was he talking about his brain? Bernie's brain was one of the best things we had going for us, right up there with my nose. From out of nowhere I got very itchy, started scratching all over the place.

"C'mon, Chet. Let's go."

I bounced right up. Bernie switched on the flashlight and followed the base of the high rocky wall, sweeping the beam back and forth over the ground. I walked beside him. Almost right away we spotted something shiny: a CD with a big chip missing. Bernie turned it over. "*The Very Best of Deep Purple*," he said. "Meaning the RV must have been parked right around here." He took a little stick with a flag on the end from the evidence bag and twisted it into the ground. We explored the area around the stick, making circles that got bigger and bigger—Bernie shining the flashlight, me sniffing for a scent—but came up with nothing.

Bernie thought. He stood very still, his face white in the moonlight, a face that could have been made of stone. I didn't like that, gave him a little bump. He gave me a quick pat. We moved on, alongside the base of Red Butte, the flashlight beam sweeping back and forth even though we didn't really need it with the moon so bright.

"Smell anything, Chet?"

Did I smell anything? Was that the question? Did it mean Bernie smelled nothing right now, not even the coyote piss? Every coyote in the desert must have been using Red Butte as a kind of giant fire hydrant. I checked out Bernie's nose, a not-quite-straight little thing: what was it for?

We kept going, first in the shadow of the butte, then out in open moonlight, side by side with our own shadows. From time to time, Bernie muttered to himself. "Two guys like that—three guys—are they even capable of thinking up . . . ?" And: "Evidence—not even a confession, maybe especially not—beats solid . . ." I took a moment to lift my own leg against the butte, heard the trickle on rock, always a nice sound.

"One way of looking at it," Bernie was saying. "But motive? Why no . . ." I caught up to him, listened to a bit more of this, and went on ahead.

We worked our way around Red Butte, Bernie muttering, me sniffing, shadows shifting in the moonlight. I felt great! We'd cleared a lot of cases, me and Bernie, some of them on nights just like this. Once there was this gangbanger, for example, who thought he could get away with—whoa. What was this? I sniffed, and sniffed again. Yes, the unmissable scent of biscuit, and not just any biscuit, but biscuit from Rover and Company. Rover and Company was run by a nice guy we knew from a recent case—his name escaping me at the moment, and also the details of the case—and I'd even gotten to do some tasting in their test kitchen. What a day! But no time to think of that now. I lowered my nose to the ground, followed the scent to a spot where the rock wall curved in a bit.

I sniffed at the ground, bare ground, kind of soft under my paws: a strong scent of Rover and Company biscuit, no doubt about it. But nothing to see, so I scratched at the ground. That brought more scent, coming in powerful waves. I started digging.

"Chet? What's up?"

I kept digging. Love digging, of course. I've done some serious digging in my time, including once "halfway to goddamn China" according to old man Heydrich, although I wasn't sure what that meant, just remembered something about the sudden appearance of a sinkhole, and his patio disappearing. This was back before the fence between our place and old man Heydrich's, in the days when—

My paw hit something that gave a little. I stopped digging, stuck my head in, got whatever it was between my teeth. Then I backed out and dropped it at Bernie's feet: a biscuit box from Rover and Company. I'd seen plenty of them, recognized it right away. This one was crushed and torn a bit, but when Bernie shook it I heard biscuits rattling around. I sat up nice and tall, the way I usually did when a treat was on the way. No treat this time. Bernie dropped the box in the evidence bag and said, "Wait right here."

He hurried back the way we'd come, actually running pretty fast, and with no limp. I stayed exactly where I was, didn't move a muscle. When Bernie returned, he was unfolding the fold-up shovel we carried in the trunk.

"Need some space, boy."

Space? I backed a butt-wriggle or two away, then without quite knowing what I was doing, butt-wriggled forward to where I'd been sitting in the first place.

Bernie stuck the shovel—this was the spade kind, pointed at the end; has that come up already?—in the ground, started digging. Had I ever seen Bernie dig before? He wasn't too bad at it, but why not pitch in, especially since digging was one of my specialties? I shoved in beside him, got to work.

"Careful, Chet."

Careful digging? What did that mean? Go slow, maybe? I didn't know how to do that, had only one speed for digging—pedal to the metal. Bernie worked with a steady rhythm, driving in the spade, tossing the dirt over his shoulder, chunk-a-thunk, chunk-a-thunk. Not bad at all. But with four paws going for me, it wasn't really a contest. Did I send that dirt flying or what? Fountains of earth, baby, fountains of earth. We dug underneath the light of the moon, dug and dug until—

Clang.

The spade struck something hard. Bernie paused; me, too. He laid the spade aside, got the flashlight, and down on his knees leaned into the hole and started clearing dirt with his hand. The other hand aimed the flashlight, and in the beam something hard and curved and yellow appeared. Hard and curved and yellow? I had no idea. Bernie went still and said, "Oh, God."

He took a few steps back, balanced the flashlight on a rock, and began another hole, working not just fast but kind of wildly, sweat gleaming silver on his skin. And his face: the look on it scared me. I sat still.

The hole got bigger and bigger. I saw new things in the flashlight beam: a glass window, a windshield wiper, a stubby rounded hood. Hey! A car. A car was buried down there. And not just any car, but a Beetle, a yellow Beetle: this was Suzie's car. What was going on? I looked at Bernie. His eyes had gone all liquid, and tears were making tracks through the dirt on his face. He tossed the spade aside, lowered himself onto the hood of the car, swept away dirt with his hands, faster and faster, grunting with the effort. Then he shone the flashlight through the windshield.

The beam was all wobbly and unsteady, but I could make out a person in the driver's seat, a dead person, as I knew already from the smell. I watched from the edge of the hole, over Bernie's shoulder. A dead woman; behind the wheel of Suzie's car; but not Suzie. It was Adelina.

TWENTY-FIVE

Early the next morning we drove to Rio Loco Ranch, following Lieutenant Stine's cruiser. We hadn't caught any sleep, me and Bernie, not with how busy things got at Red Butte, cops and heavy machinery showing up from all over the place. Not getting enough sleep hardly ever happens to me. I like to have a nap every morning and afternoon, plus a long night of shut-eye—goes without saying—and sometimes an evening nap as well, especially after a big steak dinner, for example. When I haven't had enough sleep, a funny feeling comes over me, like something very strong is pulling my eyelids down. I was feeling it now, in the shotgun seat, maybe not sitting as tall as usual.

We went past the corral—empty today, couldn't smell the white horse anywhere—and came to a putting green I hadn't noticed before. Putting green grass is just about my favorite surface, as I may have mentioned before. All of a sudden, I felt peppier. And not so much because of how my paws couldn't wait to feel that putting green, but on account of who I saw there: Princess! She was on the leash and running, head up high. Nance held the leash and ran along beside her—walked, really, on account of Princess's legs being so short. The count sat in a chair with a clipboard on his lap and a steaming cup in the cup holder, smiling and clapping. He wore his gleaming riding boots; that short whip thing—his riding crop—lay on the ground beside him. We parked and walked over to them—me, Bernie, Lieutenant Stine.

They turned toward us, stopped what they were doing. Princess saw me and started barking. You might have thought she was angry if you didn't know her; Princess had turned out to be kind of fierce, just as fierce as some of my huge bruiser buddies, like Spike and General Beauregard, or even fiercer, but I knew she liked me.

"Yes?" said the count, his quick dark eyes scanning us. "What is it?"

We moved to the edge of the putting green. The lieutenant and Bernie stopped there, so I did, too. "Prepare yourself for bad news," Lieutenant Stine said.

Nance covered her mouth with her hand. The count said, "What bad news?"

The lieutenant glanced at Bernie, maybe thinking Bernie would say something, but he didn't. Lieutenant Stine faced the count. "Your wife is dead."

Borghese rose from his chair, slow and unsteady, almost lost his footing. The cup toppled out of its holder and spilled on the green.

"She was murdered," the lieutenant said. "I'm sorry."

Borghese lowered his head, put his hand over his eyes. He wore a thick gold watch; it gleamed in the sun. I sat. Princess sat, too. No one moved. A horse neighed, not far away. The count lowered his hand, turned toward the sound. In a low voice, Nance said, "Come," and she and Princess walked toward Borghese. Nance touched his shoulder. The count gazed into the distance. Nance was taller than the count, and stronger-looking. She took her hand away. His eyes closed for a long moment. Princess's eyes, huge and dark, were on me.

"We have three suspects in custody," Lieutenant Stine said, "thanks to Bernie here. Bernie and Chet."

"Is . . ." The count cleared his throat, started over. "Is one of them Sherman Ganz?" He didn't turn to look at us.

"No," the lieutenant said.

"Sherman Ganz had nothing to do with this," Bernie said.

Now the count turned his face toward us, his eyes sweeping over me and the lieutenant, settling on Bernie. "You found Princess," he said, "and I am grateful for that. But on other matters, no more opinions, please."

Bernie's face got that stony look. The lieutenant said, "We checked for a connection between Mr. Ganz and the suspects and found none. No phone calls, no texting, no emails, no canceled checks, never been seen together, zip."

The count was silent for a moment or two, eyes still on Bernie. Then they shifted to the lieutenant. "Murdered how?" he said.

"Gunshot," said the lieutenant. "We're waiting on ballistics." He flipped open his notebook. "Any of these names known to you? Herman T. Crandall, aka Crash; Wardell Krebs, aka Disco; Thurman Barger, aka Thurman Brown, aka Ted Brown."

The count shook his head.

"You, ma'am?" said the lieutenant.

Nance shook her head, too. At that moment, Princess spotted something on the green and scarfed it up. Something edible? What could that have been?

"It's possible they've used other names," Lieutenant Stine said. "I've brought some photos, but if you'd prefer a later time . . ."

The count held out his hand. Lieutenant Stine reached into an inside pocket of his jacket and stepped onto the green. Bernie followed; and me, too.

The lieutenant showed Borghese the photos. "No," said Borghese. "Strangers to me."

Bernie moved in closer, pointed at the photos. "These two have less hair now and this one's beard is fuller. Also—"

"Hair or no hair," the count said, leaning back a bit from Bernie, "beard or not—strangers, completely strangers."

"And you, ma'am?" said the lieutenant, angling the photos toward Nance.

"So evil-looking," Nance said. "I would remember faces like those if I'd ever seen them before."

"And have you?" Bernie said.

Nance gave him an annoyed look. "Didn't I just say?"

"Not exactly."

"Then I'll make it simple," Nance said. "N.O."

N.O.? I knew that one, had heard it many times.

"What about Suzie Sanchez?" Bernie said.

"Another unknown name," the count said.

Nance touched his arm. "The reporter," she said.

"Ah, yes," the count said. "But we had no comment."

"When was the last time you heard from her?" Bernie said.

The count made a shrugging gesture, hands spread, eyebrows raised; he had lots of big gestures, an interesting guy to watch, interesting in a way that somehow made me want to give him a quick nip.

"Think," Bernie said, his voice not very pleasant; maybe he

was feeling the same thing as me. Lieutenant Stine put his hand on Bernie's arm.

The count tilted up his nose; a big bony nose, also interesting. "I beg your pardon?"

"I know this is a bad time," Bernie said, sounding a little less harsh. "But we've got another open case out there."

"Of this I know nothing," said the count.

"And the last time we had any contact with the reporter—Suzie something?—was at the corral when you were here," Nance said. "So now, if you don't mind—"

"We wish to be alone," Borghese said.

"Of course," said the lieutenant. "We'll be in touch about, uh, the delivery of the . . . of Mrs. Borghese."

"Contessa," said Borghese, his tone sharpening. "The Contessa di Borghese."

Up there, up above my head, things went on that weren't too clear. Down here on the putting green, Princess and I were close together, kind of by ourselves. I lowered my head to give her a friendly little bump. And what was this? She nipped me on the nose? And it hurt!

"Chet?"

"What does it mean?" Lieutenant Stine said. Later that morning: we met at a bench outside the sheriff's office in the town Bernie called Nowhereville. Bernie and the lieutenant sat on the bench; I lay in the shade underneath. Still no sleep, that force dragging down my eyelids getting stronger and stronger. I'm pretty strong myself, but because all my strength was concentrated on pulling my eyelids back up, I might have missed a bit of what was going on. I'm pretty sure I caught Bernie saying:

"What does what mean?"

And after that, the lieutenant said something about Adelina being in Suzie's car.

"Isn't that what we're working on?" Bernie said. "What it means?"

"Sure we're working on it, but what do your instincts tell you?"

"Nothing."

"Come on, Bernie. Won't hold you to anything—this is me. And even when you were on the force, despite all the . . . well, friction—your instincts were good."

"Friction?" Bernie said.

"Aw, Bernie, do we have to? How about after we clear this case, I'll stick my chin out and you can take a free swing?"

"How about I do it now?"

I opened my eyes. Yes, they'd closed and I'd been on my way to dreamland—which for me is almost always the canyon behind our place on Mesquite Road, where I have the kind of adventures I have in the canyon in the daytime, or even better—when I got the idea that Bernie and Lieutenant Stine were about to throw down.

And what was this? Lieutenant Stine sticking out his chin? He had kind of a big chin anyway, already sticking out quite a bit, but now it was way way out there. Bernie made a fist, drew back his arm. I started scrambling out from under the bench, with no particular idea in mind except I liked Lieutenant Stine. He'd been the source of so many crullers I couldn't even count them—not quite what I mean, since I always stop counting at two. And why shouldn't I? Two is enough.

But back to Bernie's fist, a big fist and I'd seen what it could do. Maybe Lieutenant Stine had, too, and didn't want to look. He closed his eyes, all scrunched up like a little kid, very strange on such a hard face. Bernie threw a punch, pulling it at the last possible instant. His hand relaxed. He gave Lieutenant Stine a light pat on the cheek.

"You're the biggest jerk in the state," said the lieutenant.

"Second biggest," Bernie said.

What the hell was going on? No idea, and no time to figure it out, because at that moment the door of the sheriff's office opened and out came Earl Ford, star on his chest, cowboy hat on his head.

"Mornin', boys," said the sheriff. "Sorry to keep you coolin' your heels—last-minute details. Let's roll."

"Roll where?" said Bernie.

"Thurman Barger's place."

"What's there?" Bernie said.

"Want you boys to see for yourselves."

We went for a drive—the sheriff's cruiser, then the lieutenant's, us last. For a while, I kept my eyes on Bernie's heels, saw nothing different. The force started up, the one that made my eyelids so heavy. Soon all of me got heavy, too heavy to even sit. I lay on my seat. Everything so heavy, and then came a heavy fog rolling through my mind. The car went rumble rumble beneath me.

I woke up. Usually I wake up in the middle of an exciting dream, but not this time. No dreams? I tried to remember any, even the leftover pieces, and couldn't. Dreams or no dreams, I felt pretty good, tip-top, in fact, except for a slight thirst. I sat up, looked around. We were somewhere new, just coming to a trailer park. Loved trailer parks—we'd had plenty of trailer park adventures, including one I'll never forget where a gangbanger with a pet gator . . . maybe a story for another time—but we didn't turn into this trailer park. Instead we kept going, past some boarded-up buildings and vacant lots, and up a rutted road to a grove of dusty trees at the end. Some buildings stood among the trees, wooden buildings more like shacks, all faded and worn.

We parked and followed Earl Ford to the biggest shack. The door opened with a creaking sound and out came the deputy, a toothpick sticking from the side of his mouth. That always caught my attention. I wanted that toothpick real bad. How to get it? Couldn't think of a way. I lifted my leg against the wall of the shack, not sure why.

"All cleaned out," Les said, the toothpick bobbing up and down. "Looks like ol' Thurman was getting set to take off to somewheres far away, maybe Alaska, accordin' to sources."

"So?" said Lieutenant Stine, sounding kind of irritated. "Why are we here?"

Les smiled, not a friendly smile because his eyes weren't part of it, more like just showing his teeth. I showed mine, but nobody was watching. "Left one little thing behind in the garage," Les said.

He headed toward another shack further back on the property. This one had big double doors. Les threw them open and said, "Ta-da!"

A rusty old pickup was parked in the garage, a dirt-floor garage full of car smells. This wasn't the white pickup I'd escaped from, looked green to me.

"Green one fifty," said Lieutenant Stine.

"Bingo," the sheriff said. "Matches up real nice with the description of the kidnap vehicle, don't it?"

"What description?" Bernie said. "Didn't the witness turn out to be legally blind?"

"Had another witness step up," said the sheriff.

"Who?"

"The count's driver."

"I thought he remembered zip."

"Now he remembers better," the deputy said.

"Sometimes happens after trauma," said the sheriff.

We all gazed at the pickup.

"Where are the plates?" said the lieutenant. He walked around the pickup.

Les shrugged. "Searched all over."

The lieutenant peered through the windshield. "No VIN either?"

"Looks like it got ripped out," Les said.

"Registration?" said the lieutenant.

"Hasn't turned up, yet," Les said.

"Maybe you can ask ol' Thurman these questions when you're back in the Valley, lieutenant," the sheriff said.

"He's not that old," Bernie said.

I didn't get that; in fact, didn't get anything about this deal with the green pickup. Whatever was happening made everybody's face look kind of mean. Not Bernie's: he never looks mean, but angry sometimes, yes, and he was angry now. If Bernie's angry, I'm angry, but who was I supposed to be angry at? Time to grab someone by the pant leg? Who? I checked out everybody's pant legs, got nowhere. All I could think of to do was growl, so I did. Bernie gave me a pat.

On the way back to the cars, Les spat out the toothpick. I made quick work of it, felt lots better.

TWENTY-SIX

Know what's interesting?" Bernie said as we drove away.

I sure did: bacon was interesting, also Frisbees, socks on the laundry room floor, squirrels trying to sneak across the front yard, the hunting show on ESPN2, a certain she-bark that came across the canyon from time to time—where did it end?

"They finish each other's sentences," Bernie said.

Huh? Missed that one, and whatever it was didn't sound interesting to me. I checked Bernie's face: not happy. He worried a lot. When he worried, I worried, but I didn't know what to worry about and it's hard to worry about nothing, so pretty soon I stopped and looked around. We were zooming down a two-lane blacktop, Lieutenant Stine's cruiser not too far ahead, low reddish hills off to both sides. Bernie reached into his pocket, took out—uh-oh—Suzie's little gizmo, forgotten the name—and started pressing the buttons again.

". . . bourbon? In case a certain someone comes shambling—" Click click. "Purchase price? Passaic Realty?" Click click. "Hello? Yes, this is she. Who are—" Click click. "Who are—" Click click "Who are—" I'd seen humans—Leda, for example—sometimes cover their ears, wished for the first time I could do the same. There was no sign the click-clicking would be stopping soon, but at that moment, the lieutenant's brake lights went red and he pulled over to the side, fishtailing a little. We stopped behind him.

Lieutenant Stine was already out of the cruiser, hurrying toward us. He came to the side of the Porsche and said, "Disco rolled."

"Where's Suzie?" Bernie said.

"Doesn't seem to know about Suzie," the lieutenant said. "The sheriff wasn't too clear on that, or a number of other things. I'm headed back there."

"We're coming," Bernie said.

Lieutenant Stine stared down at him. Bernie stared back. "Just try not to screw it up," the lieutenant said.

"It's already screwed up," Bernie said.

Back in Nowhereville. "Whoa," said Les, as we went into the front door of the sheriff's station. "We didn't say nothin' about this guy." He pointed his chin, one of those too-small chins some humans have, at Bernie.

"He's with me," Lieutenant Stine said.

"And the dog?" said Les.

"What's the problem?" Bernie said. "Afraid of dogs?"

"Hell, no," Les said. But he was: I could hear it and smell it. I got that funny feeling at the roots of my teeth, like they needed lots of pressure on them.

We followed Les inside, around a long counter, past some desks—one of which must have had a tuna sandwich in a drawer, the smell of tuna being pretty hard to miss—and down a hall. At the end was a small room with the sheriff sitting on one side of a table and Disco, now in an orange jumpsuit, on the other.

"The PI's coming to this party for some reason," Les said.

"Now, now, Les," the sheriff said. "Bernie here's on the good side. Been doing some checking—he's got an excellent rep." The sheriff gestured at me. "So does the dog, here, name of Chet, I believe."

"The dog has a rep?" Les said.

"Grade A," said the sheriff.

One of those sudden breezes sprang up behind me, like a fan getting switched on. I knew rep. The sheriff was turning out to be not so bad.

Bernie sat at one end of the table, Les at the other, the sheriff and Lieutenant Stine in the middle. I sat on the floor beside Bernie, the fan behind me switching off. All eyes were on Disco. Disco's own eyes, little brown ones, were darting around in a way that reminded me of the eyes of this huge rat I'd once cornered in an alley in the bad part of Pedroia, and that's bad. Also, Disco didn't have his long gray fringes anymore; he no longer looked like a hippie, just a bald old man.

The sheriff leaned forward and rubbed his hands. I always noticed when humans did that. It made me watchful, no idea why. Had I ever seen Bernie do it? Not that I could remember.

"Disco here and me been gettin' to know each other," the sheriff said. "Ain't that right, Disco?"

Disco nodded the tiniest nod, hardly a movement at all.

"Interest you in another Pepsi?" the sheriff said. He turned to Bernie. "Mostly this is Coke country," he said, "but Disco turns out to be a Pepsi guy."

Bernie said nothing and his face was blank.

"Yeah," said Disco, his voice not much above a whisper. "Pepsi."

"Les?" said the sheriff.

Les rose and left the room.

"Feel like tellin' my friends here how you come by that handle—Disco?" the sheriff said.

"Told it already," Disco said.

"But these folks didn't get to hear and it's such a good story."

Disco licked his lips. He had a pointy tongue, white and dried-out looking. My own tongue felt nice and moist at that moment. Disco looked at Bernie. His eyes shied away, moved on to Lieutenant Stine instead. "Know those disco balls?" he said.

"Familiar with them," said the lieutenant.

"I . . . uh, stole one," Disco said, and went silent.

"C'mon now," said the sheriff. "You're not makin' it live." He smiled at Bernie. "Ends up that the disco ball heist is the oldest item on Disco's rap sheet, step one on a long life of crime."

"Wouldn't, um, say a life of crime," Disco said.

"No?" said the sheriff.

Disco gazed down at the table.

"Tell the story," the sheriff said.

Disco kept his eyes on the tabletop, spoke in a low voice. "I hated disco," he said, losing me completely. "Disco sucks, you know? Drove me nuts, couldn't believe it was happening—like they were stealin' our future. And then this club, the Electric Pumpkin, my favorite—Quicksilver Messenger Service played there, man—" Disco's voice got stronger, and he raised his head. "—and then one night the Pumpkin goes disco, just like that, no discussion, no warnin', finito. So I went in there—"

"Bust in there," said the sheriff. "After hours." He laughed. "Meanin' in broad daylight."

"Bust in there," said Disco, "and ripped down that fuckin' disco ball and smashed it to goddamn smithereens." His hands, not big or powerful, curled into fists and his jumpsuit sleeves fell back. He was wearing handcuffs.

Silence in the room. Can't speak for anyone else, but as for me I wasn't even trying to understand what Disco's little speech was about, in fact was having thoughts of those hunting shows on ESPN2 and how much I wanted to go hunting and Bernie was such a crack shot but we'd never been hunting, not once. Why was that?

Meanwhile, the sheriff was saying, "And forever after, everyone called you Disco—stuck with the name, so to speak."

Disco shrugged. "I got used to it."

Les returned with a can of Pepsi, cracked it open, set it on the table. Disco took it in both hands and drank.

"Moving on to the kidnapping," the sheriff said.

"Again?" said Disco. "We been through this already."

"New customers," the sheriff said.

Disco's eyes flickered over to Bernie, then to the lieutenant, settled again on the tabletop. "Starting where?" he said.

"The idea," the sheriff said.

Disco licked his lips again. Lips all cracked and that dry white tongue: hard to take my eyes off the sight. "Thurman had the idea."

"Speak up," said the sheriff.

"Thurman had the idea." He went silent.

"Which was?" said Bernie.

"Hey," said Les. "We'll do the asking."

"Now, Les," the sheriff said. "Gotta be more flexible. And Bernie here has a rep, as I mentioned."

Me, too: I had a rep. My tail did some sweeping of the floor.

Bernie hadn't seemed to pay attention to any of the back-and-forth between Les and the sheriff; he watched Disco. "Which was?" he said again.

"Ransom," said Disco. "Kidnap for ransom."

"How much?" Bernie said.

"Like two or three mil."

Bernie leaned back, crossing his arms over his chest. He did that sometimes; nothing good for perps ever happened after. Meanwhile, Lieutenant Stine leaned forward, also interesting, what with Bernie leaning back.

"But there was no ransom demand," the lieutenant said.

Disco glanced at the sheriff. "Yeah," he said. "It all got messed up."

"How?" Lieutenant Stine said.

"Like, uh . . ." Disco took a deep breath.

Lieutenant Stine turned to the sheriff. "You honestly see this asshole in front of a jury?"

"Won't never get that far," the sheriff said. "He's nervous, that's all. Don't be nervous, Disco."

"All buddies here," said Les.

"Won't get that far means, uh?" Disco said.

"Everybody pleads," said the sheriff, "like I explained. But the lead singer does short time, maybe no time, depending on performance."

Disco's voice got a little stronger. "Things were goin' good, the snatch and all that, but—"

"Who was the target?" the lieutenant said. "The woman or the dog?"

"The both of them. Thurman said the dog was valuable, so we took her, too."

"Who drove?" the lieutenant said.

"Thurman. We headed right to Clauson's Wells—there's this cabin Thurman knew about. Took turns guarding her, the three of us, and on Thurman's shift—me and Crash were zonked in the RV—she got aholt of his gun and—"

"Which gun?" said the sheriff.

Disco nodded. "Yeah, sorry. The .44. The woman gets aholt of the .44, pistol-whips Thurman, and takes off with the keys to the truck. Thurman comes out of a daze—got a bad temper, Thurman—and pops her with the rifle." Disco shrugged. "Pretty much it."

"Shrug like that again," Bernie said, still sitting back with crossed arms, "and I'll beat your head in."

Disco's eyes opened wide. Everyone else whipped around quickly to Bernie.

"Don't know about down in the Valley," the sheriff said, "but hereabouts we don't treat prisoners like that."

"I'm sure Bernie was just speaking metaphorically," the lieutenant said.

"Huh?" said Les.

"And maybe was a little pissed off at the notion of the story ending how it did," the lieutenant went on. "Leaving out any remorse concerning the victim or any details of what happened after. Such as—"

"Suzie Sanchez," Bernie said. His voice got low and harsh, his real dangerous voice which I'd hardly ever heard. "Did she get popped, too, you son of a bitch?"

Disco shrank back in his chair. "Don't know nothin' about her, like I told the sheriff."

"Explain about the car, Disco," the sheriff said.

"Car?"

"Beetle," said the sheriff. "The yellow beetle."

Disco nodded. "I didn't know nothin' about it and I didn't ask. Thurman drove up in it and put her, you know, inside. Then we went over to Red Butte and me and Crash dug the hole and Thurman pushed the car in and we covered it up." Disco started to shrug again, glanced in alarm at Bernie, stopped himself.

"Why Red Butte?" the lieutenant said.

"Thurman's idea—far from Clauson's Wells and nobody was gonna look there."

"You ever have any ideas of your own?" the lieutenant said.

"It was all about the money, man," Disco said. "No one was sposta get hurt. Would never have gone through with it if we'd knowed Thurman could wig out the way he did."

"Here's what I don't get," Lieutenant Stine said. "You kept her little dog, Princess. Why? Might as well hang a guilty sign around your neck."

Disco glanced at the sheriff. "Yeah, we knew. The pooch kind of followed us, me and Crash. We told Thurman we'd get rid of her, but the thing is, we just couldn't."

"Couldn't kill the dog—is that what you're saying?" the lieutenant said. "But you can kill a human being?"

"Not me. Not a human being."

The lieutenant pointed his finger at Disco. "You," he said. "In the eyes of the law, you, just as much as if you'd pulled the trigger."

"Disco understands that," the sheriff said, "which is why he's cooperatin'. Correct?"

"Yeah," said Disco. "Cooperatin' to the fullest."

Silence. I heard some small creature scratching inside the walls.

"There you have it," said the sheriff. "Any questions, gentlemen?"

"What's the point?" Bernie said.

"Excuse me?" said the sheriff. He gave Bernie a hard look. Bernie gave it right back.

"Okay," Bernie said, "here's a question for our dog lover."

"Always had a soft spot for 'em," said Disco.

"Then," said Bernie, "knowing Thurman's true character—this is after the murder of Adelina Borghese—how come you sold Chet to him?"

Disco looked at me. I looked back at him. "Sorry, fella," he said. Hey! He was saying sorry to me? Didn't that make him a good guy? Why was he in cuffs? Disco turned to Bernie. "The money."

"There's a surprise," said Bernie, rising. I rose, too. "That's it for us. Lieutenant?"

"I'm done."

"Thank you, gentlemen," said the sheriff. "Any follow-up questions, don't you hesitate."

We went outside. The air felt great.

"Well?" said the lieutenant.

"You tell me," Bernie said.

"I'll go back, bounce this off Thurman and Crash."

"They won't say a thing," Bernie said. "Disco got there first."

"Then we're still left with a case that looks pretty makeable to me," the lieutenant said.

"Yeah?" said Bernie. I glanced at the station, saw Les watching from a window.

We hopped in the car, took off. "Here's all we've got," Bernie said, "one little thing. Suzie was alive when her car got buried.

Otherwise she'd have been in it. And if she was alive then, why wouldn't she be alive now?"

I didn't know, was still trying to figure out if Disco was a good guy or a bad guy. After a while I remembered something about the munchies and how he hadn't shared that last Slim Jim. So didn't the answer have to be: bad guy?

TWENTY-SEVEN

Once in a while, we got together with the Valley DA, Cedric Booker. Not sure what a DA is, but something important, so I was always on my best behavior, easy to do with Cedric, because he liked me and I liked him. We met Cedric in a little park downtown, not far from the courthouse, the same one where I'd made my only court appearance. Cedric was an interesting guy, the tallest human I'd ever seen up close. A long time ago, he'd starred on the Valley College basketball team, might have gone pro, Bernie said, except he couldn't play with his back to the basket, whatever that meant. The truth is, I've never had much interest in basketball, on account of the ball being impossible for me, as I may have mentioned already. Did I also get into the story about the Police Athletic League game and how I softened up that ball a little? If not, some other time.

Cedric and Bernie shook hands. Cedric towered over Bernie and Bernie's hand practically disappeared in his. Seeing Bernie looking up at someone hardly ever happened, was kind of fun.

"How's Exhibit A?" Cedric said, reaching way down to give me a pat. "Got something for you."

Something for me?

"Always amazes me how high he can jump," Cedric said, brushing something, possibly a tiny clump of dirt, off the shoulder of his suit jacket. Uh-oh. And was that a small tear in the fabric?

"Christ," said Bernie.

Cedric laughed and produced a tennis ball, hidden until then in his other hand. A real fresh one: I could smell it. Then he reared back and threw—very far, but not quite as far as Bernie. Bernie had a great arm, had pitched for Army, which if I haven't mentioned already I should have.

I took off. Is there anything better than chasing tennis balls? Grabbing perps by the pant leg, maybe, but that was it. Some days I'm faster than others, no idea why—always fast, you understand—and today was one of those fast days. Was I zooming or what? I caught up to that ball on its last low bounce, just before it was about to start rolling, scooped it up and whirled around in one motion, and flew back across the park, ears flat back, skidded to a stop, the turf rippling up in green waves and making a lovely ripping sound, and dropped the ball at Cedric's feet.

"Ballistics report came in," Cedric said, bending to pick up the ball. I heard a crack that seemed to come from his knees, had heard it before when humans bent down. Forced to get around day after day on only two legs: spare me.

"And?" Bernie said.

"Thirty-ought-six," said Cedric.

"Got the weapon?"

"Hasn't turned up yet. Stine's looking. So's the Rio Loco sheriff." He hurled the ball again, maybe farther than before. Far as you like, Cedric! Zoom. I was off. But what was this? One of my guys, member of the nation within, bounding in out of nowhere, making tracks for my tennis ball? Just like the Porsche, I've got an overdrive—that's what Bernie says. I shifted into overdrive—my paws hardly touching down at all, a hard-to-describe feeling—tore across the park, sprang at the ball, now rolling, at the exact same instant this other dude—kind of big and ugly, with long long legs and lots of drool—was leaping, too. Then came some confusion and clouds of dust, and when that was pretty much over, I trotted on back to Cedric with the ball and dropped it at his feet.

Cedric looked down at it and said, "Should have brought another ball."

"You haven't answered my question," Bernie said.

"Which one, Bernie? I count half a dozen so far."

"What if no weapon turns up?"

Cedric sighed. "Sometimes it is what it is," he said.

"What's that?" said Bernie. "A koan?"

Koan. Rang a bell. We'd worked on the Bert and Stacie Cohen divorce a while back, one of our very worst jobs—would I ever forget what happened after that diamond ring got flushed down the toilet?—and if they were involved in this—especially Bert—I wanted no part of it.

"What's your IQ?" Cedric said.

"No idea," said Bernie.

"The army must have tested it."

"Then maybe you can find out through the Freedom of Information Act," Bernie said. "What's your point?"

"There's such a thing as being too smart," Cedric said. "That's my point."

"Meaning?"

"Meaning we've got a confession, we've got Princess, found in possession of the suspects, thanks to you, we've got the body, also thanks to you, dug up at one of their known hangouts, and we've got the vehicle used in the kidnapping, the green one-fifty. No case is perfect—whether you believe that or not—but the decent ones all get to some tipping point and it's my judgment that we're there. In short, Bernie, don't overthink. The case is solid." Cedric picked up what was left of the ball and threw it once more, not very far this time, and it didn't bounce at all, just landed with a soft thud. I ambled over to get it.

Not far at all, so I could hear their conversation quite easily. "No VIN, no plates, no registration," Bernie said.

"Brought the Borghese's driver—" Cedric flipped open some device, pressed buttons. "—Rui Santos over for a look. He ID'd it, also had no memory of plates on the kidnap vehicle."

"How come he didn't ID it before?"

"That happens."

"What about Nancy Malone, the trainer?"

"Thought the color was right, otherwise couldn't say. Still seemed a bit traumatized, in my opinion."

"In what way?"

"A lot of crying, that kind of thing."

"Nance?"

"Anything surprising about that?"

"Doesn't strike me as the type."

"The type who gets upset by a violent crime happening right in front of their eyes? What's the other type?" Cedric gazed down at Bernie. Bernie gazed up at him. "Not everybody's as hard as you," Cedric said.

"If you think I'm hard, you're in the wrong job."

"Don't push me."

"I'm not pushing you, Cedric. I'm trying to hold you back."

"From what?"

I didn't like the sound of their conversation, hard to say why, soon found I'd chewed up the remains of the tennis ball and maybe swallowed them. Right away I didn't feel too good.

"From making a big mistake," Bernie said. "Suzie Sanchez is missing, remember? That means mistakes, real big ones, are still possible."

"I don't need you looking out for me," Cedric said. "And I don't need reminding about Suzie. We offered Crash a deal this morning—reducing the charge down to involuntary manslaughter for any information."

"And?"

"His PD was in the room, of course—Crash and Thurman lawyered up right away—and practically told him flat out to take the deal, but Crash said he knows nothing, never heard of Suzie. Then he went into a rant about what he'd do to Disco if he ever got his hands on him."

"Maybe he's telling the truth," Bernie said.

"You're saying whatever happened up in Clauson's Wells Thurman did on his own?"

"That's possible, but it's not what I'm saying."

"Then what?"

"Do one thing for me," Bernie said. "The Rio Loco sheriff gets nowhere near either of them, Crash or Thurman."

"Can't promise that," Cedric said. "But I'll be in the room."

"And let me know if he or the deputy even asks to see them."

"Taking the little scrap you had with them personally?" Cedric said. "That won't help you think straight."

Silence. Bernie stuck his chin out a little; Cedric did the same. "Also," Bernie said, "if that rifle turns up, I need to know."

"That's three things, Bernie. You said one."

I went behind a trash barrel and puked up what was left of the tennis ball, felt better.

We drove in silence for a while. Then Bernie said, *"Like two or three mil.* Christ. That's the whole story right there." It was? I didn't get it, waited for more. But no more came. How about some music? But that didn't happen either. Bernie's hands were tight on the steering wheel, knuckles sticking out. "Gotta stand back," he said, "see the big picture. Why do I always have to keep reminding myself of that?" Bernie was great at asking questions, could make people squirm, always good for us. Sometimes, though, like now, he made himself squirm. That was bad. I shifted a little, put a paw on his leg. "Chet—I'm driving."

I took it off.

"Sorry, boy," he said, and gave me a pat. "This case is just so . . ." His voice trailed off. Outside the shadows of the downtown towers slanted across the street, making me feel hemmed in. "Big picture," Bernie said, as we turned a corner and came to a huge domed building I recognized: the Metro Arena. "Big picture—Suzie wasn't in that car. Meaning she's out there, Chet, I can feel it."

I'd been in the Metro Arena once, back before the hockey team left town, me and Bernie working on a case involving some crazed fan. Hockey: the strangest game I've ever seen, made no sense, plus all the fans turned out to be crazed, and we maybe didn't even end up finding the right one and clearing the case, which hardly ever happens. Also, I got to go on the ice, supposedly a treat. Ice! Once was enough, let me tell you. Plus the players smelled very bad and the puck was none too tasty.

The Metro Arena parking lot was huge, almost empty at the moment, with rows of tall metal lampposts going on and on. For some reason the sight of all those lampposts made me uneasy. As soon as we got out of the car, I marked one of them, then another and another and an—

"Chet! For God's sake."

We walked toward the big doors at the front of the arena, but before we got there a small door opened and out came Aldo. He carried a suitcase, wore a jacket and tie. Ties were interesting, especially swinging freely the way they did sometimes, kind of inviting. Bernie had a tie for wearing to court, a nice tie decorated with saguaro cactuses. It hung in the closet, just out of reach.

Aldo saw us and paused.

"Going on a trip?" Bernie said.

He nodded. "They canned me."

"The count?"

"And Nance," Aldo said. "Mostly Nance. They're inside now."

"Doing what?" said Bernie. "Things don't start till tomorrow."

"Rehearsing the opening ceremony," Aldo said. "The whole show's being dedicated to Adelina's memory. I heard—" Aldo's voice went funny and his eyes got wet; a bit surprising, what with Aldo being a big strong guy. "I heard you caught the killers," he said. "Thank you."

Bernie nodded. He had all kinds of nods; this one meant nothing, just moved the conversation along.

Aldo brushed his eyes with the back of his sleeve. "A botched kidnapping? Is that the story?"

"There's a confession to that effect."

A taxi pulled up. "Will they get the death penalty?"

"I'm the wrong one to ask," Bernie said. "But probably not."

"Life in prison?" Aldo said.

"That's more likely."

Aldo looked up at the sky, the normal downtown sky, hazy blue. "Knowing that doesn't make me feel any better," he said. "Not even if they got the death penalty." He brought his gaze down to Bernie. "Does it make you feel better?"

"Punishment for criminals?" Bernie said. "Yes."

Aldo watched Bernie for another moment or two, then looked at me. I was standing at Bernie's side, remembering my only ride in a taxi, a ride that would have gone much better if the driver hadn't left his lunch lying out on the front seat; my first encounter with pepperoni—the smell turned out to be too much for me.

"Your dog is great," Aldo said. Hey! What a guy after all! He opened the back door of the taxi. And damned if I didn't smell pepperoni right away!

"Where're you headed?" Bernie said.

"The airport," Aldo said. "I'm moving back east."

"Suppose I need to get in touch with you," Bernie said.

"For what?"

"Maybe you'll think of something you forgot to tell me."

"That won't happen."

"What if I think of something I forgot to tell you?" Bernie said.

Aldo took out a card and handed it to Bernie. Then he got in the taxi and rode away, pepperoni scent lingering in the air. Bernie and I went into the arena.

TWENTY-EIGHT

We went down a long, dark tunnel—not too fond of tunnels—and came to a railing high above the arena floor, rows and rows of empty metal seats all around. A blue floor, no ice. I was just noticing that when a horrible sound filled the air, part blare, part squeak.

"It's all right, boy," Bernie said. "Just feedback."

The sound faded at once; had Bernie somehow made it go away? And feedback? Did that have anything to do with food? How was that possible? Food was one of the best things going. I didn't get it, but strangely enough at that very moment, with my mind on food, I spotted part of a pretzel, one of those big soft ones, under a nearby seat. Easy pickings, and I picked it—not quite as soft as I remembered, but I hadn't had a pretzel in way too long—and joined Bernie at the railing.

Down below on the arena floor stood a small group of people, more than two, plus one of my guys, whom I recognized partly from her being such a little fluffball, more from how she held her head in that determined way: Princess. And the people? I picked out the count, with that big nose—big for a human—and the mustache beneath it; and Nance standing beside him, somewhat taller, holding the end of Princess's leash.

Another tall woman, this one blond, had a microphone in her hand. Her lips moved, and just after that a voice boomed out through the arena, her lips and the words not quite lining up, making it hard for me to understand. "I'll just say, and now to open the Great Western Dog Show, please welcome our mayor, blah blah, blah blah. Then the mayor will take the mic—"

"After the boos," Bernie said, very quiet.

"—and he'll say this year's show is being dedicated to the memory of Adelina Borghese and—"

The count leaned forward and his lips moved although I heard no sound.

"My apologies," said the blond woman. "Countess Adelina Borghese, and after that, he'll pass the mic to you. And then—"

The count reached out, took the mic from the blond woman. "The Countess Adelina *di* Borghese," he said. "She would appreciate very much this show. The countess was a famous friend to the world of dogs and—"

The blond woman reached out for the microphone. I heard her say, "No need to for the whole speech now, sir, we're only—"

But the count pulled the microphone away from her, and went on. "And so in her name, I, Count Lorenzo di Borghese, officially am the opener of the Great Western Dog Show. Let the competition begin!"

Down of the floor, everyone just stood there, looking kind of uncomfortable in a way that's hard to describe; everyone but Nance, who clapped her hands, making a very faint sound. The count returned the mic, made a little bow to the blond woman.

"When that's done," she said, "I'll introduce the—"

Bernie backed away from the railing. I backed away, too,

stopped listening. Bernie had spotted a man sitting at the end of the arena nearer to us, but lower down. A small, white-haired man dressed in black, with a stud sparkling in one of his ears: I'd seen him before, but where? He rose, started walking down an aisle toward the arena floor.

"Rui Santos," Bernie said, "the driver." Down on the floor, Nance had moved away from the others, was walking toward Rui. "How come we didn't interview him already?" Bernie said. Couldn't help him with that. "I'm losing it," he said.

Bernie losing it? No way. We were doing great on this case, had cracked it, in fact. Weren't the perps behind bars? But where was Suzie? That was a worry. Perps in the can meant the case was cracked, yes or no? My mind went back to me and Princess with Adelina in the cabin, and Thurman with the choke chain, and some other things a bit too dim to remember, and I thought maybe we hadn't cracked the case after all but couldn't get past that.

"Hey, Chet, what's wrong?"

Nothing. Nothing was wrong. I realized my tail had drooped down low, got it raised up high again, stiff and ready for wagging.

Rui waited at the end of the aisle by the lowest row of seats. Nance, still crossing the floor, started to raise her head, maybe to look up into the stands. Bernie ducked behind a seat; I didn't have to, was pretty much down at that level already. We peered over the top of the seat. Nance reached Rui, handed him an envelope, the big padded kind. That padding doesn't turn out to be edible, a story for another day. Nance turned and walked away. Rui turned, too, and began climbing the stairs. We stayed down, eyes on Rui. He came to our level, but at the next aisle over, and headed into one of those tunnels leading out of the arena, not glancing in our direction.

Very quiet, Bernie made this little sound, kind of tchk-tchk. We rose and headed toward the same tunnel, me completely silent, Bernie as silent as a human could be. Just before we entered the tunnel, I glanced back down at the floor, saw Princess's big dark eyes. They seemed to be looking in my direction.

Following people without them knowing was one of the best things about our job. Once we tracked this real bad guy deep down into Mexico, maybe not strictly legal, whatever that means. Mexico! Let me tell you. Gunfights—I'd never seen so many. And my guys, not all but some, are different in Mexico. They run in packs, stay away from humans except for getting food. Some real tough customers, red-eyed dudes, lean and mean. I tried to make friends, but they were having none of it. Got into some scraps down in Mexico, and so did Bernie. The Mexican vet had to stitch me up; she stitched up Bernie, too.

We walked through the tunnel. It was dark, with Rui just a human shape against the light at the end, and then gone. "I think you know something I don't," Bernie said, his voice low.

Me knowing more than Bernie? No way. Well, no way except for possibly knowing more about how the world smells and sounds, and the taste of certain things, like sticks in the yard, chair legs, chew strips. Maybe not chew strips: I had this faint memory of a party sometime after we'd cleared the Gulagov case, a party with funny hats, popping corks, and Bernie gnawing on the end of a chew strip, just to give it a try. Was Bernie the best or what? I moved a little closer to him.

Some humans look back when you're following them and some don't. According to Bernie, the ones who don't are toast, which I didn't quite get. Toast is good, nice and crunchy on the outside, although the toaster itself can be pretty dangerous, especially this one time Bernie stuck a knife down inside it, not sure why. Where was I? Oh, yeah: Rui. He turned out to be the kind of human who didn't look back.

We followed him down the tunnel, real easy guy to tail. No looking back, left behind an oniony breeze, and wore hard-soled shoes that clicked loudly with every step. Bernie wore old beat-up high-tops and hardly made a sound, and I, of course, was silent.

Rui led us down a ramp and into the parking lot, still practically empty. Bernie and I stepped behind the corner of a Dumpster. Dumpsters came up from time to time in our line of work, and I've got a story or two to tell about them, not now. I'll just take a second to mention Dumpster smells: fascinating.

Meanwhile, Rui was on his way to a black limo, not far away, clickety click, clickety click. He opened the door, tossed the padded envelope inside, and got in. "Let's go," Bernie said, and we ran to the Porsche, also not far away but in the other direction. It might surprise you that over a short distance Bernie can run quite fast for a human, even with his bad leg. True, I was sitting tall in the shotgun seat by the time he reached the car—eyes on the limo, which was now almost at the exit—but I hadn't been waiting long.

Bernie turned the key. Love the sound of our engine, low and rumbling, almost like some powerful creature, all set to burn rubber. What a smell that is! But this time we didn't burn rubber, instead drove slowly across the lot. Way too slowly, in my opinion. The limo had left the lot, was no longer in sight. "One-way street," Bernie said. "And the day I lose a stretch limo is the day I hang 'em up for good." I batted that one around in my mind, so confusing, and let it go.

We left the lot, drove onto the street, and picked up the limo right away, waiting at a traffic light; all my worrying for no reason. My money's on Bernie, always was, always will be, although

I don't actually have any money and neither does he. What was the latest problem with our finances? I got that feeling in my head when I come close to remembering.

"One little problem," Bernie said. "Rui's had two chances to see the car—at our place and at the strip, so we can't count on—" At that moment a van swerved over from the next lane and got in front of us. Normally Bernie doesn't like that one little bit, sometimes honks the horn, a sound I can't stand. But not this time. This time he said, "Thanks, buddy."

We shadowed the limo, with the van in between, and sometimes other cars as well. Kind of tricky, with all the traffic lights, but Bernie's a real good driver, if I haven't mentioned that already. After a while, the limo took a freeway ramp, and so did we. Stop-and-go traffic on the freeway, the limo a few cars ahead in the next lane, Bernie's hands relaxed on the wheel, not usually the case in stop-and-go. Once in a stop-and-go situation this huge trucker had shaken his fist at Bernie: big mistake, buddy boy.

We rode away from downtown, passed the giant longhorn bull sign, got onto another freeway, even more packed than the first one. "They're talking another million people in the next ten years," Bernie said. "See where this is headed?" I had no clue. The sun was setting. Everything, including Bernie's face, got red and hazy. "Only one aquifer for the whole valley," he said. "When that dries up, we die of thirst, end of story." Oh, no. That was scary, especially with Bernie's hazy red face. I got thirsty right away.

Traffic thinned out. Night fell, a hazy night in the Valley, but clear once we climbed into the hills. The limo had big red taillights, easy to see. On the far side of the hills, the limo slowed and pulled into a gas station. "Check those prices," Bernie said, voice low. "No limo driver gasses up at a place like this."

Did I know what Bernie was getting at? Not at all, but no

problem: he had his job and I had mine. The limo went by the pumps and around to the side of the building where it was all shadowy. Bernie cut the lights and kept going, parking by a tow truck in a dark corner of the lot. From there we had a good view of the limo, building, pumps, everything.

At first, nothing happened. Then the window of the limo slid down and cigarette smoke came drifting out, and almost at once I could smell it. Bernie got fidgety, reached toward the glove box—forgotten cigarettes sometimes lay crumpled up in the back—and stopped himself. After that we just sat still, watching the cigarette smoke rising in tiny clouds. Hard to beat this, me and Bernie on a stakeout, although exactly why we were running a stakeout on Rui the limo driver with the bad guys already in the can wasn't clear.

All of a sudden a bright light shot across the sky. The sight made Bernie smile. "Shooting star," he said. "Not a star at all, of course," he added, losing me right away. And a while later: "Number of stars in the Milky Way Galaxy—two hundred billion, give or take. Number of galaxies in the universe—at least a hundred billion. See what this means?" No one can be expected to make sense all the time, especially on long stakeouts. I was about to put a paw on Bernie's knee when a dusty SUV appeared, driving past the pumps and around the building, where it parked cop-style beside the limo, driver's door to driver's door. Rui wasn't a cop: that was my first thought; and only.

The SUV driver's window slid down. A hand reached out. Rui's window slid down a little more and I caught a glimpse of him, cigarette glowing between his lips. He laid the big padded envelope on the waiting hand. The windows rose; the limo and the SUV started up and headed toward the road, limo going one way, SUV the other. We tailed the SUV, Bernie's decision, but I agreed: who was in there?

The SUV wound down through the hills on the other side of the Valley. Bernie kept a few cars between us at all times, but then the SUV turned onto a back road, paved but narrow, with no traffic at all, and Bernie cut the lights. No problem for me: I could still see fine, but Bernie leaned forward, squinting, and his hands gripped tight on the wheel. The SUV seemed to be pushing a cone of light through the darkness; just a little light in all the great big darkness, and we were part of that darkness. That made me sneeze for some reason, and then I felt great, wide awake and rarin' to go.

After not too long, the lights of a town glowed off to one side. "Nowhereville," said Bernie. The SUV came to a crossroads, headed toward Nowhereville, with us in the darkness behind. A few houses appeared by the side of the road. The SUV slowed and swung into the driveway of one of them. Bernie pulled over and stopped, switching off the engine. It got real quiet. I heard a door close, and then a light went on in the house with the SUV.

We got out of the car, walked along the side of the road, entered the driveway, Bernie glancing inside the SUV on the way by. The pavement felt warm beneath my paws, but the backyard was cooler, hard-packed, scrubby. Light shone in a window at the back of the house. We crept up to it—Bernie crouching, me at my normal height—and peered over the sill.

Beyond the glass—cold against my nose—lay a kitchen. A man sat at the table, sideways to us. He opened the big padded envelope, took out wads of cash, and began counting, his lips moving silently. A lean man with pale eyes and a cowboy hat: I'd already gotten to know him a bit—Earl Ford, sheriff of Rio Loco County.

TWENTY-NINE

Wads of cash, and the counting took a long time. After a while, Sheriff Ford squirmed in his chair a bit, like he was uncomfortable, and took off his gun belt. He laid it on the table, went back to counting. I got bored and glanced at Bernie. His face was hard. He didn't look at me, only laid his hand on my back, very light. That meant: get ready. But of course I was ready already, just not sure for what.

Bernie took his hand away and drew our .38 Special from his waistband. The .38 Special meant business. I felt the hairs standing up on the back of my neck, a real good feeling. Bernie rose, slow and calm. We'd taken down a lot of bad guys, starting in ways like this. But a sheriff was a kind of cop, right? And so—

I hadn't gotten any further than that when the sheriff suddenly glanced up at the window. His eyes opened wide, mouth, too. At almost the same time, his hand darted toward the gun belt. Bang. Smash. Bernie fired through the glass. The gun belt shot off the table and fell to the floor. Bernie's a crack shot: I know I've mentioned that, but maybe you didn't believe me. Nickels spinning in the air—I've seen him drill a whole bunch, ping ping ping, just the two of us out in the desert, having fun.

But no time for that now. Earl Ford dove for the gun belt. Bernie kicked out the window and we both leaped through, me first. All this action, plus gunplay and shattering glass: who could ask for more? Not this dude, amigo.

The sheriff turned out to be pretty quick, grabbing the gun belt, rolling over and ripping off one shot—CRACK, louder than the .38 Special—the gun still in the holster but the muzzle sticking out, before I was on him. I got his wrist, made him drop the gun belt, heard a real scary growl, realized it was coming from me. Earl Ford cried out in pain and fear, and I had no problem with that: I could smell him now and he had the bad guy smell and lots of it. I looked at Bernie, expecting him to be right beside me with the .38 Special, and—oh, no. Bernie, still only partway across the kitchen, was slowly sinking to the floor, the .38 Special loose in his hand, and blood coming from one side of his head.

I forgot everything I was doing and ran to him. Oh, Bernie! He was on his knees. I started licking at the blood, trying to make everything all better. "No, Chet," he said, leaning away from me, feeling his head. "Grazed me, that's all."

Then came more commotion from behind. I swung around and there was the sheriff, grabbing the gun belt again, whipping out the gun. What had I done? I got ready to spring, but way too late. The sheriff aimed right at Bernie. Up came the .38 Special. Bernie shot first. The sheriff staggered backward and dropped his own gun. A red hole appeared high up on the inside of his gun arm. He didn't make a sound, only gazed down at the wound, and as he did red came spurting out, a little spurt, and then another. "Oh, God," he said, clamping down on the wound with his other hand. Blood leaked out from between his fingers, dripped down on the wads of cash. He looked up at Bernie, now rising to his feet. "Help me, man," he said. "I'm gonna bleed out."

"Then you'll have to talk fast," Bernie said. "Where's Suzie Sanchez?"

Earl Ford was turning white, blood trickling from his arm. Bernie was bleeding, too. I got a real bad feeling, but what to do? The next thing I knew I was barking.

"Letting me die?" the sheriff said.

"Up to you," said Bernie. And then, "Easy, boy." I went quiet.

The sheriff sat in the chair, landing hard, like his legs had given out beneath him. He kept pressing on the wound, but it did no good. "Can't stop this by myself," he said. "What kind of man are you?"

Bernie stuck the .38 Special in his waistband, went to the sink, tore a strip off a dish towel. "Where is Suzie Sanchez?" he said.

"Jesus Christ," said the sheriff. His voice got high and small, like a whimper.

"You live or die," Bernie said. "Your call."

The sheriff licked his lips, his tongue bone white. "She's dead."

Bernie's face, so hard already, hardened some more. He almost didn't even look like Bernie now. "Who killed her?"

"I don't know."

Bernie dropped the strip of dishrag on the counter.

The sheriff's gaze switched to it. "I swear I don't know," he said. "I swear on my mother's memory."

"Didn't know her," Bernie said.

The sheriff gazed at Bernie. Those pale eyes, so tough and full of rage: but all of a sudden they changed completely and tears rolled out. I kind of understood what was going on, had seen and been part of a lot of one-on-ones in my world, the nation within the nation. Humans had an expression for this, an expression I understood pretty well: top dog.

"Don't know who killed her," Earl Ford said. "She was already dead by the time we got to Clauson's Wells."

"Is that where the body is?"

"But I had nothing to do with it."

Bernie was silent for a moment. Then he said something that made me feel cold all over. "Here's a nasty thought—I could put a slug in your other arm."

The sheriff spoke quickly. "Les took care of all that, the body and so forth. But I can show you."

Bernie stood motionless by the sink, his eyes on Earl Ford. Blood all over the place now—the money, the table, dripping over the edge and onto the floor. Bernie picked up the dishrag strip, crossed the room, and tied it tight above the wound. At the same time, he looked the sheriff in the eye. "This comes off just as fast—remember that," he said. Bernie swept up most of the bloody money, stuffed it back in the padded envelope, and said, "Let's go."

"Where?"

"Clauson's Wells."

"But what about my arm? I know a doc just down the road."

"It's not as bad as it looks," Bernie said. "Trust me." He dabbed at the side of his head with his sleeve, checked it: hardly any blood at all; his own bleeding had almost stopped. He took the sheriff by the back of his collar and lifted him to his feet. "That SUV an automatic?"

The sheriff nodded. "Why?"

"You're driving."

* * *

The sheriff drove, although Bernie, in the shotgun seat, had to turn the key. I rode in back with the padded envelope. No problem, not being in the shotgun seat myself, hardly any problem at all. I could do this. Lots of room in the backseat, couldn't complain about that, and what was this, wedged under the armrest? A flip-top box, the kind fast food burgers came in? Fast food: one of the greatest human inventions. Humans could rock sometimes, for sure. But I wasn't thinking about all that in the backseat of the sheriff's SUV, too busy flipping open the flip top, and there, inside, a nice grayish burger, no bun, with only a bite or two missing. A moment later: no burger at all. Very tasty; at the same time, eating it made me realize how hungry I was, kind of strange how that works. I sniffed around for more burger—more anything in the food department—detected none.

Meanwhile, there was talking in the front seat. "Start with the money," Bernie said. "Payment for something you already did or that you're going to?"

The sheriff didn't answer. I could see the side of his face, green from the dashboard lights. He smelled green, too: a weird kind of thought I'd never had before.

"Got to be one or the other," Bernie said.

The sheriff kept silent.

"A real easy knot to undo," Bernie said. "One little tug."

The sheriff took a deep breath, began talking in a very low voice.

"Speak up," Bernie said.

"You're smart," the sheriff said, a bit louder. "You can figure it out."

"That's not going to work, Earl," Bernie said. "Try some—" Bernie's cell phone rang. He answered. "Janie? Have to call you back. Kind of busy right—"

He listened. I could just hear the sound of Janie's voice—one of my favorite voices—but couldn't make out what she was saying. Have I mentioned Janie? She's the best groomer in the Valley, has a great business with a great business plan: Janie's Pet Grooming Service—We Pick Up and Deliver. Loved Janie, and she hadn't picked me up in way too long. She even brushes my teeth! The fun we have with that, let me tell you.

"Post-it note?" Bernie said. "I never saw a Post-it note. What did it—" His voice rose. "A lump?" He listened; I heard Janie talking fast. "What kind of lump?" Bernie said. "Where?" He listened some more, then clicked off. "Stop the car," he said.

"Huh?" said Earl Ford.

"Pull over. Stop the goddamn car."

The sheriff pulled over, parked at the side of the road, a quiet desert road with no traffic. Bernie twisted around, looked at me through the space between the front seats.

"Chet? You okay?"

Okay? I was a lot better than just okay. This was pretty exciting stuff. Had we ever taken down a sheriff before? Not that I could remember. I just hoped Bernie knew what he was doing, but of course he did.

Bernie reached through the space, patted my head. Always very nice. Very, very nice: all the exciting stuff—taking down a sheriff, bloody wads of cash, gunplay—slipped my mind for a few moments, my tail sweeping back and forth on the seat. Bernie patted down my back—hey, this was great, even though I had a vague idea we might be a little pressed for time right now—over to my side, where he patted some more before his hand went still. His eyes were on me, big and liquid in the night.

"Chet?" Bernie's voice was soft and strange, even sounded a

bit scared. Impossible: had I ever heard Bernie scared before? No way. Nothing scared Bernie. "You okay, boy?"

What was going on? I wagged harder so he'd get the message: I was feeling tip-top, couldn't be better. Bernie withdrew his hand—have I mentioned how nice his hands are, big and strong?—and turned around. "Drive," he said.

"I'm not feelin' so good," Earl Ford said.

"Drive."

The sheriff pulled onto the road and drove. No traffic, a quiet night, a pair of glowing yellow eyes in the distance, and then just the darkness. I watched the back of their heads, Bernie's and the sheriff's. The shape of Bernie's was much nicer.

"I'm not hearing you," Bernie said.

"Huh?"

"The money—payment for work done or work to do?"

The sheriff was silent. Bernie reached for the dishrag strip. The sheriff shrank away, the SUV swerving across the road, tires squealing. "You'd do that to me?" he said, steering back to the other side. "Be murder, pure and simple."

"But you wouldn't be around to argue the case," Bernie said. "Here's what you're missing—you can tell us the truth and live, or not tell and die, but we'll find the truth anyway. Got that?"

The sheriff nodded.

"Don't think you do," Bernie said. "Say it."

"Say what?"

"The situation—what I just told you."

"What the hell? Now you're playing games with me?"

"You're not that lucky. Say it."

A long silence. Then the sheriff said, "Tell the truth and live, not tell and die."

"But?"

"But you say you'll find the truth anyway."

"Count on it," Bernie said. "In fact, we're so close now we may not even need you. Get the implication?" He gave Earl Ford a long stare, again hardly looking like Bernie at all. But he still smelled exactly the same, so I was cool with it.

"Payment for work done," the sheriff said.

"Which was?"

Another long silence.

"It's over," Bernie said. "Aren't you smart enough to see that? I thought Les was the dumb one." The sheriff's head moved, a kind of flinch. In the nation within the nation we had flinching, too. "But you've still got some wiggle room," Bernie went on, "assuming two things. One, you didn't murder anyone yourself. Two, you survive the night."

"I didn't murder anyone," Earl Ford said.

"Who did?"

"All I know's we got a strong case against those three guys—there's a confession, for Christ's sake."

"There you go," Bernie said, "hurting your chances on number two. Disco, Crash, Thurman—accessories after the fact at the most, more likely just frame-job saps. So, one more time, who did the killing?"

The sheriff took another deep breath, like he was going to say something important. And maybe he would have, but at that moment Bernie's phone rang again.

"Cedric?" Bernie said. He listened for a moment and then said, "Not much." More speaking from Cedric, nothing I could make out. "Lester?" Bernie said. "Interesting." And then: "Wouldn't hurt to look into Adelina's will, whether she had a prenup, that kind of thing." Cedric's voice rose on the other end. "Why?" said

Bernie. "Because your case is blowing up—that's why." He closed his phone, put it away.

The sheriff drove. Bernie had been asking all sorts of questions, but now he was silent. Fine with me: I hadn't understood a thing. I concentrated on the smell of blood, most of it coming from Earl Ford, a little bit from Bernie.

The sheriff spoke first. "Something about my cousin Les, that call?"

Bernie turned to him, blinking a bit, as though he'd been lost in thought. I'd seen that happen, but not at times like this. "Missed that," he said.

"The phone call," Earl Ford said, sounding impatient, which made me like him even less. "Was it about my cousin Les?"

"The asking questions part of your life is in the past, Earl," Bernie said. "From now on it's answers only. Who did the killing? Adelina first."

"You can believe me or not," the sheriff said. "I don't know—she was dead, too, by the time we got to Clauson's Wells."

"What made you go there?"

"Got a call about some trouble."

"From who?"

"Anonymous."

"Have to do better than that," Bernie said. "You're up against all that cash in the backseat."

I placed my paw on the padded envelope.

"Came from the trainer."

"Nance?"

"Yeah."

"What did she say?"

"Been an accident. More like a suicide, actually."

"Adelina shot herself—that's the story?"

"Yeah."

"The ballistics came in, Earl—you didn't hear? Single shot to the forehead, thirty-ought-six."

"It's still possible."

"Nope," Bernie said. "Her arms weren't long enough. Who killed her?"

"Not me," said the sheriff. "That's all I know."

"And Suzie?"

"Don't know that neither. Never even saw the body."

"How come you know where she's buried?"

"Les told me."

The moon rose. We bumped along a desert track. Ramshackle shadows appeared in the distance, silvery at the edges: Clauson's Wells.

Bernie peered at me over the headrest. "You okay?" Asking me that again? I was fine, couldn't have been better, unless I'd been up front in the shotgun seat.

THIRTY

We drove along the empty main street of the ghost town. A rat skittered through the headlight beams, disappeared underneath a broken sidewalk board. Don't like rats, not one little bit. They stink, simple as that, and something about those long skinny tails—maybe the thought of chewing on them—makes me queasy, if that's the word for when you're about to puke.

The sheriff parked in front of the saloon. Bernie pulled the keys from the ignition and put them in his pocket. "Flashlight?" he said. The sheriff pointed his chin at the glove box. Bernie opened it, found the flashlight, then looked more closely and took out a pair of steel handcuffs, the tiny key in the lock. The sheriff glanced at the handcuffs, didn't look happy. We got out of the SUV, Bernie first, then Earl Ford, then me. I stayed right behind the sheriff in case he got up to any tricks. We stepped onto the sidewalk—the sheriff groaning a bit—and went through the swinging doors into the saloon.

Bernie switched on the flashlight, shone the beam around. The busted-up staircase; coyote turds—none fresh; the long bar with the cracked mirror behind it: nothing had changed. We followed the sheriff around to the other side of the bar. He pointed down to the floor, his finger, long and crooked, trembling slightly in the flashlight beam. Bernie shone the light on the floor. It glinted on a thick metal ring screwed into one of the wide floor planks. Then the beam rose slowly up to Earl Ford's face, now all shiny with sweat. Sweat, human sweat, is a real interesting subject—something we know about only by observation in the nation within, one of the many reasons for being happy just the way I am—and I promise to go into it another time, but right now Bernie was talking.

"You put her down there?" I'd never heard his voice quite like this, so deep, harsh, unsteady.

"Not me, man," said the sheriff, raising his hands like we had a gun on him. "I told you—it was Les."

"But you stood right beside him."

"That's not true," the sheriff said, a drop of sweat dripping off the end of his nose.

"Where were you?"

The sheriff didn't answer, just stood there dripping sweat.

"Up in that cabin?" said Bernie. "Was that where Adelina got killed?"

"Not by me," Earl Ford said.

Bernie shifted the beam slightly, settled it on the sheriff's wound: no bleeding that I could see, the dishrag strip still knotted tight. "Open up," he said.

The sheriff reached down with his good arm, grasped the ring, and pulled. Nothing happened.

"Harder," Bernie said.

Earl Ford tried again, grunting this time, with a sharp sound of pain at the end. But nothing happened.

"You're not trying, "Bernie said.

"Best I can do—I'm right-handed. And I'm not feelin' too good. Got a bullet in me, for Christ sake, and—"

"Shut up."

Earl Ford shut up. Bernie glanced around, poking the light here and there. A rusty chain hung from the back of the bar. Bernie tugged on it, then said, "C'mere."

"What for?" said the sheriff.

"Was that a question?" Bernie said.

The sheriff didn't answer, stepped forward. Bernie clamped one handcuff around the sheriff's good wrist and the other to a link in the chain. Then he bent down, grasped the ring in the floor and yanked at it. A square section of the floor opened up, a small door, really; and it didn't just open but got torn right off its hinges. That was Bernie. He tossed the door aside—trapdoor, was that the name? I had a faint memory from some DVD in our pile at home, back from a period where we'd gotten into horror movies, a brief period because they turned out to be too scary for both of us.

I went to the edge of the hole in the floor. Bernie shone the light down inside. I peered into a square hole with wooden walls and a wooden floor, not too deep or big, but plenty big enough for a human body. Wasn't that what we were expecting? Suzie's body? Maybe I hadn't understood, because she wasn't down there. All I saw was a rusted-out beer keg and a huge thick spiderweb with something shiny caught in it.

Bernie spun around, grabbed the sheriff by the scruff of his neck and jerked him over to the hole, stretching the chain out straight. Earl Ford gazed down.

"Christ Almighty."

"That's all you've got to say?"

"Les told me he dumped her there. That's all I know."

Their faces were very close together, the sheriff still sweating even though cool air was rising up from the hole; Bernie's face dry. "You're a liar," Bernie said.

"Not about this."

Very slowly, Bernie let go of the sheriff's neck. Then he crouched down, put one hand on the edge of the hole and dropped into it with a spinning, vaulting kind of move I had no idea he could do.

"No, boy," he said, not even looking back up at me. How did he know I was just about to jump in, too?

Down in the hole, Bernie plucked the shiny thing out of the spiderweb. He held it up. Two things, actually, two shiny things on a tiny ring. Hey! I knew what those were, had two of my own.

"Princess's tags," Bernie said.

"News to me," said the sheriff.

"Know what this tells me?" Bernie said. The sheriff was silent. "Tells me who the kidnappers were, two of them, anyway. Care to try your luck, Earl? Guess right and the prize is we don't leave you here."

"Here?"

"Meaning in the hole. All by yourself, trapdoor nailed down tight."

"You wouldn't do that."

Bernie pocketed Princess's tags, pulled himself up. He unlocked the handcuff from the chain by the bar, jerked the sheriff toward the hole. "Hop in," he said.

"Me and Les," the sheriff said. "We did the snatch."

"Let's go pick him up," Bernie said.

Earl Ford driving, his good arm now handcuffed to the wheel; Bernie riding shotgun; me in back, and the moon hanging low in the sky. The sight made me want to do some howling, no idea why, but I knew this wasn't the time, and so sat absolutely still, except for a bit of picking at the seat upholstery.

"How much money's in the envelope?" Bernie said.

"Didn't finish counting," the sheriff said.

"Humor's tricky, Earl. I'd lay off it."

Silence. I can feel things about humans sometimes. For example, whenever I'm with Bernie and Suzie I'm pretty sure they like each other a lot. And Bernie's feelings for Charlie are huge, all good except for some sadness mixed in. Right now in the SUV I could feel hate, and plenty of it, going back and forth between Earl Ford and Bernie. Hadn't often felt such powerful hate between men, and those times I did, violence broke out soon after. I shifted slightly, giving myself a clear shot through the space separating the two front seats.

"Seeing some patterns here," Bernie said after a while.

"Don't know what you're talkin' about."

I was totally with the sheriff on that one. Patterns: I'd heard Bernie talking about them before, but what were they? Something you could see? I looked around, saw no patterns that I knew of.

"Here's one pattern," Bernie said. "This repetition of unexpected burials."

"Don't get you."

"No? We dig up Suzie's car and find Adelina. Then where you tell us Suzie's supposed to be, we find Princess's tags. There's a pattern, kind of a sick one, so my guess is we're looking for someone sick. See what I mean?"

"No."

"Then maybe you weren't much of a cop."

"I am," the sheriff said, his voice low. "I'm a good cop."

"You're not a cop, Earl."

The sheriff turned to Bernie and his voice rose. "I was, then, you bastard. I was a good cop."

Did I like hearing people calling Bernie names? No. But I knew this was a kind of interview, and Bernie's interviews were one of the best things we had going. Also I didn't have a clear idea of what was bad about bastard.

"I accept that," Bernie said. "You were a good cop. And then what happened?"

The sheriff didn't answer. He faced front, eyes on the road, his face—the side of it I could see—green from the dash, with a deep groove in the cheek I hadn't noticed before.

"Possible answer," Bernie said. "Your cousin Les happened. Correct me if I'm wrong."

The sheriff said nothing.

"Les came back from the army, dishonorably discharged and all fucked up," Bernie said.

"He was already fucked up," said Earl Ford.

"But you hired him anyway."

"Military guys make good cops—you know that."

"Not military guys like him."

"Hindsight," the sheriff said.

"Always this easy on yourself?"

More silence. Soon lights appeared, the moon got dimmer, and we rolled into Nowhereville, the town quiet, no one around.

"You know Cedric Booker?" Bernie said.

"The Valley DA? Talked to him once or twice."

"That was him on the phone, the call about Les. He's done some digging—backs up that idea of yours."

"What idea?"

"About Les being fucked up even before the service. Wouldn't mind hearing the story in your own words." The sheriff turned up a side street, a street with a few lamps at first and then none.

"Talk," Bernie said. "Chet and I are in a hurry."

We were?

The houses got smaller and farther apart and soon we were in open country. The ground rose and the road began to curve, back and forth. Trees appeared. Eucalyptus: I could smell them—almost taste them, in fact, eucalyptus twigs being my favorite.

"I want a deal," the sheriff said.

"You're not alone," said Bernie.

"He's my cousin. Our mothers were sisters, very close. They died in a wreck."

"I'm listening."

Glad someone was; way too complicated for me, all this talk, plus I had no idea where it was headed.

"You could put in a word," the sheriff said.

"Depending on how it all plays out."

"Fair enough," said the sheriff. "The fucked-up part was behind why Les went in the service in the first place."

"Judge gave him an ultimatum?" Bernie said.

The sheriff shot Bernie a quick glance. "Cedric tell you that?"

"Not exactly."

"Then how'd you know?"

No answer from Bernie.

"Yeah, that's what happened. First offense—first real offense—and he was only twenty-three."

"Not a kid."

"No."

"And the offense?"

"Some girl," the sheriff said. "But he didn't do anything to her, not really."

"Oh?" said Bernie. I'd heard that kind of oh from him before, an oh that sounded not very interested, but after all the cases we'd worked I now knew better.

"Didn't hurt her is what I mean," said Earl Ford. "Barely touched her."

"But?"

"A very pretty girl—met her in Vegas, I think it was. Didn't have any interest in Les, but he thought all she needed was time to get to know him."

"Is that a euphemism for locking her up in his basement?"

"Wouldn't call it locking up, but he kept her for a weekend. Unharmed—hope Cedric mentioned that part."

"Cedric didn't have much in the way of details," Bernie said. I saw a low light up ahead, twinkling through the trees. "How did you hook up with the count?" Bernie said.

"That was Les, too. He met the trainer—"

"Nance?"

"—yeah, Nance—at the Rio Loco Gun Club. She was the instructor."

Then came a long silence. I could feel Bernie thinking, a heavy pressure in the air, pushing and pushing. The low light grew brighter, and I made out a house, a garage, and maybe a barn in back.

"Nance killed Adelina?" Bernie said.

The sheriff nodded. "Wasn't supposed to be that way, not from what she told us. The idea was just to stir up some publicity about the dog show."

"You believed that?" Bernie said.

No answer.

The sheriff slowed down, turned up a long dirt driveway.

"Crazy thing was the dog ended up running away. We looked everywhere. The count was bullshit."

"Cut the lights," Bernie said.

The sheriff cut the lights. I looked around, could see just fine with the moonlight: big trees; a tipped-over tractor and some other machinery; a small house with a glow in one window.

"Les has a front-end loader?" Bernie said.

"Had a little construction business at one time."

"Handy," Bernie said.

The driveway went over a rise that led to the garage. Bernie pointed. "Pull in." The sheriff parked on the far side of the garage, away from the house. Bernie took the keys from the ignition, grabbed the flashlight. "You're staying here," he said.

"Like I have a choice?" said the sheriff, clanking the handcuffs softly against the wheel.

Bernie and I got out of the SUV. The first thing Bernie did was pop the hood. Uh-ho. Did that ever lead to anything good? Bernie reached in and yanked out a wire. "In case he thinks of honking the horn." Bernie held the wire up, shone the flash so the sheriff could see. Wow. That was Bernie, smartest guy in the room.

We walked around the garage, stopped at the corner, and gazed across the yard at the house. The glow came from the front. We headed for the back, the moonlight glinting on the .38 Special in Bernie's belt, and my ears up, high and stiff.

THIRTY-ONE

We'd done this kind of thing before, me and Bernie, sneaking up on a perp's house in the night. Bernie always liked to do a little recon first, so I did, too. That meant crossing this crummy yard, all weeds and stone, getting out of the open real quick, then standing in the shadows at the back of the house, just listening.

Didn't know what Bernie heard, but I heard TV voices, very faint, coming through the wall. I could even make out a few words, like "red zone blitz," which meant football. We watched a lot of football at home. Bernie preferred college football to pro football, had once gotten into this big argument about it with a perp we had tied up in the back of a beer truck. Kind of strange, and maybe a story for some other time.

We moved along the back of the house, rounded the corner to the far side. Bernie put his ear to the wall. Did he hear anything? Maybe not. I still heard the TV voices, but fainter now. Bernie took another step or two, peered into a dark window. It was too high up for me, so I peered into another dark window, down on ground level.

At first I saw nothing, just a lot of darkness behind dusty glass. But then I got the feeling—does this ever happen to you?—that someone was watching me. An uncomfortable kind of feeling: I twisted my head to make it go away, but it wouldn't so I kept staring through the ground-level window and pretty soon the darkness on the other side wasn't quite as dark. I realized I was gazing down into a basement. Moonlight shone faintly on this and that: the handle of a paint can; the teeth of a rake; and what was this? A pair of eyes? Yes, a pair of eyes, silvery in the moonlight, and round the way human eyes are round. The hair on the back of my neck went up.

"Chet?" Bernie spoke very low, so low I almost couldn't hear him. He crouched down, looked at me. I have this kind of muffled bark I can do, soft and quick, a sound that doesn't even leave my throat. I did it now. "Shh," said Bernie. He aimed the flashlight at the low window, flicked it on and off real quick.

But what I saw in that basement, frozen like a photo in the sudden light and then gone: oh, boy. Suzie. Yes, Suzie, her eyes dark and shiny like the countertops in the kitchen—no one had eyes like Suzie—and maybe blinded now by the sudden light. Suzie, beyond doubt, sitting with her back to a wall. And one other thing: she was chained there, the metal links easy to see. Oh, and one more: she had a strip of duct tape over her mouth.

Bernie made a hissing sound; had I ever heard him do that before? And maybe I made a sound of my own—an angry growl—because Bernie again said, "Shh."

He got down on his knees, pressed on the window, not hard. Nothing happened. There were all sorts of windows out there; I'd never opened any of them—never even tried. Screens: a different story, although you couldn't exactly say I'd opened any of the ones I'd gotten through.

Bernie pressed harder on the window, then gave the frame a tap with the palm of his hand. The window remained closed. He took off his shirt, folded it up small, laid it against the glass. Then he raised the flashlight, and swung it like a hammer, butt end first. Behind the shirt, glass shattered, but not loudly, and after a silent pause, tinkled down on the hard floor below. We stayed still, listening. A TV voice said, "Fourth and goal from the Aggie three." Bernie reached through the hole in the glass—it was mostly hole now, with a few jagged shards still stuck in the frame—fiddled with something out of sight inside, a look of concentration on his face. Then he pushed again on the frame. This time the window swung open.

"No, Chet," Bernie said, not loud but kind of urgent. And also too late: I'd already jumped through.

Always been a pretty good lander, in case you haven't guessed. Maybe a bit more light would have helped, but I hit the floor the way I like—front paws first, then bunching up my body real quick before my back paws touched—coming down with hardly any bump at all. And the truth is all that stuff—front paws, back paws—I don't think about; it just happens.

Behind me I heard Bernie clambering through the hole. I went right to Suzie, nuzzled against her. She made a sound, not crying, kind of complicated and hard to describe, but I knew she knew who I was: Chet! Chet the Jet! And Suzie was alive! Were we expecting that? Didn't think so, but maybe I'd gotten it wrong.

Bernie's light flashed on. He hurried over and knelt by Suzie, including her in the circle of light without shining it in her eyes. No bruises, no blood, but she didn't look good. That was easy to see, and so were those chains, hanging from a ceiling pipe and fastened to clamps on both wrists. Bernie knelt in front of her—actually more to the side since I was in front of her, sort of partly on her lap—and very gently, slowly working his thumb and first finger under one corner—peeled the duct tape off Suzie's mouth. Their gazes met and even though Bernie wasn't a crier and I was pretty sure the same went for Suzie, I expected crying to come next.

But it didn't. Instead Suzie licked her lips—all dry and cracked—and in a rough, scratchy voice said, "What took you so long?"

"I'm an idiot," Bernie said.

Bernie an idiot? No way. He touched her hair, smoothed it out. Then he glanced around. Not much to see: a mostly empty basement with rough stairs, no railing, leading up to a closed door at the top. Bernie rose and gazed at where the chains were attached to the ceiling pipes. Copper pipes: copper had a special smell I knew from a case we'd worked once in copper-mining country. Bernie raised his hands, got a good grip on a copper pipe, and started to pull. At that moment, a car horn went off outside. Honk honk—honk honk honk—honk honk.

"Christ," Bernie said. "Did I pull the wrong wire?" The smartest guy in the room, except maybe when it came to what's under the hood. But no time to think about that, even if I knew where to start, because right away heavy footsteps pounded up above. A door slammed. Honk honk—honk honk honk—honk honk. Bernie tugged at the pipe. It bent but didn't give. The pounding footsteps returned. Bernie gave the pipe a huge yank, tearing it out of the wall. Water sprayed down. The door at the top of the stairs burst open. Lights flashed on. And there, gazing down, stood the deputy sheriff, Lester Ford, his crooked nose throwing a strange shadow across his face. He had a baseball bat in his hand and a gun on his hip. His eyes got real narrow and he reached for the gun.

Meanwhile, I was already on my way up those stairs, charging full speed. Lester didn't have time to clear the gun from the holster so he swung the bat at my head. He connected, got me a good one, but on the shoulder, not the head. Knocked me sideways, but I kept my footing, claws scratching deep into the stairs, and then I sprang and did some connecting of my own. We rolled down the stairs, Lester yelling, me growling my fiercest, and landed hard on the floor, me on top. Bernie stepped up, put the muzzle of the .38 Special right against the tip of Lester's nose.

"Don't shoot," Lester said.

"Did you touch her?" Bernie said, his trigger finger bone-white. "I'm going to kill you."

"No, I swear."

"Suzie?" Bernie said, not turning to look at her, his face real close to Lester's.

"Nothing like that happened," Suzie said, in this new weak, scratchy voice of hers. "Not yet."

The .38 Special stayed where it was, pressed to Lester's nose but no longer quite steady; and now Bernie's face was as bone-white as his trigger finger. Something real bad was about to happen. I heard a little high-pitched sound. Hey! That was me. Bernie glanced my way. Then he took a deep deep breath and lowered the gun.

We left Les chained up nice and tight down in his basement and went outside, Bernie's arm around Suzie the whole way. The moon was gone, who knows where.

"You limping, Chet?" Bernie said.

Maybe I was a little. I took a few more limping steps, felt pain in my shoulder. Then all of a sudden, on the very next step, the pain vanished and I was fine. I ran around a bit for no reason.

"He looks okay," Suzie said.

We found Earl Ford still cuffed to the wheel of his SUV. Bernie threw open the door, pretty angry.

"Glad to see the lady's alive," Earl said.

"Don't want to hear it," Bernie said. He unlocked the cuff from the wheel, pulled Earl out of the SUV.

"My arm," said Earl.

"Least of your worries."

"I could bleed out."

"Not from that wound."

"How do you know?"

Bernie didn't answer, just led Earl into the barn. I stayed by the SUV with Suzie, pretty sure that was what Bernie wanted me to do. Suzie gave me a pat, looked me in the eye. "Good to see you, Chet," she said. "Can't begin to tell you."

Good to see Suzie, too. I got the feeling this case was going well. We'd found Princess, and now Suzie. Then I remembered Adelina and the ants, and wasn't so sure. I tried to think back over the details, but everything got hazy. I pressed my head against Suzie's leg. "You're the best," she said. She leaned down so our faces were on the same level. Oh, no. Suzie didn't look good, not good at all, especially her eyes. And there was a strong strange smell—kind of like milk gone bad—a smell of being so afraid. Poor Suzie. I gave her face a nice big lick.

And all at once her face got misshapen like it was coming apart and she started sobbing, wet tears streaming down. I licked and licked, trying to lick them all up, so salty. She went to her knees and held on to me. I stood strong, took her weight no problem. Suzie shook for a bit but then she stopped and the crying stopped and I could feel strength coming back to her body. She rose, wiped her face on the back of her sleeve, then leaned down again, this time kissing me, right on the nose. That tickles, but I love it.

Bernie came out of the garage, talking on his cell phone. ". . . and the other one's in the basement," he was saying.

He listened for a moment. Behind him I saw a faint band of milky light, low in the sky. The end of night, a real quiet time. I could hear Cedric on the other end of the phone. "You'll be there, I assume?"

"Nope," Bernie said, and clicked off.

"Where are you going to be?" Suzie said.

"Wrapping things up," said Bernie. He gave Suzie a long look. "But first we'll take you to the hospital."

"Hell, no," she said, wiping her face again.

"Sorry, Suzie. It could be dangerous."

"That's a joke, right? Under the circumstances?"

"Can't let you."

"I'll sue."

"For what?"

"Restraint of trade," Suzie said. "This is a big story."

Bernie was still for a moment, his face hard, the way it had been all night. Then he smiled, a big smile that brought him back to the usual old Bernie.

Which was good. The only bad part was how I ended up in the back of the SUV again, Bernie driving, Suzie now in the shotgun seat, my spot. But I was cool with it, especially after I got myself right up to the edge of the backseat, putting my head actually in the front, between Suzie and Bernie. Suzie's hand rested on the console and his hand lay on hers. And then my paw was on top of both! How had that happened?

"Chet?"

I backed up a little.

"That was Cedric on the phone," Bernie said.

"Figured," said Suzie.

"You know Cedric?"

"You're funny, Bernie."

"Huh?"

"I worked the crime beat for two years. Go on."

"Um," said Bernie. "Cedric says Adelina and Borghese had a prenup. In the event of divorce—"

"—he got zip."

"How'd you know that?"

"Research." The milky band of light was turning orange: a brand-new day. I always liked watching that happen, and maybe missed some of the back-and-forth between Suzie and Bernie, kind of hard to understand anyway. Suzie said something like, "But her predeceasing him was a different story—he got it all. The moment I found that out I should have crossed Ganz off the list. Instead I heard about him owning that ghost town and went there on a hunch. Which turned out to be right, except for the Ganz part."

"What happened?"

"I heard barking, up in that cabin. Thought it was Princess, of course, and started there on foot. Then these two guys stepped out of the shadows."

"Earl and Les?"

Suzie nodded. "I called your number, couldn't think of anything else to do. Later, when they had me tied up, I heard him telling Earl and Les to get rid of me, and Les said he'd handle it."

"Who's 'him'?" Bernie said.

"Borghese," Suzie said. "Haven't you figured this out yet?"

"They're in love?"

"They even finish each other's sentences."

"I noticed that," Bernie said.

"You did?" said Suzie.

Bernie shrugged his shoulders. For some reason, that made Suzie laugh. Then she leaned over and gave him a quick kiss on the cheek. I didn't know what the hell was going on.

The sun was up by the time we drove past the corral—the white horse watching us over the fence rail—and the putting green and parked in front of the big house at Rio Loco Ranch. "The deal is you stay here," Bernie said.

Suzie didn't answer.

"Deal?" said Bernie.

Suzie nodded, a very slight motion, almost none at all.

Bernie and I got out of the SUV. A beautiful morning, the air still, the house quiet. Sometimes, early in the morning like that, with the air so still, you can hear small sounds from far away, or at least I can. At that moment, I heard a faint clink, the kind of clink silverware makes on a plate. The sound came from somewhere behind the house and I headed in that direction. "Good boy," Bernie said, coming with me.

We went around the house, through a big garden with lots of flowers, past some orange trees—oranges dangling from branches out of reach—and came to a huge swimming pool with a patio beside it. An umbrella stood on the patio, a table underneath. Seated close together at the table, legs touching, the count and Nance were having breakfast. Scrambled eggs, bacon, toast, orange juice, coffee: I smelled it all.

By the time they heard us coming, we were almost on them; we could be real quiet, me and Bernie. They looked up, first Nance, then Borghese. Then they moved farther apart from each other, the coffee slopping over the edge of the count's cup.

"Morning," Bernie said.

The count placed his cup in the saucer. "Mr. Little?" he said. "To what do we, uh—"

"Owe this visit," said Nance. Her purse lay on the table. She drew it closer.

"It's about the case," Bernie said. We stood by the table, Borghese and Nance on the other side. The sun shone on a big glass jug of orange juice: a beautiful sight.

"The case?" said Borghese.

"What case?" said Nance.

"The three culprits are in jail, no?" Borghese said.

"And you've been paid," said Nance.

"They won't be in jail for long," Bernie said. "At least not for this. That was so lucky, how fall guys kept popping up for you. Even Ganz—were you going to murder Adelina anyway, or did it only become irresistible when he sent that photo?"

"What is this nonsense?" said Borghese. "I'm afraid we must ask you to—"

Borghese cut himself off, gazed past us. So did Nance. Their eyes opened wide. I turned, and there, emerging from the orange trees, came Suzie. She had a little camera in her hand, now raised it to snap a picture.

Bernie had turned, too. "Suzie," he said. "Get back."

"Freeze," said Nance.

Uh-oh. We both spun back around, me and Bernie. Too late. Nance had slipped a little handgun out of her purse. Her skin, so dark from the sun, and her eyes, shrunk down to points: she looked a lot like those dangerous gunslingers from the Westerns in our DVD pile, except she was a woman. She pointed the gun right at Bernie's head. "I missed your dog, but that was at long range," she said. "I won't miss now."

The muscle in Bernie's jaw got hard and lumpy. "You were shooting at Chet?"

Hey! I remembered that, a real bad memory that made me mad. I leaped. Most of the time I'm a very good leaper, but this wasn't one of my better leaps, in fact maybe my very worst, my legs letting me down for some reason. I cleared the table all right—the gun swinging over to point my way—but crashed into that big jug of orange juice. Did the gun go off? Not sure, but the jug went flying, splashing orange juice all over the place, including—hey!—in Nance's face.

"Ow," she said, putting her free hand to her eyes.

The next moment, Bernie had her, twisting her arm up and behind, making her say, "Ow," again, this time louder, and drop the gun. We'd taken down women perps before, but never this roughly. In this case I was all for it. Bernie kicked the gun away.

Meanwhile, Borghese had taken off, was running across the lawn. The count turned out to be a poor runner, one of the very worst human runners I'd ever seen. I had him by the pant leg in no time. Case closed.

Lieutenant Stine, a SWAT team, and a bunch of other cops soon arrived. By that time, we'd found the thirty-ought-six under some hay bales in the barn. Normally we tend to hang around in situations like that, accepting congratulations, free drinks, lots of pats, that kind of thing. But not this time. This time we were in a big hurry. Why? No clue.

Not long after, we pulled into the vet's parking lot. The vet? I was fine, shoulder all better, not a scratch on me. We went inside, me, Bernie, Suzie. The vet's name was Amy, a big round woman with a nice voice and careful hands, but I always started shaking the moment I entered the waiting room, and this time was no different.

They laid me on a table. Bernie stroked between my ears, very nice. Amy felt along my side. A lot of talk went on over my head—something about biopsies, whatever those were—and I thought about the tray of bacon we'd left untouched on the count's table. I felt a tiny jab high up one leg, and then nothing.

Woke up feeling tip-top, out in Amy's waiting room. Bernie was saying something like, "If you had to guess?"

Amy looked away from him. "We'll have the results in two days," she said. Then they saw I was up and at 'em and gave me some pats. We left. I had no idea what that was all about, just felt glad to get out of there.

We went home, listened to a message from Chuck Eckel. "Big news," he said. "Some peasant just stumbled on the biggest tin deposit they've ever found in Bolivia. Gonna drive the price down to practically zero. You'll make a shitload."

Bernie didn't seem thrilled. I wasn't either. It sounded kind of disgusting.

The next day we went to the Great Western Dog Show at the Arena. I sat with Suzie, the whole place packed. And where was Bernie? Down on the floor with Princess! There were a whole bunch of tiny dogs, some fluffballs, some not, but I only had eyes for two—Babycakes, with Mr. Ganz, and Princess, with Bernie. They got paraded around one by one. Babycakes did her little move, one paw raised, waiting patiently to get going. What crap! Then, last, came Princess, running in her blurry-legged style, Bernie kind of shuffling along beside her.

"He's adorable," Suzie said in a quiet voice.

Huh? Who? What? Missed that completely.

Down on the floor, all the dogs waited at their stations, a human standing beside each one; only the humans looked nervous. Then a big, scary-looking old woman in black started walking slowly past each one, staring at them. Now my guys looked nervous, too. She spent an extra long time gazing at Babycakes, who raised her goddamn paw again, and at Princess, who stuck out her little pink tongue right in the scary woman's face. And then—and then! The scary woman extended her arm and pointed right at Princess!

Applause. Clapping and cheering. Princess, now wearing a blue ribbon, took Bernie on a victory run. He had this huge smile on his face and she had her head up in that determined way. Had I ever seen anything so exciting? I wanted to be down there so bad.

And the next thing I knew I was! I ran around crazily. Princess got free and ran around with me. Then all of them—all those midgets—were on the loose. Somehow that blue ribbon got eaten, possibly by me. We went wild.

ACKNOWLEDGMENTS

Heartfelt thanks to my friend, Alan Cohen, my agent, Molly Friedrich, and my editor, Peter Borland.